THE WEST HOUSE

Erik Dussere

Regal House Publishing

Published by
Regal House Publishing, LLC
Raleigh, NC 27612
All rights reserved

ISBN -13 (paperback): 9781646030101
ISBN -13 (epub): 9781646030378
Library of Congress Control Number: 2020930425

All efforts were made to determine the copyright holders and obtain their permissions in any circumstance where copyrighted material was used. The publisher apologizes if any errors were made during this process, or if any omissions occurred. If noted, please contact the publisher and all efforts will be made to incorporate permissions in future editions.

Interior and cover design by Lafayette & Greene
lafayetteandgreene.com
Cover images © by ThereIsNoNe/Shutterstock
Credit for author photo: Anna Carson DeWitt

Regal House Publishing, LLC
https://regalhousepublishing.com

The following is a work of fiction created by the author. All names, individuals, characters, places, items, brands, events, etc. were either the product of the author or were used fictitiously. Any name, place, event, person, brand, or item, current or past, is entirely coincidental.

Lyrics and dialogue used with permission from the following:
Lyrics from "Like a Rolling Stone" (Bob Dylan) (Special Rider Music)
Lyrics from "That's Not Me" (Brian Wilson/Tony Asher) (Hal Leonard LLC)
Dialogue from the film *The Big Sleep*
(with thanks to the estate of Raymond Chandler/RCW Literary)

Printed in the United States of America

For Stephanie and Liv

PART ONE

June – July
1993

1.

Sometimes when you cross a line, you know it.

The traffic had finally relaxed its grip somewhere east of New Haven and now it was full dark, the air cooling, distant shapes of hills and houses gone blurry in the summer night. Taking the exit, the rearview was bright with the glare of lights from the highway. Ahead was a deep wooded darkness. The interstate went on its way without me, and by the time I reached the stop sign at the bottom I had passed into an entirely different landscape.

Traffic and streetlights a fading memory, I found myself navigating narrow roads that seemed to twist and ramble endlessly, blind-cornered corridors overhung with trees and lit only by the moving pool of the headlights. Beside the road, a low wall made of stacked stones followed my progress, often broken by intersections and driveways but seemingly continuous, a long rough ribbon that let me know I had arrived. The wall was a sign that read not *Welcome to* but *Here be New England*, a sign for a place that looked askance at the civic boastfulness of signs, a message meant to be legible only to those with environed knowledge and good sense enough to read it.

I had never driven here before, had not been to this part of the country since I was old enough to drive. In fact I had no real memory of it at all; this was a homecoming to a place I had never known. But after only one wrong turning I found the driveway I was looking for, the black mailbox without name or house number but with a small frayed ribbon of red and gold tied around the post. I turned into the driveway, which could have been mistaken for yet another of the narrow local roads, and slowly navigated the quarter mile of blacktop as it wound among trees, bushes, and boulders, finally widening at the end and stopping at a freestanding garage. The house loomed in darkness on the left. Parking in front of the garage, I unfolded myself slowly, stretched in the glow of the light, and pulled my duffel bag from the car.

After the long, loud rush of the highway, the night here was so still that I stopped and stood next to the car for a few moments. Moths swooped and fluttered around the light, and the air was full of the massed white noise of unseen insects. Dark shapes of trees rose high all around, and stars were thick in the sky, layer upon layer, all the luminous strata revealed in the absence of streetlights.

I walked to the screen door at the back of the house and hauled my bag into the kitchen.

The old man was sitting with his elbows on the kitchen table. He looked up at me, his eyes hidden by dark glasses and his face locked in an unreadable frown. His head was large and ungainly; it looked like something sculpted in clay but not finished or fired, with a lumpish nose and a slightly dented bald dome. The dark hair, mixed with gray, seemed after decades of ruthless combing to have retreated to the back of the head, where it now hung limp. Smooth, skinny ankles showed bare above his shoes, but his torso was thick, solid. With the dark glasses and the pugilistic expression, dressed in sweatpants and a beaten-up windbreaker, he could have passed for an aging gangster living in witness protection. Even with his eyes hidden, I could tell that he was glaring steadily at me.

"Did you shut that screen door?"

"Good to see you too, Frederick," I said, easing the bag off my shoulder and onto the linoleum. If he was going to talk to me as if we saw each other every day, I was going to respond in kind. I had been in the house for only thirty seconds and already I had to be on my toes.

He pointed a thick finger at me. His middle finger on the right hand was missing, a smooth stump. "Look," he said. "You don't shut that fucking door, it bangs around in the wind."

I turned and opened the kitchen door to show that the screen door on the other side was closed and latched.

"All right," he said grudgingly, still frowning. He took the accusing finger away, slid a cigarette out of the pack in front of him, tapped it four times on the table, and lit it. He looked me up and down through the curling smoke, a curt appraisal. I was in shorts and a T-shirt, and the sweat on my back, from long contact with the car seat, was beginning to cool in an unpleasant way. The duffel bag sagged on the floor beside me.

"All right," he said again. "You can get started tomorrow. Right now you better go change your clothes. The neighbors want to get a look at you."

2.

That was how I met Charlotte West.

Still dazed from the hours in the car, I found myself walking down the dark driveway with a flashlight, on my way to the neighbors' house. I had quickly brought my things to the room I would be staying in, a small apartment above the garage, splashed water on my face, and changed into dry clothes before setting off into the night.

As I stumbled for the third time over an unexpected buckling of the asphalt I wondered grimly how the long day had brought me to this particular place, navigating through a half mile of dark Connecticut, most of it driveway, in order to pay some sort of social call on people I did not know and probably would not like. Certainly the old man didn't seem to like them much. My impression was that he did not have or want any friends, but he had explained to me that he had run into this neighbor, Franklin West, at the post office the day before. West apparently had caught Frederick off guard by insisting that I, the unknown young visitor, come to visit him at his home sometime.

I was sure that it was entirely the old man's idea to get this chore out of the way by packing me off immediately upon arrival. I should have protested, should have argued—but you didn't, somehow, with Frederick. I hadn't seen him since I was a boy and would not have recognized him on the street, but I had spoken to him on the phone and knew well that most of the time it was easier to agree or to do what he demanded than to argue. He liked to argue and harass and chastise, so every conflict avoided was a kind of victory.

At the end of the driveway I turned left onto the dark road. Second house on the same side of the street, Frederick had said.

I could hear the whispering movement of leafy tree boughs

high above, although there was no breeze where I walked. The frogs and insects made a complicated rhythm that accompanied me along the stone wall, until I reached the second mailbox and turned onto yet another long driveway. I had grown up in the suburbs, among lawyers and dentists, families richer than my own, with money for travel and large televisions and endless home improvement, but the money here was different. Older. Money with history, expressing itself by hiding itself, taking the form, for instance, of long driveways that provided privacy and implied a way of life both superior and self-effacing.

Frederick was an accidental inhabitant of this world, an immigrant who had come to America as a child and had worked for years as a factory laborer and building contractor. He had also been a scandal, at least in my family. My father's aunt, five years dead now, had betrayed her distinguished bloodline by marrying him. Maybe it was a marriage of love, passion. But more likely it was her only way of saying *no*, however indirectly, to her family and its history and to the tyrannical and overbearing father who represented them both: *No, I will not be the vessel for bearing this tradition forward.* She had had no children, so yes, her childless marriage to an impoverished nobody whose ancestors were themselves impoverished nobodies somewhere in Germany was a kind of refusal. But it had been a passive refusal; her brother's, my grandfather's, refusal had been more difficult, more direct. As a man he must have felt a different kind of patriarchal insistence, of name and blood conjoined, and so had to say his *no* out loud, had to tell his father that he wanted no part of the family and its ideas about what he should do with his life and whom he should marry. Father and son had quarreled loudly and bitterly, the break had been absolute, and as a result none of the money in the family had ever trickled down into my branch of it.

But my father's aunt, Frederick's wife, had inherited her share. And she must have been clever in her dealings with her father, or perhaps he just neglected to find his way around the legal proscriptions involved in marriage and inheritance. Because now

Frederick, the former laborer, was provided for handsomely through his wife's trust and continued to maintain his illegitimate compound in the wooded heart of Yankee Connecticut. If my grandfather's victory had been in gaining his own freedom from the weight of family and tradition, his sister's posthumous triumph lay in having installed this interloper, this wrong husband, wrong widower, and planting him like an insistent weed in a carefully tended garden.

But perhaps the garden could simply accommodate the occasional eccentric weed. What is disturbing in a son-in-law might seem like harmless variety in a neighbor. And over time the old man might even have begun to adapt himself to his surroundings. It must be a burden, after all, having to represent a cause, a resounding *no*, that is not your own.

So maybe it was fitting that I was going to be living with him this summer, because I felt that I, too, was there to carry out someone else's business. My father's business.

The first call had come out of the blue two years ago, during my brief visit home that summer, my father standing with the phone in his hand and an expression of curious concentration, telling me that his uncle Frederick was on the phone and that he had asked to speak only to me. The call was brief and strange, coming from an old man I had never really met, but who had apparently decided that he wanted to find out more about me. He continued to call once every few months, at my dorm room now, often late at night, me listening to him talk, to the exhalations of smoke far away, and I would imagine him sitting in the dark, a disembodied voice, because I had no picture of him to recall. Maybe even then he was cultivating me, knowing that his eyes were failing and that he would need someone to come there eventually, someone he trusted at least a little bit, because soon he would not be able to read anymore.

When he did propose that I come for the summer, I felt only a mild surprise and curiosity, and so I was not remotely prepared for my father's reaction, the uncontrolled eagerness that lit in his eyes when I told him. I had never seen that expression on his face before, and didn't like or trust it. Eagerness, in a man who had never looked eager in all the days I had lived in his house.

I don't remember the words we exchanged then, because all I remember is that look in his eyes and the two terrible things I learned when I saw it. First, that I did not like my father, and never had. Second, that he wanted desperately for me to go. He wanted me to go back to the place in which his own inheritance—the one he felt was rightly his—had been lost, and he wanted me to curry favor with the old man so that I might inherit his money and so restore the balance. Yes, I saw that. Saw it, and told myself that I would go, not to please my father but to disappoint him.

The neighbors' house was visible now at the end of the driveway; it was taller, narrower, and more carefully maintained than Frederick's, with lights shining from second-story windows and a small garden, which I passed through on the brick pathway to the front entrance.

I paused there and switched off the flashlight. On the door was a bronze knocker and below it a plaque with what appeared to be a coat of arms. I knocked and then stood in that atmosphere of expectant mystery that surrounds all such moments, the literal experience of the threshold, where the hidden life of the house and the family is made vulnerable to the incursions of the outside world.

The door opened and inside stood a woman, silhouetted against the brightly lit interior. Dark hair, something forbidding in the posture.

"Do I know you?" she asked.

I hesitated, feeling desperately young at twenty-two, like a child who has been sent to fetch something and then, arriving, is chastised for asking for it. "No, you don't know me—but, I'm going to be—"

There was a movement behind the woman in the doorway, and another silhouette appeared. My eyes were adjusting and I could begin to see the man's curious face peering out at me—a square, handsome face framed by carefully trimmed gray hair. "Ah! You must be the young man already," he said. "Come in, come in."

3.

My father never told stories. I don't mean bedtime stories, although it is certainly true that even trying to imagine him sitting at the edge of a bed and making up a tale for his children's amusement is, quite literally, impossible. What I mean is that he never told a story or an anecdote or spoke about his past. Not once, if he could avoid it, did he say a word about the place he grew up, his parents, his childhood here in Connecticut. But I am not my father's son. As soon as I saw her for the first time, I started to tell myself stories about who Charlotte West was, where she was from, wildly, helplessly inventing stories that proliferated and twined themselves around the West house like a thicket, remaking it and her in the multiplying images I created in my head.

But first I had to step inside.

Blinking, still a bit dazed, I took in the interior surroundings before the two people came fully into focus. The entryway led directly into a high-ceilinged living room, with a large patterned rug laid over the wood floor, lamps and chairs and sofa carefully arranged. There seemed to be a nautical theme at work here, but a quiet one—I noticed a lamp made from a ship's lantern, scrimshaw engravings, a couple of paintings of boats and men on the high seas. The room did not look as if it got much air and light even during the day, and this, combined with the decorative touches, did provide a subtle sense of being in the interior of a ship. Later, in retrospect, I felt that a tendency toward preciousness in the decor was being held in check by a stronger controlling spirit, as if a tasteful hand had firmly refused to allow certain things. No coffee table in the shape of a lifeboat, no anchor-motif wallpaper.

The man was shaking my hand. He was slightly shorter than I

was, in late middle age, with a solid build and the sort of crushing grip that I had always associated with business suits, although he was wearing slacks and a slightly rumpled gray sweater.

"Frank West," he was saying. "And my wife, Charlotte." She looked at me without betraying any sign of interest. "So you are the young man who will be staying with Mr. Hardt this summer? And you are family as well?"

"Kesey," I said, by way of introduction. "Kese for short. I'm a sort of grand-nephew. By marriage—we're not blood related."

Frank West patted me heartily on the shoulder. "Nonetheless, we shall treat you as an *honorary* blood relation," he said. "Let me get you a drink. You've just finished your college years, so you must be of age."

He moved off to a corner where a liquor cabinet stood and busied himself with glasses and bottles, while Charlotte West stood against a mantelpiece gazing in my general direction. I could see now that she was younger than her husband by some years—I would have put her in her middle forties—and that she was unforgettable. Her eyes were wide and dark above a strong nose and full lips, all set within the frame of her black hair, which had just enough gray and just enough disorder to make her look a little bit wild. The black of the clothes she was wearing blended seamlessly with her hair and with the shadows of the room; she seemed to linger just outside the light cast by the lamps. There was something about her that made me want to look more closely, a foreignness whose source I could not trace. She was like one of those European accents that Americans respond to helplessly, the remnants of old-world caste systems that we can never understand. The phrase that came to my mind was *highly bred*, as if it had taken many generations of people who were used to having servants to produce her. Her face was complicated and hard to read—haughty, maybe, and disaffected, and perhaps a just a little bit sad—a puzzle that could keep you worrying over its pieces for long hours, a place where you could lose yourself.

In fact, I had forgotten that I was staring at her when she spoke at last. "What exactly is your summer employment at Mr. Hardt's place?" She spoke with precise elocution and just a little archly, as if she were forcing herself to take an interest in the pool boy, or whatever I was.

I stared blankly for a moment, suddenly aware of my heart's beating. "Well," I said. "I don't know if you know that the—that Frederick has been having trouble with his eyesight lately." She widened her dark eyes slightly, neither an assent nor a denial. "He's hired me to stay with him over the summer and do his reading for him—or, I mean, to him."

I had been concentrating on meeting her gaze, and Frank West startled me by turning toward us, spreading his arms wide. "Here I am," he proclaimed loudly. "An old man in a dry month, being read to by a boy!"

I stared for a moment in alarm, wondering if he was genuinely unhinged. But he came forward and handed me a heavy-bottomed glass half filled with scotch and ice. He clinked his own glass against mine, smiling as if he expected a response from me. When I remained speechless, he said, "But surely you know your Eliot? I hear, after all, that you are soon to go on in your studies, to graduate school pursuits? A fine future. I am deeply envious of you, young man, with all that lying before you."

I hesitated, unsure what exactly had passed in the conversation between him and Frederick. I had no idea where this talk about graduate study had come from, and wondered for a moment whether either of them even knew that my degree was in journalism. There was something in West's tone that made me pause, too—a genuine envy, perhaps, for the boy and his future, but with a curdled sour something underneath it. His wife had raised her eyebrows slightly, not fond, not censorious, but just watchful.

"I don't actually know what I'll do now that I've graduated," I said, taking an exploratory sip from the glass. The scotch tasted harsh, heady, and debilitating. The flavor of adulthood. "Anything's possible."

"It would certainly be nice to think so," Charlotte West said drily.

She was a woman who had no fear of an awkward pause. We

stood uncomfortably for a moment, until Frank West finally spoke. "Well," he said, "When Frederick told me that he was to have a young visitor for the summer, I told him that he must send you around to us since, after all, the company of a rather gruff older man, set in his ways, day in and day out, must inevitably become tedious for a young person. So although we can offer little in the way of true entertainment or of distraction, we thought at least that it might be useful to you to know that there are friends in the vicinity. And of course Charlotte felt the same eager sympathy, isn't that so, my dear?"

"Yes, Franklin," she said in a tone that was flat but not actively contemptuous. She was looking at me in the same flat way, and for a moment I thought of Benjamin Braddock and Mrs. Robinson, the young man just out of college and the bored idle older woman. But no, there was no desire or entreaty or even that kind of boredom in her gaze, which had assessed and dismissed me in the moment of first opening the door, which seemed only to be waiting for me to leave, and in the meantime watching me carefully for signs of danger or threat, though I couldn't guess why. A bored and idle woman, certainly, but one who had no interest in seducing anyone anymore and certainly no interest in seducing Frederick's pool boy—or perhaps she knew, without especially caring, that she already had.

"And of course we were curious to meet you as well," West said. "Frederick says so little about himself, so rarely goes out socially, he is really a sort of man of mystery. I must admit that I was curious. So it is a pleasure to make your acquaintance."

I tried to smile in a friendly way and took another drink. I had the feeling that West only listened to himself for a few words— and you had to give him credit for that, the momentary check of self-awareness, like a brief stumble before the runner hits stride—before he settled into a steady flow of meaningless talk. Yet while he did all the talking, I could feel my eyes drawn, again and again, to Charlotte West. The small movements of her eyes or mouth as she listened were far more compelling than anything that her husband could say.

"You have a lovely house," I said, looking at her. Then, demonstrating my admiration by surveying the room, my gaze snagged on a small recess in the opposite wall, an alcove that displayed a large black-and-white sketch. Stepping closer, I saw that it was a large family tree, elaborately framed, and lit from above by a small rectangular lamp.

I leaned in, intrigued, and for some moments I was lost in concentration, eyes wandering through the tangle of lines and boxes, names and dates, all rendered beautifully in black ink and sloping calligraphy. It took a few moments to orient myself amid all that information, all the tangled bloodlines, all the Marthas and Johns reduced forever to their names and the dates of birth and death, their family names floating in between the male and female boxes, the squares and circles, as if they were separate and abstract entities with no connection to the people who carried the names for their brief allotment of years—*Mary b. 1832 d. 1880*—as if the names owned them, rather than the other way around.

My eye was drawn to the top of the document, the top square, which was drawn more darkly and ornately in what looked like a rendering of a plaque: *Elder William Brewster b. 1566 d. 1644.* Next to the box was a small drawing of a ship. I bent down to the bottom, skimming over all those generations, and found what I was looking for: the floating name *West* and, on either side of it, square Franklin and circular Charlotte Lenoir, linked by a line, with another line descending to a circle reading *Eleanor b. 1974.* I was looking around idly to see if this was the most recent birth to have been recorded, when West spoke from just behind me. "I won't deny that I'm very proud of this, young man. I suppose that I should say, welcome to the history house."

On a display stand below the framed genealogy was a glass case containing what looked like a very old, or possibly burnt, piece of wood. Not a log or stick—something that had once been shaped to some human purpose but was now just a broken fragment.

"What is this?" I asked.

"That," he said with evident pride, "is a piece of the ship

Mayflower, which as you of course will know sailed from England and landed on these shores in the year 1620."

I must have looked surprised, because he added, eagerly, "The provenance of the piece cannot be verified absolutely, I fear. But I have done my best, and its authenticity is a certain thing in my mind, at least. There are a number of people from old families in this area of the country, but few can trace their lineage so precisely, and even fewer can respect the connection properly."

I looked back to the family tree. "I see. So this William Brewster, your ancestor—he's the *Mayflower* connection."

"More than an ancestor, but your word *connection* is well chosen." *Actually it was your word*, I thought. "This is a connection to history, this chain of *blood relations*. For me it stands in for the history of America itself, it links those of us in the present day to the origins of this great country, to the moment when it came into being as the dream of those visionary English travelers. It gives shape and weight to our lives, don't you think, to these twentieth-century lives that so often seem reduced and insubstantial? Here, come with me for a moment." He led me across to the other end of the living room. I glanced at Charlotte West as I followed him, feeling nervous and hot under her gaze. She watched us with slow eyes and said nothing.

One whole wall of the room was bookshelves, fully stocked and carefully dusted. American literature and American history, biographies of presidents and regional publications on towns in New England next to Melville and Emerson and Hawthorne.

West patted the volumes fondly. "As you can see, this is the place where I pursue my, well, my *American studies*. The organization is somewhat chaotic, as you see, but I am sure that to a scholar like yourself this will appear in the proper light," he said. I was not at all sure what the proper light was, or what made me a scholar, besides having attended college. Left to himself in this house, poring over old books, he had acquired the autodidact's insecurity about the academic world. He spoke with assurance, but beneath the surface, I felt, there was an undercurrent, a sunless place where he drifted, watching himself and aware that there was in his talk something ineffectual and pathetic. So his self-awareness had a bitter edge, almost imperceptible, lingering in his pauses and intonations like the faint acrid smell of something long ago burned.

"I find that to study my own family, my own inheritance, is to study in miniature the history of the nation," he was saying. "The *Mayflower* brought the people who made America, and America in turn made the Wests. I have researched many of the individuals on that family tree, the illustrious and the humble both, and catalogued the accomplishments of each—for posterity if not for publication. Future generations of Wests will have that to consult. They will be informed about their history. I hope that they, too, will be proud of it."

I opened my mouth, but was saved from making a polite reply by the sound of quick feet coming down the stairs.

West and I walked back, past the *Mayflower* shrine, to the front entryway. At the foot of the stairs, a girl in her teens was putting on shoes while Charlotte West stood by. The girl looked up, and then stood up, brushing off her skirt.

"My daughter Eleanor," West said. "Ellie, let me introduce Kese. He is spending the summer down the road with Mr. Hardt."

We said our tepid hellos. She resembled her mother only slightly. She had shoulder-length hair, dull brown in color although from the look of it expensively cut, and was dressed for going out. Her eyes were lazy and her face was open and uncomplicated—young, you might say, but it was hard to believe that that face would ever have either the hauteur or the unsettling appeal of her mother's. Ellie did not linger but grabbed a purse she had hooked over the banister and headed out and down the brick walk, followed not long after by sounds of a car starting and driving away. I was thinking that it was time for me to be going, too, and envied her swift and efficient escape.

"We shall lose her soon," West said. "Ellie has just graduated from high school, and now her last summer before college is upon us. I am afraid that there is little entertainment for young people here. Ice cream stands. The beach. What else I don't know. But it will be hard to see her go." He looked helplessly at his wife—an appeal, it seemed, to share his sense of their impending loss—but her face remained tight and impassive.

Without noticing that I had been drinking it, I had finished the scotch, and was feeling bolder and blurrier than usual. Bold enough to speak directly to Charlotte West.

"Mrs. West," I said. Again, her eyes widened slightly. Her manner was detached but those dark eyes seemed expectant, alert, suddenly—or as if an alertness that was always there was being brought to bear on me. "That family tree. I guess the West family has been gathering and keeping that information forever, but what about your family? Don't you want someone to tell your story?"

West put his arm around her shoulders, but instead of leaning toward him, she seemed somehow to retreat into herself, to become more still and solid. I noticed for the first time how tall she was, how nearly the same height they were. "My dear, as you know, as I have said—I would be happy to do the research—if you wanted—"

She smiled, a curious twist of the mouth, not looking at me but looking in my direction. "No, Franklin." It was quietly said, but the *no* was definite and absolute. "Your family is the one with the history. There's no point in framing my family and hanging it on a wall. No one would be interested in that."

4.

I made the walk back beneath the murmuring trees, making a game of not using the flashlight and so stumbling more often, to find on my return that the light in the kitchen was out, the old man apparently gone to bed.

I walked up the six wooden steps and the brief path that led to the back of the garage. There was a terraced hill in back of the house and the garage was built into it, so that cars were parked on the same level as the house, but by walking up the steps you came level with the apartment above, its door on the back side. Behind that was another low stone wall, and beyond it a sparse woods, perceptible in the dark only as a deeper looming.

I turned a light switch in the small apartment—one room, the ceilings sloping down on either side, and in the front a small alcove with a window facing the driveway, the bathroom door on its left. The room was neat but musty, the smell of mildew everywhere and mottled gray patches low down on the walls and behind the towel bar in the bathroom. I think I was disappointed, somehow, in the absence of luxury here. Without actually having any idea what to expect, I had in fact been expecting—what? Something more grand than the world I had grown up in. Some hint, I guess, of the better life that my father always seemed to feel he had been robbed of when his own father cut all ties to the family money. So this is it, I thought, running my fingers over one of the rough, thin towels laid out on a chair. When I pressed it to my face it smelled faintly sour.

A narrow bed was built in on one side under the slanted roof, and the room showed evidence of boarders or relatives who had stayed there in the past. There were bookshelves lining the walls, a dresser and a small table. My bag was on the floor, clothes strewn around it where I had changed hastily earlier in the evening.

I was thinking about the Wests while I brushed my teeth and undressed. Strange that they had offered themselves—well, that Frank West had—as contacts or companions. Maybe it was a sincere gesture, but more likely it was a rare opportunity for him to show off his family tree and his sacred piece of rotted wood. A piece of the ship itself. That strange half-religious belief that history lives on in objects and that you can commune with the spirit of Robert E. Lee by looking at a pair of spurs he once wore. George Washington slept here. Or maybe it was even simpler than that and he had invited me out of bored curiosity: the desire to see the new person, to break the unchanging procession of dull days and make the old things seem bright again by trotting them out for the new-minted acquaintance before his newness is all sucked away and he, too, is dull and spent.

Which I was. Turning out the light, I went to the bed and then fumbled with the sheet, unable for some reason to find the corner of the sheet in the darkness, the thing that would orient, give me my bearings as I prepared to enter sleep. Finally I gave up and climbed onto the bed. Lying there in the darkened room with the ineradicable smell of mildew and the frogs and crickets loud outside, I thought finally, drifting off, of Charlotte West, beautiful and strange, standing in the shadows and watching me with an expression on her face that I could not read.

5.

I woke to a pounding.

A dull measured crashing, like the work of some powerful machine, was shaking the whole room. Heart beating fast and shallow, I jumped up and cracked my head against the low slanted ceiling above me. I dropped and buried my face in the pillow, too barely conscious to even feel the insult of the pain. Sunlight filled the windows, shone through the skimpy flyspecked curtains, and all the bright cheer of the waking day seemed to be mocking me as I lay there, unwilling to move again.

The crashing stopped briefly, then began again, with a persistent rhythm. One Two Three Four. One Two Three Four. I hauled myself up, pulled on a pair of shorts and stumbled out and down the steps, around to the front of the garage, squinting and groggy in the morning sunlight. The old man was standing in the open garage, next to the car, powerful torso and skinny legs, holding the sturdy wooden broom with which he had been bashing at the low ceiling of the garage. Dislodged bits of flotsam lay scattered on the concrete. He looked irritated, but I felt immediately certain that he was enjoying himself. He held up a set of car keys. "All right," he said. "Get some shoes on. Time to go to work."

I went back up to put on shoes and a shirt, feeling grimy and unshowered. We climbed into his big old Range Rover and I took us down the driveway. He stopped me at the entrance to the main road, leaned out the window and pulled two newspapers from their plastic holsters beside the mailbox, and pointed left. I drove on, squinting against the morning sun, while he directed me along the winding roads, and it occurred to me that until my arrival he must have been driving himself around with his bad eyes.

We stopped again at the post office and he got out to fetch the mail from his P.O. box inside; out of some unknown paranoia, he had never had it delivered to the house. This daily ritual of the old man's must have been how he had run into Franklin West. I waited in the humming car in the parking lot, shading my eyes, sun streaming through the windows, watching tiny old women extricate themselves from huge cars and then go shuffling into the building, younger men and women, in entitled middle age and preppy clothes, holding the doors for them.

Frederick climbed back into the passenger seat with a bundle of mail and said, "All right. Let's get something to eat."

Five minutes later we were opening the door of the local diner, the kind of place that has vinyl-upholstered booths and a counter with swiveling wooden-backed stools in a row. A stocky man with dark hair and an olive complexion came smiling to meet us. "Mr. Hardt," he said. The man's accent, Greek maybe, caught on the syllable and pulled it down deep into his throat. "Good to see you again." He gave me a meaningless wink and a grin, saw us settled at a booth, and moved smoothly away. A waitress appeared with menus and I ordered French toast and coffee. I didn't drink coffee, but it seemed like a good day to start.

Waitresses in checked uniforms maneuvered among the tables, angling hips and elbows with brisk grace as they moved by. A man wearing a bandana and an apron, ensconced in the hiss and smoke of a grill, was visible through the long slot in the wall where order slips sat in a row and hot dishes cooled. Only half of the tables were occupied and few of the patrons were young—I was getting used to being the youngest person in any room—but the constant clatter of silverware and murmur of voices gave a musical hum to the breakfast hour.

The old man pulled an ashtray in front of him, tapped a cigarette on the table briskly, and lit it, the disposable lighter looking small and incongruous in his thick fingers. He leaned back and breathed out the smoke, a sigh. "So," he said. "What did you think of Franklin West?"

"He quoted T.S. Eliot to me."

"That fucking idiot," he said, without heat. "That guy is always saying he needs to *educate* me to some goddamn thing or other. He tells me he's going to educate me to Faulkner, he's going to educate me to Melville. Christ."

He smoked, meditating. "T.S. Eliot," he said with contempt. "You like him?" He didn't wait for an answer. "I bet you don't know he was born the same year as Raymond Chandler. Huh? Now that was a goddamn writer. Not like these idiot mystery books they write now where every book has a fruit in the title or some fucking thing and a new one comes out every year. *A Peach of a Murder. Murder Goes Bananas.* It's drivel, is what it is. Drivel for idiot housewives."

I was on the lookout for my French toast.

"Is that what you want me to read to you, Raymond Chandler?"

He took a drag, exhaled, smoke rising and taking shape in the slanted sunlight. "It's an idea. Sure. It'd be an education for you."

The breakfast arrived and we ate a while in silence, me wincing slightly at the bitterness of the coffee, adding milk. I said, "Did you ever try listening to audio books?"

He put down his coffee cup. "Those books on tape. Yeah. Didn't like them." He paused, leaned back away from his eggs. "You'll be reading the newspapers, too. I want to know what's going on in the world. Plus local stuff. The real estate. What's going on with that big thing the Pequots have got going."

"The Pequots?" I said.

"Indian tribe, local. Out past New London. They've got a big new casino. You'll be reading about it in the papers. What did you make of that wife of his?"

"What?"

"The wife. That Charlotte West."

"Oh," I said. I had the feeling that I needed to answer very carefully, as if I had a secret that I was hiding. I was blushing already at the mention of her name. "She didn't say much. She seemed—I don't know. Proud, maybe?"

He snorted, but it sounded like agreement. "Sure. She's got a lot more to be proud about than that idiot husband, but I guess she knew what she was doing when she married him. She got a lot of people riled up when she first came here. When they got married, too. Everyone gossiping about her but no one having any clue what they were gossiping about, everyone just riled up because a woman comes into town acting like she owns it, and they don't like that. Don't like her because she gets them all hot and bothered, don't like her because she marries a rich respectable Asshole Born and Bred. They don't like her because she makes everyone else look like pale window dressing and because the fact is that, deep down, they really like the goddamn way that not liking her makes them feel. People hate everything that's got a little life to it. They're just waiting for it to burn itself out. That way they can keep on feeling smug. Of course I could never stand to be around her much; she's a goddamn piece of work. But she really tweaks my balls, you know?"

I had my mouth open, but before I could grope my way back to a question, there was a bustle of activity in the front of the restaurant. A man had come in and pushed up to the counter, planted both hands there. He wasn't old, but his clothes were old-fashioned, out of date. He was dressed in a tan-colored suit, a white shirt in a faded print showing at the collar and wrists, and a fedora hat, the kind that everybody wore in forties movies. He spoke loudly, addressing himself to the man behind the counter or to anyone else who might be listening. "Hey, you there, do you know Eddie Slope? You know where I could find him?"

The man at the counter, the one who had seated us, leaned forward and spoke to him, looking around uncertainly. They talked for a moment in lower voices, there were gestures and headshaking. The newcomer stood back from the counter, took a quick confused look around at the tables, pushed his hat back on his head, and walked out again.

As soon as the door had closed behind him, the dark-haired man at the counter looked around, smiled, and shrugged. He caught Frederick's eye and wobbled his head back and forth comically: *crazy*. The noise in the place had died down—people hadn't been staring, exactly, but their politeness had not prevented them from focusing their attention toward the counter in front—and now it rose again, the conversations somewhat louder. I turned back to the old man, who stared past me, eyebrows raised in thought.

"Eddie Slope," he said. "Jesus Christ, I haven't heard that name in twenty years. He died in a car accident out on the Post Road, that long ago."

6.

There was a steady routine to the days, an old man's routine. We would get in the car, pick up the papers at the bottom of the driveway, get the mail at the post office, have breakfast. Then we would come back to the house, sit at the kitchen table and go through the newspapers. First I would read out the headlines. If Frederick was interested enough, I would read the story while he sat back, considering, sometimes chewing thoughtfully on a pill from one of his several prescription bottles. The stories he most often wanted to hear were the ones that allowed him to pass scathing judgment on the people involved. All were brought to the bench and given a tongue-lashing by the justice. *Fucking idiots. Jesus, the garbage people say. Ignorant bastards.*

Then we would move on to the real estate section, to which he gave careful attention, listening closely and often taking the paper and holding it close to his face, raising the dark glasses to reveal intent rheumy eyes. He kept close watch over which houses were on the market, how much they were listed for, who was selling and which agent was offering. Sometimes later in the day we would drive by the properties that were selling and look at them from the road. I came to dread these real-estate reconnaissance trips, driving the endless miles of back road which felt to me like one incessant tedious maze of twisting asphalt, while around us the landscape was always the same, the acres of forested swells, dotted here and there with huge boulders mottled over with green mosses.

My vague plan for the future was to work as a reporter, so even in college I had read the newspaper every day. But with nothing else competing for my time, I was now paying attention to the news in a way I never had before. There was an earthquake in Japan, conflict with Iraq, and the Unabomber had tried to blow up a professor at Yale. There was the woman who had taken a knife and cut her abusive husband's penis off, after which she drove away and flung it out the car window. The old man couldn't get enough of that story, which inspired him to flights of comic dismay. Sometimes out of the blue he would look wistfully off into the distance. "John Wayne," he would say, shaking his head. "His name had to be John Wayne. Jesus, it's better than the movies."

There were local stories as well, quite a few of them about the Indian casino that the old man had mentioned. It had opened as a bingo parlor a few years before but was now expanding into a Las Vegas-scale palace in the heart of the Connecticut countryside that took in an endless flow of gamblers. Local residents were concerned about what they considered the garishness of the casino itself, and also about the remora accumulations of crass commercialism that, they feared, would gather around the great beast, the neon signs and chain restaurants and the overnight mansions that newly wealthy tribal members were now in a position to build. It was easy to see where the concern would come from, since the main street here contained not a single business that advertised itself as such. There must have been strict regulations about signage, and quaintness preservation groups. So now the Indians, displaced for centuries so that white people could populate the land and make money, were encroaching on the dream of purity that white people's money dreams when it becomes old enough to call itself taste. Plenty of entertainment value for the old man there, too.

"Here's one, Frederick," I said, opening the paper one morning. "That real-estate guy, Donald Trump. He went on the radio saying the Pequots aren't real Indians. Says he's more of an Indian than they are. The radio host got into it, too. Sounds like he thinks the Indians are too black or something. Does that make any sense?"

He squinted at the article. "Donald Trump. Fuck him. Worried about the casino competition. Real estate developers, Jesus."

For lunch we ate sandwiches, and in the afternoons he would often nap, leaving me an hour free—but no matter how tired, I could not bring myself to take a nap and thus surrender completely to the septuagenarian rhythm of the days.

In the evening we would eat while watching the news on television, Frederick sitting a foot from the screen. Afterwards sometimes we would watch a movie rented from the local video store, but more often I read to him.

We had started with *The Big Sleep*. Between the kitchen door leading outside and the steps leading up to my garage apartment there was a paved patio with a few lawn chairs, and on that first night I sat down there in the fading light, opened the old paperback and began to read about Philip Marlowe and Los Angeles and General Sternwood among the hothouse orchids. I read and slapped at mosquitoes around my ankles, while the old man sat by and smoked or lifted weights on a barbell, huffing out his thick chest in the New England dusk.

I understood early on that my job was not really or not only to be a reader, that I was something more like a paid companion. I could be used to run errands or to take notes on Frederick's stock purchases, but I was also there to drive lazily around on a summer afternoon, or to be available to be talked at, or to discuss a plot point during *The Wild One*.

So, yes, I was bored. In my free time during the day I would sometimes drive into town, which was not much of a change, but at least I could choose my own directions and stop and walk around wherever I wanted to.

It was there that I saw Charlotte West one day, walking on the street. I was on the other side and she did not see me. She looked straight ahead and moved with unswerving and unhurried purpose, elegant in her dark clothes, composed despite the wiltingly humid afternoon. I watched as she passed two women in white tennis dresses who were walking the other way, not slowing down as they acknowledged each other in passing but not seeming to hurry either, with that imperious air that seemed to be simply a part of her, a product of birth and breeding. Afterwards the two women in white put their heads together in gossipy collusion and I was struck by the contrast between them and her, thinking that if they disliked her—as the old man had suggested that many people did—I could understand their envy. Common ducks ruffled by the passage of a dark swan, spinning in her wake.

When I looked back down the street for her, she was gone.

7.

That night I found myself standing outside the West house, looking in.

Most nights, after the old man had gone to bed, I would lie in bed and read or stare at the ceiling, listening to my old Walkman. The little room above the garage must have been cleaned from time to time—otherwise it would have been all dust and cobwebs by now. Over the years guests and relatives had come through and left belongings behind, and the room had served, too, as a storage area for things that were not needed but that were not yet junk. It had become an apartment furnished with the random secondhand, the things once wanted and now forgotten, and I suspected that Frederick had not even been in the room in the years since his wife had died.

There were the books on the shelves, record albums. There was a collection of board games in boxes that were falling apart, stacks of magazines telling the news of other decades, a Rubik's Cube that would not turn and remained unsolved, a snow globe sitting by the bedside on top of a deck of Bicycle cards, a flyspecked box of poker chips tucked away on a slanting shelf under one of the eaves.

But that night I was too hot and too restless to take any interest in my odd little apartment. I paced the room, damp with sweat, not seeing anything. Instead I gazed at the image, still strong in my mind's eye, of Charlotte West walking down the main street in town that afternoon. Watching her walk past, so self-contained and so serenely unaware that I was watching her. The more I dwelled on the memory, the more I wanted to see her that way again. Then I stopped pacing. Stopped suddenly in the middle of the carpet, closed my eyes, wiped the sweat from my face, and stood there with my forehead pressed hard into my palm.

"Shit," I said aloud. I couldn't pretend anymore that I didn't know what I was going to do.

I took up my flashlight and went out the door, quietly closing the screen behind me.

There was no breeze and the muggy night was stifling, but it was a liberation just to be out in the dark, the night, with its million unseen speaking creatures. I stepped up and over the low stone wall and walked away from the house, into the woods behind. A sickle blade of moon turned tree limbs high up into faint shadows against the sky, but at ground level the darkness was profound, and I felt my way ahead carefully. Vines and roots tripped me and I could feel an occasional raking branch or a clump of burrs catching at my clothes, but for the most part the going was surprisingly easy. The trees were spaced far enough apart that it was not hard to weave among them. It felt as if I was actually following a woodland path. I used the flashlight sparingly and moved slowly because I knew that there would be another house somewhere to my right as I went forward and I was listening closely for any sound of dogs.

None reached me, and I had seen no sign that the Wests had any pets. Working by instinct and guesswork, I veered to the right in a long arc and eventually found the trees thinning as the back of the West house became visible in dim outline, pale windows looming out of darkness.

I moved out of the woods and crept quietly through the back-yard, keeping in shadow and watching the windows, wondering which one Charlotte West was most likely to appear at. I stood for long minutes in the darkness among the sounds of the wood-ed night, feeling foolish but also unable to leave, gazing up at the lit windows on the second story. An occasional shadow moved across the walls or corners, but no human figure showed itself. The mystery of inside and outside. Inside the inhabitants were passing somehow another evening. Outside I stood in darkness, the lawn around the house a solemn clearing and the vast sur-rounding forest a frame for this tableau of uncertain meaning.

I went back several more times over the course of the next few weeks, compelled by the ritual of retracing my path through the woods, the shallow-breathing moments standing and watching. Looking at the house, moving discreetly from place to place at the edge of the lawn to see the different sides, different windows, I saw, without truly noticing, how completely separated the three members of the household were. Often the daughter was not there at all, but even when she was, there would be three lights at three different windows in the large house, the lights spaced as if to create maximum distance. No voices carrying through the still summer night, no laughter, no visible activity, each of the three isolated, held together only by the confines of the house, a steep-gabled shadow against the sky.

But I was too completely caught up in my own intense and baffled fascination to feel the sadness of that household, too profoundly pulled and held there to notice anything beyond the pleasure and shame of being there watching. What did I want?

Once Charlotte West did appear at a tall, thin window, silhouetted there just long enough to close it against an unusually cool evening, and I felt my pulse racing. But mostly I was content to be soothed by the approach, the being there, the closeness to her, the momentary reprieve from days and nights governed by a routine that was not my own and that was already pressing toward me again, only a brief night's sleep hovering between me and the next round of papers, mail, breakfast, papers, mail, breakfast, papers, mail, breakfast.

8.

It was after breakfast one day that I met Duke.

The sun was anemic behind muggy walls of cloud when the old man and I stepped out of the garage, leaving the big old engine radiating heat behind us. I tucked the papers under my arm and shaded my eyes, squinting out at the lawn, where a figure in dark clothes was doing something to one of the hedges.

"Who's that?"

The old man adjusted his baseball cap and craned his neck forward. "That's Duke," he said, as if only a fool would have to ask. "Why don't you go and introduce yourself. You might learn a thing or two." He took the papers from me and headed toward the house, and I walked down the easy slope of the lawn.

As I approached, the man lowered the large hedge clippers he had been wielding and nodded a hello. He was my height, about six feet, wearing a black T-shirt and jeans that were permanently stained by grass and dirt. He had close-cropped reddish hair, slightly receded, with what looked like a permanent stubble of the same color and length on his face, a prominent and slightly squashed nose in an appealing face, and if anyone had asked I would have guessed he was in his late thirties.

We said hello, a little stiffly. "So it's Duke?" I said. "Were your parents John Wayne fans?"

He didn't smile but didn't seem bothered, either. "Can't say they were. Or are. The full name is Deucalion," he said. "Deucalion Emmett. But Duke's easier to say." He put aside his clippers, took a case out of his back pocket and removed a thin hand-rolled cigarette, then squatted down and lit it, squinting. I raised my eyebrows, recognizing the sweet smell of pot. He held it toward me, a question. I waved off the offer, but, feeling awkward at our height difference, sat down on the grass.

He took a drag, paused for the exhale. "Greek name. My uncle Noah, he named me. He's kind of the black sheep of the family, belongs to the local freethinkers—sort of atheists, you know? Well, when I was born he came up with this name from somewhere, and he convinced my pop that it was a name from the Bible. My pop, he swears by the Bible, you know—he swears by it, but he doesn't exactly *read* the Bible. So Uncle Noah pulled a fast one on him, and I don't know if he ever figured out the truth, but even if he didn't, I think he regretted it. He thinks I'm too much like Noah, not enough like him. Which is fine by me."

I ran my hand idly through the grass, considering. "Does the name mean something?"

"Maybe all it means is the joke's on my pop. Which means that I'm the joke, I guess. I'm sort of a case of mistaken identity. The rest of my family, they don't like me much and I don't like them much. Don't see them if I can help it, except for Noah. Didn't go into the family business like my brothers. Car repair shop."

"So you—do this instead?" I asked.

"I keep the lawns looking good, keep the trees trimmed and the bushes and grass from taking over. 'Course I do indoor work, too, drywall, painting, whatever. But mostly I like working outside. I've been working for Frederick, and for his wife when she was alive, for a while now. Going on ten years, maybe. I guess I'm not too ambitious. Looks like maybe you're not, either."

That caught me off guard, and I felt hot as I said, "What makes you say that? My *ambition* is to be an investigative reporter."

He regarded me mildly. "No offense meant. Guess I just thought it takes one to know one. And this seems like a pretty quiet spot to launch a newspaper career from. Why are you here?"

He had me there. For a moment we were silent. "I guess I wanted to see the place where my father grew up, even if I never liked him much. Family history."

Duke nodded. I guess he understood something about difficult fathers.

"Do you do any lawn work for the West family, a couple of houses down?"

Duke had been looking off down the driveway, but now turned back to me. "Sure, I know them. Nice place. Some of those trees are a bitch."

I plunged ahead. "Do you know anything about Charlotte West?"

He raised an eyebrow, paused to take a last drag. "What did you have in mind?"

"Well, Frederick said something the other day, but he doesn't—it's hard to get a straight story out of him." Duke nodded like that wasn't a surprise to him. "But I get the impression that she's not from around here, and there was something that happened when she arrived in town, some scandal or—something?"

"You could say that." He stubbed out the last bit of the joint on a rock and replaced it in the case, then stood up. "I better get back to work. Why don't you come out to the house sometime? I'm up near Uncas Lake and I usually take my Thursdays off. I don't know anything that everybody doesn't already know, but it might take a few minutes to tell." He paused. "I guess it must get pretty dull, just hanging around here reading the news to old Frederick. Might be a good idea to get out of the house, have a beer maybe. Couldn't hurt to have a couple hours off." He picked up the clippers. "Why so curious about her?"

"I don't know," I said. I did know, but I couldn't have put it into words even if I had wanted to. There was desire, yes, but that was only a part of the fascination. She had that aura of mystery around her, and there was a part of me that was always looking for a problem to work on, something to investigate. It was a quality that had made me good at schoolwork and at assignments for the college paper, although maybe not so good as a boyfriend, or even a friend, sometimes. I lived too much inside my own head, and I was much too ready to grab hold of a loose thread and pull until the weave revealed itself, even if that meant destroying the garment. And now, with no assignments or stories to write up, I was just drifting along through the aimless, slow-passing summer, listening to the gears of my thinking while they turned and turned without purpose.

"I guess it must get pretty dull," Duke said again, and went back to his work.

9.

So that Thursday afternoon I paid a visit to Duke's place.

I had asked the old man for the afternoon off and he had given me directions. "That's a guy who really knows what's what," he said, waving a cigarette in my direction while I stood with a hand on the screen door, waiting for him to finish so I could be on my way. "His whole family, they're a bunch of swampers. But Duke's all right."

So I drove on up the Neck Road, heat rising from the asphalt in steamy waves. As I got closer to the lake the woods closed in and the world became darker, cooler, greener, while the roads were rougher and less clearly marked. It didn't help that none of the street signs matched the names the old man had given me, but eventually I found the mailbox labelled "Emmett" and turned off down a gravel drive, at the end of which was a small house that looked sturdy and lived-in. It did not have a lawn, but seemed instead to stand in a clearing, as if it was continuous with the woods and would accommodate itself to them. Some neatly stacked lumber was visible in back, and a deck ran along one side of the house. On the wooden steps that led up to the front door, a cat lay stretched out, opening a languid eye as I turned off the engine and left my old hatchback parked next to a much larger and apparently very new black sedan.

But no one was home. The cat grudgingly left its sunny spot on the steps while I knocked at the door and peered in the window at an entryway with jackets, work boots, and shoes neatly hung or placed, beyond which seemed to be a kitchen, but there was no sign of life or movement. I stepped down. The clearing around the house was still except for the shufflings of birds and squirrels and another cat staring wide-eyed at me from behind a tree, ready to dash. The afternoon sun came in dappled through the gaps in the leaves and although it was still early summer there was something already, perhaps permanently, autumnal about the whole hushed scene. I walked back over to the black car next to mine and was holding my hand at the window for shade to see inside when an explosion cracked open the idyll.

A gunshot.

I ducked down on all fours between the two cars, breathing hard, adrenaline on the move, as the echo faded, followed by another shot, and then another. Dry leaves and gravel were rough against my hands. I crouched there, waiting.

After a minute or two I decided that no one was actually trying to kill me, and I gathered up the presence of mind to determine that the shots, though thunderously loud, were coming from somewhere on the other side of the house and did not seem to be getting closer or farther away.

Standing up slowly, I held my hands over my ears and moved cautiously away from the shelter of the cars. There was a pause in the shooting while I walked slowly around the front of the house and then turned to follow along the left side, keeping close to the wooden deck.

Another shot, definitely closer.

I flinched, and then, looking through the sparse trees, I could make out a figure, maybe a hundred feet away. I was disoriented by the booming shots, feeling them like rough muffled blows against my chest, but as far as I could tell the figure seemed to have its back to me.

At the next pause in the shooting I yelled out and moved closer, waving a raised hand. I shouted again, and saw the figure turn around, removing something shiny and red from its head, some kind of ear protection. It waved back at me. I walked forward, pulling myself up self-consciously from my wary crouch and walking more naturally as I picked my way among fallen branches and ground vines.

I think I had been expecting either Duke or some stereotype of a hillbilly hunter, in orange and camouflage, with a three-day beard, a sunburn, and squinting eyes. But the man who was holding out his hand to me was thirty-something, black, with a shrewd gaze and a handsome narrow face slightly creased around the eyes with the hint of an ironic disposition, a readiness to be amused. Despite the heat he was wearing a thigh-length tan jacket that was somehow both outdoorsy and stylish. The immediate impression was of a man both comfortable in his skin and careful about his way of presenting himself. "Wasn't expecting company," he said. "Or at least I wasn't expecting you. Friend of Duke's?"

I explained that I had come out on Duke's invitation.

"Kese," he said, as if committing the name to memory. "Name's Clinton. I came out to see Duke, too. But mostly just had the itch to do a little target practice, somewhere no one would be bothering me about it. Want to take a few? Happy to share, if you know how to handle one of these."

He indicated the rifle, a streamlined and expensive-looking thing.

"No, thanks," I said. "I don't like guns."

He smiled, a little roguishly. "Liberal do-gooder, is that it? Suit yourself." He did not sound like a Yankee, and in fact it was hard to detect an accent of any kind; he sounded like he could be a radio announcer. "I guess I'm done for the day, anyhow. I hope Duke shows soon, but with him you just never know."

He adjusted something on the gun and picked up his things, and together we walked around to the front of the house. Clinton sat down on the wide front steps, and I leaned against the siding; there was something about him that invited social ease, if not intimacy, so I asked how he knew Duke. He leaned back against the front door and looked at me as if he were deciding something—or, more accurately, as if he were performing the act of deciding something.

"Duke and me," he said, "Duke and I are tribal brothers."

He said it consciously, knowing that this was going to require further explanation. I suspect that I looked skeptical, as I tried to envision Duke and Clinton joining one of those middle-aged man societies, Masons or Elks or whatever, without success.

"Tribal brothers," I said.

He plucked a piece of grass and rolled it between his fingers. "You've heard of the Pequots, one of the local Indian tribes?"

"The casino," I said. "I've been reading about it in the papers. A big casino on a small reservation, making lots of money."

"Right. So all right, let me give you a little history," he said, leaning forward again with his eyes in the middle distance, getting ready to tell a tale. "You ever drive anywhere in this country, ever look at a map? You've probably noticed that every damn river or town or rock has got an Indian name. Connecticut. Massachusetts. That little lake over that way?" He pointed back behind the house. "Named after Uncas, he was a Mohegan warrior chief. All those Indian names hanging on out there like ghosts on the landscape. Ghosts, because you just don't seem to meet a whole lot of actual living Indians, do you? I sure never did, or when I did I didn't know it.

I was beginning to feel like this was a spiel that Clinton had been working on, like he was trying it out on me. But I didn't have anywhere to be just then, so I settled myself on the steps next to him while he talked.

"There were lots of tribes in Connecticut when the ships started arriving. The *Mayflower*, the other ships. The white folks' settlements get started, get bigger. Doesn't take many years before the real conflict starts. Complaints, skirmishes. Battles.

"For the Pequots, the big one was in 1637. A couple years earlier they'd had a smallpox epidemic, I figure you can guess how that happened, so there were already a lot fewer of them to fight the English soldiers, plus there was that Mohegan dude, Uncas. He had a grudge against the Pequots, so he came in with a bunch of Indian fighters to help the whites. The campaign goes their way, big win for the English, they celebrate by setting fire to the Pequot village, hundreds of people burned to death.

"The Pequots fought a little bit with the colonists, off and on, for a few more decades, but mainly it's just a pretty sad story for the next three hundred years. The whites don't let the Indians use the sea coast for catching fish anymore, keep them up on their landlocked reservation in the swamp. On the res, everybody's poor. Trapped. So the population keeps going down, and so the state makes the reservation smaller and smaller, and—I mean, can you imagine being a young man, your age, wants to make his way in the world, faced every day with all that shame and inertia and no chance of seeing that it'll ever be any different? So by the time we get to, say, twenty years ago or so, the reservation is about a tenth of what it was and the population is about, oh, *one*—depending on how you count it. Mostly it's just this one old lady. Looking like zero isn't far away.

"Then this young guy, the grandson of the old lady, after she dies he gets the idea to make something out of the reservation. Guess he went through the old rhyme, like, doctor, lawyer, got to Indian chief and decided that was his best bet for a career.

"He moves himself and some family to the res, trying to keep the tribe alive, gets lawyers working on it—and the lawyers have some ideas, too. The last twenty years or so some Indian capitalists have found useful little loopholes that they can squeeze some money through.

"That's how the casino got started. And it's not in some Nowhere, North Dakota, it's right here where all the people are. Practically spitting distance of New York and New Jersey. It's doing huge business. All of a sudden you've got a very rich, very small Indian tribe, which means that *anyone* who thinks they've got a Pequot great-grandma is knocking on the door wearing a feathered headband and trying to look like Sal Mineo."

I opened my mouth to ask a question, but he held up a hand.

"White guy. He played Indians a couple times in the movies. See, the thing is that there isn't a single full-blooded Pequot anywhere anymore. Even the new leaders of the tribe *might* be able to claim they're one eighth if they monkey around with the family tree just right. So to keep the whole business more or less fair, anyone who can prove they've got a fraction of Pequot blood can claim membership. A whole new kind of one-drop rule, except that this time you get a handsome salary instead of a whipping. And that's where I come in. Or did, just about a year and a half ago."

He finally paused. Speech over, time for questions from the audience. "So you're part Pequot." He nodded. I was still trying to place that flat accent he had. "Have you always lived around here?"

"No, never. Not until recently. Born and raised in Michigan. I was working in a paper mill, but can't say I ever had any love for the work. This was a better deal no matter how you looked at it. And if you're wondering, which you are and no shame in it, the answer is yes, there are quite a few black Indians."

"Or—black people with a fraction of Indian blood," I said.

Clinton was unfazed. "What's a black person? What I'm telling you is that it's not that simple. Racism, strange bedfellows. Over the years, as those Pequots filtered out of the reservation, a lot of them wound up in black neighborhoods, lots of times because they weren't welcome among white folks. Not that you could convince some of the other tribal members that we're all, you know, people of color. Who would have thought that you'd have to be white to be an Indian?" He spread his hands, miming exasperation. "So, yeah, there's some racial tension there. I say, give it some time, we'll get past it. It's just going to have to be a little melting pot of our own."

"So does that mean you're a wealthy man now?"

He smiled. "Yes, indeed. At this rate there's definitely going to be some Indian millionaires around here. I plan to be one of them." He looked me up and down. "Did you ever read *Moby Dick*?" he asked.

"Yes, for a class a couple of years ago."

"Never finished it, myself. But I know the gist. Captain Ahab out on a boat, hunting down a big white whale that took his leg off. Story's told by a guy on the ship who doesn't do much himself, mostly just watches and listens."

"That sounds like the one I read."

"And do you remember the name of the whaling boat? The

Pequod. Old Melville named it after our little tribe." He lifted his rifle from where it leaned beside him and squinted, pretending to aim it at my car. "Look out, white whale! Here comes the little *Pequod* with a big harpoon. Here it comes. Boom!" He lowered the rifle, turned to me. "Thing is, it turns out that white whale is a big piñata, full of money. Prick it with a harpoon and the dollars all come bursting out and you just grab all you can."

He pulled out a thick shiny leather wallet and laid it on the wooden step, fanning out a large sheaf of twenties, so many it seemed absurd to carry them that way at all. I whistled.

"If you're going to have all that cash on you, wouldn't it make more sense to carry fifties or hundreds?"

He looked at the bills, bemused, and picked one out to display the whole front face, the numbers and patterns and symbols, the portrait of the man in the center done in tiny layered pop-art lines, his skin that eternal sickly green. "I like carrying twenties. Call it a symbol. Andrew Jackson, the great Indian-hater, and now he has to watch, totally helpless—horrified, I hope—getting passed across drugstore counters and real estate desks, while we use him to buy back some of what he thought he was taking from the Indians forever all those years ago."

We both looked up at the sound of unhurried tires on the gravel drive. A battered old pickup truck drove up and parked alongside the two cars. Duke emerged with a bag of groceries and regarded us for a moment, the two of us sitting on the front steps, Clinton still resting a hand on his rifle, holding the splay of twenties in the other.

Duke gave us a look like *what did I miss here?* But all he said was, "Door's not locked."

10.

Before doing anything else upon his return, Duke had picked up two large battered metal dishes that lay in the grass near the house and filled one with water, the other with cat food. There had been a rustling and then in moments the plate of food was swarmed with feral cats, black and white and mottled and tabby, silently tucking in.

In the kitchen, too, there were smaller dishes on the floor. The cat that had been lying on the steps when I arrived was lapping water.

"Any given time, there's one or two of them that give up the wild life and come inside to live here," Duke said, taking three bottles of beer from his bag of groceries and setting them out for us. "There's just the one here at the moment. Her name's Mutt."

"Lovely feminine name," Clinton remarked.

"She hasn't complained yet." Duke reached over and tweaked her tail. "She's got six toes on both her front paws. Seems like a lot of the local cats do."

I crouched down and picked the cat up. She purred in an exploratory way and then watched as I examined one of her six-fingered paws, pushing under the soft tame pads to splay out the claws hidden there. "A six-fingered cat. She's the opposite of Frederick," I said. "Duke, have you ever asked him how he lost his finger?"

Duke was watching the cat in an absent way. "That middle finger? I heard once that he showed it to the wrong guy when they were having an argument about something, guy chopped it off with a hatchet. But of course I always thought Frederick had more sense than to get in an argument with someone holding a hatchet, so who knows."

"Maybe his wife was like that woman down in Virginia," Clinton suggested. "Mistook that finger for his, ah, *member*, cut the thing off and threw it in the woods."

"I didn't think things like that happened in New England," I said.

"Lots of things happen here that can't."

"I guess you came to hear about a couple of them," Duke said to me.

Clinton smiled. "He's been hearing about a few already."

"Aw, Clint. Don't tell me you've been giving him the whole history of the Connecticut Indians." Duke rolled his eyes over to me. "He's been learning all that like he was cramming for a Pequot citizenship exam this whole last year or so. Soon he's going to be giving speeches."

"Duke, just because you've lived here all your life and this is all old news to you, have a little patience for those of us who are playing catch-up." Duke snorted. Clinton appealed to me: "Do you know that Duke here does yardwork for three different families that can trace themselves all the way back to the *Mayflower*, no less? He's deep into this place. Could probably be an honorary member of the Daughters of the American Revolution and all that."

Duke leaned back unperturbed, smiling with one corner of his mouth. "Funny thing is, these days it turns out there's a lot more money in Pequot blood than there is in Mayflower blood."

"Two ships doing battle on the high seas," I suggested.

Clinton broke into a grin, reaching over to clink his bottle against mine. "The kid learns fast," he said.

"So you're part Indian, too?" I asked Duke, trying not to make the question sound incredulous. With his red stubble and slightly ruddy complexion, which surely had never even seen a suntan, it was hard to imagine. I found, too, that I was looking around the modest little bachelor house for any sign of hidden riches. Although it was neat and clean, nothing in it looked as if it had been purchased in the last decade except for the groceries in their bag on the faded countertop.

He nodded. "My mom's side."

"There are plenty of white-looking Pequots in the tribe," Clinton added, "but even so, no one is as white as the Paleface Indian here. He's a whole different kind of red man." Then he seemed to catch my other thought as well. "I sometimes wonder how many of those folks he works for know that they've got a millionaire handyman lawn boy."

"You've got to appreciate the way Clint has with words," Duke said to me. "He's going to be a big man in tribal politics one of these days."

Clinton considered it, rubbing at the loose corner of the label on his bottle. "Maybe," he said. He looked like he might say more, but didn't.

We sat in silence for a moment, and then Clinton finished the last of his beer and stood up. "Time I was on my way, and it seems like you two still have some business. Nice to meet you, Kese. So long, Paleface." He shook both our hands and headed out the door. After a minute the car outside hummed to life and went crunching down the drive, leaving us at the table in silence and an afternoon sunlight that shifted with the movement of the leaves outside.

Duke got up and fetched a joint from the cabinet above the refrigerator, then sat down and lit it. I waved away his offer again. He tipped one of his shoes off onto the floor and used it as an ashtray, the cat padding over to sniff at it with interest. "Well," he said, "I know you came by because you were curious about Mrs. West, so I'll try to tell you what I can. But like I said, what I know is just what everybody already knows."

11.

In fact, no one knew how or even when Charlotte Lenoir had arrived in town. Certainly Duke did not know, sitting there telling it in the faded kitchen with the smoke lightly curling toward the ceiling and the cat settled next to him in an empty chair. He told it, but it was not his story. It was the story that everyone knows, still unfinished, taking shape between us in the smoky air, still being made, and made as much by my own intent listening as by Duke's telling.

No one knew. She appeared there as a mystery woman, a walking paradox, seeming to come from nowhere and yet displaying a pride and determination that could only have been hardened in the heat of some memorable past. No one saw her arrive, or if they did they did not remark or remember the date and time. Nonetheless, she did arrive, and she must have had an idea of some sort, even if it was not a plan exactly, and it began with the women, apparently. Because by the time anyone knew she was there, she was already living with Mary Woodhouse.

How that happened was another mystery. Maybe they had just been brought together by some fate or force that pulled like to seeming like: two women, both of them young and both alone. But the similarity ended there. Mary belonged to a family as old and respectable as any in town—and so, her father used to say, as any in America. Her growing up as an only child in a large white secluded house had been idyllic, but also lonely. She was a pleasant, dreamy girl who was seen at church with her parents on Sundays and said hello to everyone in her shy abstracted way and did charity work and had beaux, dates, of course, from time to time but nothing serious, not yet, even into her twenties, and then one day her parents died in a car accident.

At twenty-four she was living in the house that she had always lived in, taking sympathetic calls from neighbors and acquaintances that came less and less frequently, and going each Sunday to hear the sermon at the Congregational church. When she was at home by herself, when there were no visitors to talk quietly with her, who knows what she did, whether she stood at sunlit windows watching shadows dapple the lawn, or did work with her hands, or watched daytime television shows, or roamed the house exploring the secrets of her parents' lives—whatever they might have been, whatever might be left of them.

Then one day she was not alone. The consciousness must have come slowly to the town that fall, because Charlotte did not accompany Mary on her weekly churchgoing or her other errands, and Mary never mentioned her visitor in her brief encounters with people when she was out. As always, more often than not she just nodded silently or exchanged a brief greeting before moving on.

But eventually people began to know that the two women were living together, the young woman they had always known, however imperfectly, the child of parents they had known, and the other one, the stranger with her French name and her disagreeable ways. She did not appear often in town, and when she did, she did not go out of her way to be friendly. Well, people were used to that. They were not effusive themselves. But Charlotte Lenoir was different. She had no deference in her. She carried herself with a fierce pride, an arrogance that was like a physical force, *like a slap right in the face*, as one woman put it, holding her hand against her cheek as if she could still feel the blow.

That pride, which had no basis at all because no one had ever heard of her or anyone connected with her before, combined with her physical beauty, was intolerable. Who did she think she was, and how had she established a household with poor Mary? Indeed, Mary herself was now the subject of an intangible but definite reconsideration on the part of the town, to whom she now appeared as either weak in the head—which would explain a few things—or as herself harboring a longstanding contempt for her apparent friends and neighbors, hidden all these years behind a veil of diffidence. Her association with Charlotte was suspect at least, perhaps even unconscionable, and the irritation people felt was aggravated by their frustration at not knowing how the strange household had come to be in the first place, how this woman had slipped under the gate unseen to turn up, unexplained, sitting too straight at their dining room table drinking their coffee, looking too good doing it, and eyeing them with her own unaccountable and unearned disapproval.

So of course there was talk, rumor. And maybe no one ever actually spoke the word *lesbian* but it was there in the talk nonetheless, a loud absence, something that could give a zingy hint of scandal to the wounded pride that everyone felt. It would account, too, for Charlotte, who seemed somehow designed to arouse all the wrong sorts of desire, so to imagine her as the seducer of weak-minded Mary provided a satisfying explanation in which all the various pieces of the mystery could be attended to, assigned meanings, and made comprehensible. So the talk went on, keeping the talkers warm through the hibernation of the New England winter, with Mary herself oblivious.

Mary must have been waiting for the spring, waiting for the first hopeful days of the year, because that March the invitations arrived, neatly handwritten with calligraphic flourishes and delivered to mailboxes all over town, for a party to be held at her house. An evening soiree that could only have as its purpose a kind of formal social introduction of the woman who had been living there at the house for the past several months. The April melting took its course, the snow receded from the lawns and the brown grasses revived, and the day of the party was warm and pleasant, the evening moving the budding branches of trees with an expectant breeze. And as darkness came on, no cars appeared in the drive and no guests came to the door.

Have you ever arranged a party, cleaned house and bought drinks and made food and changed in a hurry, choosing clothes you rarely have the chance to wear, and then, arranging coasters or putting a plate out to cool in a state of high anticipation, looked around the empty house or apartment and had the sudden awful feeling that no one would come? It must have been like that, the two women waiting there as the long minutes passed and absurd nervous fancy began to be a dreadful certainty, Mary growing more and more agitated and unhappy, Charlotte, with a drink in her hand, calm and unsurprised and absolutely still. She would have stood there, unblinking, like a gunfighter prepared to take on all comers, ready and able to defeat each foe in single combat with her quick and heatless grace, realizing now that no one would arrive and that she would wait alone on the deserted dusty street until her guns rusted away, maybe even realizing that they were the wrong weapons after all.

There must have been collusion. The women had talked among themselves and decided and convinced those who needed convincing that no one would attend this party. It must have been a close decision, you would think, propriety and xenophobia edging out curiosity and politeness, but it was made, and as dark settled on the trees only dim candles burned in the windows of Mary's house and all was quiet.

Seeing the scene this way, filling in details to round out Duke's telling, I found myself wondering, much more than how or when, *why* she had come here at all. An attractive young woman with a certain indefinable something, with a strong will and strong ambitions, however obscure their content—she should by any logic have gone to New York City to try her luck in theater or business, gone to Hollywood to force someone to discover her in a drugstore on Sunset. At the very least she should have turned true gold digger and married for millions, had a mansion built for her and lived in it like the queen of America. What could she possibly gain or achieve here? It made no sense for her to come to this sleepy corner of New England to do battle with small-town Yankee prejudices and be cut by the locals, be left alone in a darkening house with her one friend, or at least her one accomplice, to lick her wounds and consider a new strategy.

She gave up on the women, which meant giving up on Mary, too. Not long after the party, Charlotte Lenoir moved out of that house and took a room at the Crampton Inn—an expensive rustic place that I knew well from the outside since the old man and I drove past it almost every day. That Sunday, Mary did not come to the church service, but there were reports of her being seen around town or at the post office later in the week. More than once she went to the Crampton and asked for Charlotte, who apparently sent down word that she did not want to be disturbed. Mary left, they said, in tears. The next week her house was listed for sale in the real estate pages, but she was already gone, having packed up all she wanted from the house she had lived in all her life and moved away, without a word to anyone except a lawyer and a real estate agent. No one ever saw her again.

It was hard not to feel the ruthlessness of it, the sense that Charlotte Lenoir was willing to do whatever was needed to keep moving forward. There was some sort of plan or goal in mind, although it was still hard to see out of what need or desire the plan emerged, what the accomplishment of it could possibly be, from what source it was fed and nurtured. These were my questions, though—questions asked in retrospect. No one in town was actually considering any of this while it was happening, since to them she was incomprehensible, a force of nature, like bad weather that requires endurance and resistance but not explanation. Only a child or a fool asks why when storm clouds gather. And only a sad and weak-minded girl like poor Mary would open her door when the wind knocks and let the gale and the ruination blow in.

So now Charlotte had retreated, and perhaps she was even forgotten for a while. She had some money with her, apparently, but it couldn't have been much, one could somehow intuit that, and staying at the Crampton was not cheap. But she must have made the calculation before taking a room, and once she was there she must have anxiously watched the outward flow of money, counting it precisely and watching the daily leak of cash out into nowhere and economizing in every other possible way. She had some goal that she needed to achieve and to do it she needed to be there, in that place. That was what the money was for, because she knew well what her real assets were, what she had to bargain with, and knew that those too would not last forever. She finally appeared again one day in high spring, a day when there were plenty of people out on the main street doing errands that were not really important but that gave them an excuse to leave the house and feel the air and see the trees in bloom. She appeared, as picturesque as anything in nature, walking down the street on the arm of Franklin West.

She picked him out like a wolf picks out the weak sheep in the herd, knowing somehow through instinct or observation that this is the one to take. So, ruthless, yes. But trapped now, too, in the delicate dance imposed upon women, in which this wolf was forced to convince that sheep that it was really he who did the picking out. She had to appear to be the demure object of his choosing, so that the luck would appear to be all on his side. But she chose well, and when she saw her opportunity she did not hesitate, apparently, although once again no one was ever able to say for sure how they had first met.

Back then Franklin West was slowly taking over his father's shipbuilding company, although it must have been obvious even then that he was never going to be the businessman that Roger West was. The *Mayflower* connections were on Franklin's mother's side of the family, which was respectable rather than rich, but Franklin's mother had married an ambitious man with energy and business sense. Growing up blue-collar in Hartford, Roger West had emerged from the Depression as a sturdy and inventive young man who filed patents and built his company and saw it thrive during the war and the boom years that followed. Franklin was the oldest son, the designated heir of West Maritime, but although he loved the idea of the company he had no real aptitude or taste for running it. Maybe Franklin was caught up even then in daydreams of his family's past greatness, looking past the dull accounts and papers that recorded the daily movement of parts and patents and the assembly of large seafaring craft, his gaze fixed instead, already, on those famous English ancestors sailing toward the American shore.

She picked him out, because he had what she needed or wanted.

He had money, he had a name, and he was unworldly enough that the aura of disapproval that Charlotte's name carried would not reach him, or maybe her looks and the force of her focused attention were enough to provide a different sort of aura.

So she chose well. There was resistance, of course, from his mother, from her side of the family, and you would think that Franklin West would have been easily swayed, would have given Charlotte up rather than face objections from his family. It must have been his father who became an advocate for her. He would have recognized in her a force of will similar to his own, and would have had sympathy, too, for another outsider who sought to find a foothold in this family, this place. Maybe Roger West, aging and becoming anxious as he began to give over control of his company, even hoped that his son, and therefore West Maritime as well, might benefit from a partnership with someone stronger. Charlotte would have sensed that, too. She would have charmed the old man, while also perhaps showing him glimpses of the steeliness in her that she never allowed Franklin to see.

They were married in the Congregational church, of course, but discreetly. Family and a few close friends. Charlotte West and her husband moved into their house, and now the town had to accept her presence there, one way or another. She had chosen her ground, dug in her barricades, and was prepared to hold it. She wasn't much liked, she wasn't much trusted, and she did not seem to care to be. She was neither humble nor friendly. It was not as if she was flaunting her victory, her position, or her wealth, but as if all three had always been hers to begin with and required no flaunting, and anyone who thought differently could go to hell.

There it was again. The thing I couldn't figure. What victory, and what did it achieve? Why would she bother to put so much energy into the campaign if the victory was to live quietly and have a husband and raise a daughter in a small town full of colonial houses, each with a front as flat as a Yankee accent? Yet there she was.

"Of course there was some talk too about the daughter," Duke said. The joint had long since been finished, and the kitchen was shaded and cool, the ghosts who inhabited the story dissipating into air.

"The daughter. That's Ellie?" I said. "What did she do?"

"Nothing she did. Some talk about her being born out of wedlock? I never did understand that part of it. After all, this was the seventies, already, so I can't see that anyone would have been getting all riled about something like that. I guess it was just one more thing to add to the list of things to always hold against Charlotte West."

12.

I was sitting on a bench on the main street in town, looking up at the Congregational church. The bottom part of it was really just a sort of large house, I was noticing, a white house with tall pillars in front and then, like a wildly ambitious afterthought, came the steeple, clockface and all, rising from the front of the house in stages like a moon-bound rocket, the last stage tapering to a cross-tipped point. There was something strangely aggressive about that long sharp steeple, as if the building was caught undecided between humility and grandiosity, not sure whether to be a common meeting house or something more ambitious, a lightning rod, maybe, that could draw down the holy spark and purify the land.

The clock said ten minutes to six.

Before driving home, I had gone to the library, with some vague idea of finding a way to verify or flesh out Duke's story, but it was closed, so I had sat down on the bench. At first I had tried reading a few pages of *The Big Sleep*, the only book I had with me, but my mind was too full of other things, and now the paperback hung neglected in my hand, one finger holding my place.

On the drive down, clouds had begun to climb up from the tree line and now the sky was growing prematurely dark. The old man might be fuming when I got back, but I needed a moment alone before I could fit myself back into the evening's routine. I looked up at the church, thinking, this is where the wedding was held, this is where at least one of the things that Duke has been telling about happened, not in some distant or destroyed place, but here, not in the past, but here.

When you boiled it down, when you looked at it objectively, it was not an especially unusual or even interesting story, barely even a story at all. A woman came to town and nobody liked her but she got married and settled in and nothing else ever happened. It didn't even seem like a story that anyone would bother to repeat. All right, but then why was I interested in the first place, and why did I find myself here, unable to let it go?

Because of her, of course. Because I had felt since the first time I saw her that there was something there, a story to be found and told—and clearly I wasn't the only one who felt it. Maybe that was just an effect, a certain way that she had of refracting the light around her, or an illusion that I was creating for myself, that illusion of a mystery to be investigated and solved that is projected onto the object of desire because investigation is the only way we have of freeing ourselves of desire in the end. In which case I might as well stop trying to convince myself that I was not interested. I was ten or twelve paces beyond interested.

Where had she come from? I wondered, if I knew that, would it make sense of who she was now and how she had chosen to live her life? I could ask her, of course, walk up to the front door of the West house and ask, but she would have no reason to answer truthfully, no reason to answer at all, and much more reason to turn me away. And it might not explain anything at all. The past was hidden in murk, a penny glimpsed at the bottom of a muddy pool. Even when you could ask the people who were there, how could you trust them when they always had secrets to keep, images of themselves and of the world that they wanted to preserve, memories that were not their own anymore? And the objects that endured, like the church pointing blankly into the gathering dark, told you nothing about the baffling parade of human events to which they bore blind witness.

"It is reassuring, don't you think?"

I had not noticed the woman, but she was standing by my side, only a few feet away, joining me in looking up at the church with the dark clouds swelling slowly behind it. I was disoriented for a moment, because although she was standing next to the bench and I was sitting on it, she was so short that we were almost eye to eye. She remained gazing straight ahead, so that I was not sure whether she had spoken to me or only addressed herself to the evening in general.

Then she did turn to peer at me. She must have been in her seventies, one of the many older women I had been seeing around town with their dark clothes and old-fashioned handbags, their huge cars from decades past. These women seemed so much a part of the town's landscape that to be spoken to by one was unnerving, as if a stone or fire hydrant had been given voice.

"Excuse me?" I said.

She looked me over, her eyes sharp and steady behind wire-rimmed glasses.

I felt once again, as I had so many times in the past few weeks, that I was being appraised. I wondered what people saw when they looked at me this way, what I was when seen from the outside.

"The church." She seemed to speak without moving her upper lip, which gave the words a curious rhythm, both drawling and curt. "You seemed to be admiring it at some length this evening."

"I guess I was," I said. "But really I just needed something to look at."

"You have things on your mind," she said, a little deadpan. "I don't think we have met before. My name is Alice Pickett. I tell you this because I cannot bear to be called ma'am. So: Alice. Do you mind if I sit down?"

She settled herself on the weathered bench. "I will confess that it was the book that convinced me to interrupt your thoughts."

"The book?" I asked.

She tapped the forgotten paperback in my hand. "Raymond Chandler," she said. "You are interested in mysteries?"

"This is the first one I've ever read."

She looked at me closely. "Indeed?" Her expression was so skeptical—as if whatever promise she had seen in me had suddenly evaporated—that I laughed. Then I explained who I was and how I was spending my summer.

She nodded. "Yes, Frederick Hardt. Well, I must tell you that he and I have never got along much. I knew his wife, of course. We were in school together." A faint smile touched her mouth and then moved on. "Well, so you are spending your summer reading aloud to an old and rather unpleasant—don't contradict me—a rather unpleasant old person. How do you like it?"

I smiled. "Actually, the reading isn't bad at all. I like it."

She turned to stare ahead again. "It is a curious coincidence. My late husband Gregory worked for some years, after his retirement, reading books to people. He would record them for the publishers so that people could listen to them on cassette tapes. You are familiar with this sort of thing? He had a lovely speaking voice. Now that he is gone I often listen to those tapes. I have a great stack of them and I listen to them while I paint at home, not noticing what the book is or what it is about. I suppose I have listened to some of the world's great literature without noticing it, since I only listen to the voice. I remember." She paused for just a moment. "I remember sometimes, before he passed away, I would be doing something around the house, some cleaning or whatnot, and I would hear him in the shower, talking to himself. Saying who knows what, maybe rehearsing a thought, or an argument he had had with me, or someone else, the day before. Sometimes I think that is what marriage is, hearing your husband talking to himself in the shower from another room while you go about your day. The thing you never thought you would remember for longer than five minutes. So when I paint I think sometimes I forget that he is gone at all. He keeps me company on the cassette player."

There was a moment's silence. What could you say to that?

"You're a painter?" I asked, finally. "I mean, you paint pictures, not your walls?"

Her eyes focused on me sharply again. "I do paint pictures, although I am not *a painter*. But, yes, right now I am on my way to my weekly painting class—there." She gestured toward the church. "Lessons in the basement, for old people like me." She wrinkled her nose in annoyance at the word *old*. "Every Thursday I come down the street and try to learn a thing or two. Have you been inside?"

"No," I said, a little worried. I did not want a tour of the place. "I'm not—religious."

"Nor am I," she said. "No, Greg used to go sometimes, but I have never had much use for churches and I suppose I still don't. The odd thing is that in my old age I find that I have a fondness for church basements." She gave me a wry look. "A young person like yourself would not find much there that's entertaining. Although you did seem to be enjoying your contemplation of the building."

"Well, as I said," I began, and then hesitated. Alice Pickett regarded me politely, waiting. "You've lived here a long time, haven't you?" I blurted.

She raised her eyebrows at the apparent change of subject. "All my life."

I plunged ahead. "And do you know Frederick's neighbor, Charlotte West?"

Something flashed behind her glasses, it seemed, or maybe I was just imagining it. I wondered then if she could have been one of those women Duke had talked about, those who disapproved of Charlotte when she first arrived in town. It seemed likely. But I wasn't concerned about whether or not Alice liked her. I just wanted to test the reality of the story, to ground it in the world.

Alice pursed her lips, but her response was measured, diplomatic. "Of course I know who Charlotte West is, young man. And her husband Franklin as well. Why do you ask?"

But I lost courage. What could I ask that would make any sense? "Never mind," I said. "Just a story about her that someone was telling me. That's what I was thinking about just now."

It sounded lame, I knew, and I was dreading more questions, but Alice only said, "Well, it must have been an intriguing story, but I must be getting on to my class." She stood, hitched her purse up on her shoulder, and paused briefly, with a considering expression on her face. Then she seemed to come to a decision.

"It seems wrong somehow for a young man to spend the summer cooped up in a dusty old house with Frederick Hardt," she said. "Perhaps instead you would like to go with me to the beach club one of these hot days. I have a membership, but I don't often have the opportunity to use it."

I started to protest, but she cut me off with a solemn shake of her gray head. "No. No discussion. It will do you good, but if you prefer, then consider it a favor to me. You can drive me there. Also"—she tapped the Chandler book in my hand again—"we can discuss mysteries."

She started off toward the church, walking a little stiffly. She turned and said, "Let me give you a piece of advice that may serve you well in later years. Don't get old."

"They say it's better than the alternative."

She shrugged. "Maybe," she said, and walked away.

The beach. So many social visits this summer; I was starting to feel awfully popular. I sat on the bench and watched Alice cross the street slowly and enter the church. The streetlights were turning on early under the lowering clouds, giving the light on the buildings and trees an uncanny glow. A feeling like an approaching storm was in the air. I shifted myself off the bench, stretched, and started back on my way to face the old man.

13.

On Sunday there was a party at the West house to celebrate the Fourth of July. Frederick had no interest in going, so I left him watching football on the television and walked over by myself. It was a hot, damp overcast day and although the walk was brief I was feeling sticky and unsightly by the time I arrived.

As the roof appeared through trees at the end of the driveway I realized that I had never seen the house by daylight. The front was flat and gray and the roof rose in two separate gables, one tall and narrow, the other more squat, framing a single attic window, and the eaves of both were decorated in white trim. The skinny windows that I had seen so often at night now appeared opaque and weirdly elongated. In front was a small portico bounded by square columns and topped by more decoration, with the event marked by a colonial flag sticking out from beside the front door, thirteen stars circled on faded blue cloth. Over to the left, mostly hidden behind low trees, there was a gazebo extending from the side of the house.

There were cars parked in the driveway, along with a catering van, and now I could hear voices and other sounds mingled, hovering in the muggy air. There were people standing, holding drinks, in and around the gazebo, so I followed the party noise around that side of the house to the backyard which I knew so well, but so differently. I knew it as a place of silence, shadow, and moonlight, unrecognizable now.

There were twenty or thirty people there, and I drifted into the crowd, trying not to look too much out of place. Women in summer dresses and sunhats, men in slacks and topsiders. I found a glass of wine and a place on the edge of the crowd, drinking slowly, hoping I didn't look like a wallflower at a high school dance.

Charlotte West was sitting in the gazebo, a little circle of people gathered around her, all talking eagerly, while she listened with polite attention, her eyes moving, slow and noncommittal, from one speaker to the next, looking not interested but merely patient. She seemed to take some pleasure in the moment, though, the opportunity to sit in queenly repose surrounded by courtiers. Looking on, I was thinking about the party that failed, the party to which no one came. Now Charlotte was the center of attention, no longer a stranger at the gate trying to find a way in.

Watching the scene in the gazebo, I only became aware slowly of that prickle of the senses that says *someone is watching you*. I looked around and finally up, squinting to recognize Ellie West. She was leaning on the railing of a second-story balcony, standing next to a window box filled with bright flowers and looking at me with something like amusement. I met her eyes uncomfortably, the wallflower exposed, feeling suddenly as if I was standing there again alone at night, betrayed by moonlight, and she had come to the balcony to watch me while I sought a glimpse of her mother. When I met her gaze, she smiled and then, to my surprise, winked at me. She stood straight and stretched her bare arms, then turned and disappeared behind the other bodies and voices and drinks on the balcony.

I drank the rest of my wine quickly and started to move toward the gazebo. There was no plan in my head. I was just moving blindly toward Charlotte West, hoping to speak to her or just be near to her. As I approached, we made eye contact briefly, the dark eyes turned on me for a moment, then flickered away. Focused entirely on her, I stumbled, and when I looked up again, Ellie was standing directly in front of me, blocking my view.

"You came back again," she said, smiling as if we were sharing a private joke. She had a flower stuck behind her ear, a lemony splash that unfortunately made her hair look dull and brown by contrast.

I smiled back, trying to hide my annoyance, but she tilted her head on one side and went on. "You must be bored."

Was it the wine I had drunk, or was there something actually flirtatious in her manner, something shy and bold at the same time? In any case, I seemed to be stuck with her for the moment.

"I'm surprised you even remember me," I said.

"I remember. You're here to help out old Mr. Hardt. It's your summer job and then you're going to be a scholar or something, Daddy says, though Daddy is usually wrong about things. Isn't it hard living with him?" I opened my mouth in confusion, but she kept talking. "Mr. Hardt, I mean? He never speaks to me and I've always been a little scared of him. I can't imagine being with him all the time."

"Once you know him he isn't as scary," I said, and then reconsidered. "No, I take that back. He's still scary, but in a different way. And I don't stay in the house with him. I can always go back to the garage."

She screwed up her face in disbelief. "The garage?"

I almost laughed. "Not *in* the garage. He doesn't chain me up there with a dish of water and a can of dog food. There's a room above it where I sleep. It's better than a college dormitory, in fact. But maybe I shouldn't say that. I don't want to scare you away from college before you even get there."

"You could not scare me out of going away," she said, enunciating each word. "I am so bored here I could scream forever."

"Is it that bad?"

"Look around you, summer boy. I've lived here my whole life. There is nothing going on, and now I'm old enough to know it. I can't even go out to a bar with my friends, unless I lie through my teeth and set up six or seven alibis."

I cocked a stern eyebrow. "A bar? You aren't even legal drinking age, young lady." To emphasize the point, I lifted a second glass of wine from the table next to us and took a large sip from it.

"Half the time they don't ask for your license anyway. Girls especially. But my mother would absolutely kill me. Usually she doesn't bat an eye when it comes to me, just lets Daddy fret and act like he can tell me what to do. But she is so strict about the bars. Not because she cares about drinking, she lets me drink wine at home if I want to, which I don't. But when she told me I couldn't go to any of the local bars, when she found out that people from school would go out to them sometimes, then she was scary. Said she never, ever wanted to see me in a place like that. Never, *ever*. And she really meant it."

"Just looking out for you, I guess." I felt foolish taking this avuncular tone—in fact, I was glad to be talking to someone who was not my elder by decades. "Do you usually get along well with—your mother?"

I hoped the question sounded innocent, just another natural part of the conversation, but she did not have the chance to answer it. Franklin West appeared, leading a recent arrival to the drinks. He put an arm around Ellie and shook my hand heartily. "Good to see you again, young man! Are you here alone?"

I made half-hearted apologies for Frederick, while Ellie ducked out from under her father's arm, made a wry face at me, and went off in the direction of the house. West turned to introduce the man who was with him as Harrison Adams. He was tall, with a handsome face that angled down to a sharp chin and gray wavy hair so carefully coiffed that he looked like a politician or an actor. West was dressed in high preppy style, a white sweater draped over his shoulders without any apparent hint of irony. His friend was pulling it off more effectively, his sharp-creased dress shirt open at the neck and looking both dapper and casual.

"Our young friend Kese here aspires to be a scholar," West was saying, while I stood stupidly on display, reluctant to contradict him. "He is staying this summer with our neighbor, Mr. Frederick Hardt."

Adams turned to look at me then. "Hardt, yes, of course." He had an English accent so upper-class it sounded like a speech impediment. "I know the house. That is a fine property. I have often thought that we could do something very handsome with it."

"Harrison does a great deal of work all over this area," West said. "His company is very well respected. Heritage Realty and

Development. They take care of all the details so that we don't have to think about them."

Adams was all false humility. "As they say, everyone likes the sausage, but it tastes best if you don't see how it is made."

"You don't look like a sausage-maker," I said. I had taken an immediate dislike to him, and wanted, I think, to needle him, to poke a hole in the smug surface.

He gave me a look that was not so much an appraisal as a dismissal. "I have others who make it for me."

"Much better that way," said West, enjoying the metaphor. "Less blood on the shoes." Something caught his eye as he said this. "Excuse me, I see that I need to play the host. Harrison, please do find yourself a drink." He moved off and left the two of us together. Adams eyed me bleakly.

I recklessly finished off my glass of wine and took a third from the row of filled glasses on the table. "You handle a lot of the real estate in town here?" I asked. I had seen the Heritage name often in my daily reading of the newspaper listings.

"We do not do a great deal of business in the immediate vicinity," he said, taking a glass of white wine for himself and obviously looking around the lawn for a more promising conversation. "But we do some. Our offices are in New London and we handle many properties near there. Mystic. Stonington. Niantic."

"That's near the Indian reservation, isn't it?" I was thinking back to my conversation with Clinton, trying to remember details. "There have been some disputes about who owns what land up in that area lately. Some property annexation, too, or something like that? Does any of that affect your business?"

It was a shot in the dark, but I did notice that Adams was now giving me his full attention, chilly as it was, and speaking more carefully, too. I felt, for the first time, that he might remember my face for five minutes after the conversation was over. I wasn't sure that was a good thing.

"Yes," he said slowly. "I would not say that it *affects* our business, but it does make up a portion of our business. We do some work with the Pequot tribe and you are correct, this is a *transitional* moment—as the casino expands, you understand. The local homeowners are understandably concerned, especially as the reservation's boundaries are extended, which means that some privately held land is indeed *annexed* as you say—legitimately annexed or legitimately purchased. The process is a delicate one, and it is in our interests to see that it proceeds in a smooth manner."

Smooth was right. Adams picked every word as if he was writing a legally binding contract, but did it so cleanly that he never missed a conversational beat. "We have an investment in the process, a business investment, and above all, as the casino expansion takes its natural course, we are concerned to make sure that no, shall we say, unscrupulous parties find a way to become involved in the monetary dealings that are involved."

I was completely at sea, feeling just as baffled as Adams was clearly hoping I would. "Unscrupulous parties," I said. "Wait. Gambling. Do you mean like, the mob?" I felt foolish saying it. "Is there even a mob in New England?"

"There is organized crime everywhere, just as there is unorganized crime everywhere."

"All right," I said. He was making me feel very young and naïve, and I didn't like it. "But organizations don't have to be criminal to be unscrupulous."

He leaned in now, speaking quietly but forcefully. I could see his teeth. "As I say, it is better for all concerned that we should be the ones to manage affairs."

"Manage affairs?" Now I really was feeling reckless. Maybe it was the wine. "You mean it's better that *you* should make a whole load of money than that anyone else should? What kind of heritage *development* do you do, anyway?"

He was unflappable. "The usual kind," he said. "Perhaps it is time that we stopped hoarding all the conversation. We are depriving the other guests."

And he turned, unhurried, and walked around the rows of glasses to the gazebo.

In the weeks to come I would sometimes wonder if I had ever

met Harrison Adams at all, and there were moments when the whole conversation seemed so unlikely that I struggled to recall what he had looked like, what he had said to me. But at that moment I was just relieved that he had gone, leaving me feeling suddenly drunk and tired in the middle of the afternoon.

14.

Frederick looked up when I came in and sat down on the couch. He was in his chair next to the television, his face nearly touching the screen. "Hey, how about a sandwich?" he said, reaching for a smoke. "You had enough of the Fourth of July, huh? They can't stop talking about it on the television. I had to turn the channel."

I stared at the screen, blank and weary. "Do you know a guy named Harrison Adams?"

He nodded, blowing smoke through his nose. "Sure. That son of a bitch has been around here a few times. Thinks he's a big man. That accent. I'd bet my life it's a put-on, but the assholes around here go nuts over it. He thinks I should sell the place, move into a retirement home so he can make it into a development and sell the houses to a bunch of yuppie cocksuckers from New York."

"I got the impression, talking to him today, that he's got his sights set higher than that these days. I don't think he's going to be coming after this little place anytime soon."

"Nobody's taking my fortress. Now how about that sandwich?" The program's end credits were running on the television, which seemed to call his attention to the time of day. "Shit, the eye medicine."

Giving the eye drops was one of the day's rituals. He would lean back in his chair, usually at the kitchen table, take off the dark glasses, and pull an eye open with his fingers while I stood over him with the medicine. He seemed horribly exposed that way, his eyes, so rarely seen, appearing vulnerable and grotesque as the red viscous socket was exposed, catching reflections from the light that hung over the table. The worst part was that I was not good at giving the drops. I was getting better, developing a method, but in the early days my hands shook and I held the small white bottle too far away and I would miss and wet his face, the drops rolling down like tears that he would wipe away, and then he would sit waiting for me to try again.

Tonight the treatment went smoothly enough, and then we ate while watching a movie. We had finished reading *The Big Sleep* two days ago. On Saturday I had made a trip to the video-rental store and picked up the movie version on tape, and we watched it now, absorbed in the dreamlike opening, the detective's visit to the mansion, the orchid-filled hothouse where the incapacitated old man asks him to drink whiskey, to smoke, and to investigate the mystery. The movie was almost better than the book: that Rorschach tangle of a plot, the jokey speed of the early sequences, and then the beginning of a descent into nightmare when Bogart is brutally beaten and left lying in an alley.

After the movie's end and a few minutes spent trying to sort out the plot—we would eventually watch it twice more before returning it to the store—I said goodnight and headed for the garage.

The night was still groggy with humidity, and although there was light to see by, the edges of things were indistinct and hazy. I felt as sweat-soaked as the detective in the hothouse. Once in my little room, I took a brief shower and then found myself fidgety and restless, looking in corners for something new to read or examine. I was thinking back to the party that afternoon, remembering with irritation the moments when I had struck a false note in conversation or missed an opportunity. I should have questioned Harrison Adams more closely, should have tried harder to follow exactly what he had been saying, because I didn't really understand what his involvement with the disputes over land ownership around the Pequot reservation was—and had he really said something about the mob getting involved? Was that a warning, or even a threat, or was he just trying to sound impressive?

And Charlotte West. I regretted that I had failed to talk to her, or even to observe her up close. Because when I looked at it honestly, when I stripped away whatever excuses I had, boredom or free drinks or spying for the old man, wasn't that the reason that I had even bothered to go to the party at all?

There was a knock at the door.

A brief rapping, so light and quick that even as I froze where I was, waiting, I wondered if I had really heard it at all.

I looked at the clock. Past eleven. My heart beating hard. Then the rapping came again, quiet but unmistakable. The old man would never come up here at this time, in the dark, and he would certainly never knock so gently. The night outside was still, and a faint breeze blew in from a fan at the window. I looked around for a weapon, something heavy, and grabbed a flashlight, which settled comfortably in my palm, the heft of the D cells like a roll of quarters in a gangster's fist. I turned the knob slowly and pulled the door open, the light from the room pouring through the screen to illuminate the face of Ellie West.

Her eyes were bright and she was flushed. "I came through the woods," she said, a little breathlessly, pleased with her own daring. She was holding her own flashlight. "You looked so aloof and set apart at the party today, I could just tell how fake you thought everything was, I could tell you saw how stupid and boring they all are. When you left." She paused, then looked straight at me. "When you left, I realized that I didn't want you to go."

I must have been staring blankly. She had changed out of her party dress and taken the flower from her hair, and she was looking at me with a quiet intensity, breathing quickly. The proposition was unmistakable, and I knew, with an absolute certainty requiring no clairvoyance, that I would never have an invitation like this again.

The sound of crickets was loud now, and I saw a single firefly drift softly upward and disappear while I watched Ellie's face through the crooked wires of the screen. A dog barked, a lonesome sound, far away, faint, somewhere out in the night. The moment was suspended, cradled like a bubble on a child's fingers, waiting to burst.

Then I opened the screen door and let her in.

She stepped inside, raised herself on her tiptoes and kissed me, both of us still holding our flashlights. A screen-test kiss, awkward but heartfelt. I leaned back to look at her, with the sense that choices were being made without my agreement, that events were happening to me while I stood by and watched, and yet feeling too, certain too, that I was doing something that was wrong.

I stepped forward and closed the door behind her. This time I locked it.

15.

We should have fallen into the bed right then. That would have been the way to do it: no talking, no hesitation or time for forethought, just a jumbling of limbs and half-removed items of clothing, sweat and lips and shifting bodies. But instead there was an expectant pause and within it we immediately became self-conscious and awkward, hands that should have been touching and holding on to shoulders and waists were left wandering in the open air looking for a perch or a hiding place. Ellie, suddenly shy, put her hands behind her back, standing pigeon-toed on the threadbare doormat.

I retreated a step into the room, tripped on the edge of the rug, recovered. "Would you like a drink?"

"Yes." She nodded once, with determination, and I retrieved two bottles of beer from my half-size refrigerator, twisted the tops off, handed her one. Slow drops of moisture were already gathering on the cold glass.

She sipped hers and then stepped forward to sit down in a wicker chair, placing her flashlight carefully on the floor and looking around the room. She was wearing a skirt and a loose white blouse over a neon yellow T-shirt, with running shoes lightly scuffed from the walk through the dark woods.

Her eyes were wide and bright as she observed the place, and as I looked at her—for the first time, it seemed. She was slim and not unattractive, flushed, legs smooth and tanned in the lamplight, the curve of breasts a sly promise beneath the blouse. But I found that rather than imagining what it would be like to take her clothes off, I was trying to find the traces of her mother in her face and body, the similarities, trying to strip away the admixture of Franklin West, the taint of his genetic contribution, in order to discover Charlotte there, her face and body, pure and undiminished.

But the truth was that she didn't look much like either of them. However hard I searched in the curve of her nose, the arch of her eyebrows, her high forehead and light brown hair, slightly wavy now in the damp night, I could find only unconnected traces. I had noticed earlier that some of her expressions and vocal inflections were like her father's, but there were no features that she had inherited wholesale from him. Her mother was there in her face, yes, but only as a fleeting presence, barely there and then gone again. It was her hands, finally, that caught and held my attention. Like Charlotte's, they were slim, tapering, pale and somehow patrician even in the act of holding a beer bottle. Those were the hands I wanted to touch me. I could feel my heart beat faster with anticipation.

"You managed to get away from the party," I said.

"It's mostly over. All the grown-ups are spilling their gin and tonics on the lawn and trying to hold themselves up straight. They'll be happier to be able to get drunk without me there." She was making an endearing stab at sophistication, I thought, and then caught myself. Stop thinking, Kese. Don't step outside of the moment. Stay here. "I told Daddy I was going to go meet some friends. If he notices that the car's still there he'll just figure I got a ride."

"But instead you took a walk in the woods." I reached forward and pulled a burr away from her skirt. She smoothed it against her legs, then took a drink, a little hastily.

She's nervous, I realized. I was, too, and trying not to show it, but she probably thought of me as older, more experienced. Well, I was older, but my little experience didn't count for much. Two girlfriends in four years of college, and neither had stuck around for very long before gently extricating themselves from me, pulling away more insistently as my attempts to hold on to them became more desperate. I had had the usual doubts, wondering if I was too dull for them, not stylish enough, not wealthy enough—there were plenty of trust-fund boys at my little school, with good teeth and good skin and good hair and an alertness about how to dress that I did not have, not to mention the cash to buy the clothes, and I had often thought, bitterly, that having money kept you in a bubble and protected you from life, made you more beautiful than the rest of us.

I wondered, too, if I might be an incompetent lover, not daring enough, not inventive or confident enough. But my experience wasn't even wide enough to tell me whether that could be it or not. My first girlfriend had been strangely shy, unwilling to take her clothes off unless it was completely dark in the room, and even then seemed to cling to what scraps she could—a bra, shirt, socks—and I had let her set the tone for our nights together. If it is possible to kiss and caress and make love in an inhibited way, then we did. With the second, well, we had really only had sex three or four times, and it had been fine and abandoned, probably because we had both been well and truly drunk every time. But nonetheless, maybe Ellie imagined that I was an experienced seducer—or at least, if I could imagine that she imagined it, then maybe I could inhabit the role.

She was looking around the room. "So there really is a garage."

"There really is. It's not much, but I call it home."

She stared at me, lips parted. "You're so *sarcastic*," she said, eyes shining with a kind of admiration. I was disconcerted, feeling misrecognized again, even if I knew that she was just flirting.

"I was surprised at how easy it was to get here," she said. "Walking through the woods, it's almost like there's a path there. But you know that already."

She was smiling at me in a knowing way again, just as she had at the party. I froze.

"I—what do you mean?"

The conspiratorial smile widened. She leaned forward. "I saw you."

This time I did not have to ask what she meant. I could feel myself blush, feel the sudden sweat on my forehead.

"Behind the house," she went on. "Standing there at night. Last week. I was upstairs in my room, listening to music with the lights out. I saw something move outside, at the edge of the woods in back, and then I saw it was a person, someone watching. At first I was scared, but he was just standing there, looking, so I looked back. And after a minute or two he stepped closer and just for a second I could see him—maybe it was from the light over the back door, or the moon. The moon was out. And it was you."

She paused, but I couldn't find any words. I was terrified, sure that she would ask what on earth I had been doing there. But instead she went on. "Then for some reason I wasn't scared anymore. I didn't think, he's a creepy stalker. There was something magical about it, like something in a dream or a movie, the moonlight, and the night was so quiet. I thought, he's shy, he's lonely. He wants to be close to me. Was that it?"

I have no idea what the expression on my face looked like, but I managed to nod, as if without speech it was only half a lie. In less than a minute I had gone from seducer to exposed voyeur.

She got up from her chair and came close to me, kissed me again. She whispered, "That's why I came here."

I put my arms around her, not knowing what else to do. It was a relief, in a way, to know that she did not suspect my real reasons for being, in fact, a creepy stalker. But the shock of being found out was still pumping adrenaline through my system, and my hands were trembling and clumsy. She had not shown up at my door out of the blue. However unknowingly, I had brought her here.

Ellie had her mouth close against my ear. She was saying, "Isn't it strange, that this place was here all along? I don't mean that I should have known that it was here. I just mean isn't it strange that all those places exist out there that you've never seen or heard about. And then you walk through the woods and then there's a building and it has a door. You open it up and there's this place there that you never knew about. And you step inside and everything is different. It's like Goldilocks and Little Red Riding Hood. Like a fairy tale."

But I was barely listening. I wanted to play the part of lover, wanted to go back to where we had been a minute before, where maybe it was possible to give myself over to simple passion—there is such a thing, isn't there? I wanted to lose thinking and consciousness. Most of all I wanted this moment to be past, so that I wouldn't have to think anymore about the night visits, so that I could close my eyes against the image of myself as a lurking creep. But she kept complicating things, making me aware of how far apart we were, how different our sensibilities, by assuming that they were the same, creating an image of me in place of me. And I kept complicating things, too; in fact, I was even worse, wanting a her that was not her.

In the end, though, the closeness of our bodies and the warmth of her breath against my ear were enough to push guilt and doubt aside. I whispered back, "All those houses in the woods are dangerous places for innocent little girls to go visiting, aren't they?"

She smiled, eyes sidelong.

I leaned in and kissed her, and there must have been some real desire there, there must have been something. Because I found that I was unbuttoning her white blouse thing, and that we were on the bed, somehow; she was tugging my shirt over my head, my head bumping on the low slanted ceiling, the full bottles of beer sitting in pools of condensation on the other side of the room somewhere, and I was popping open her lace-trimmed bra where it clasped in front—so much for those movies in which nervous young men fumble behind the backs of their eye-rolling dates, seeking blindly for hook and eye—while she arched her back to free herself, lying back on the sheets in the dim room, both of us having discarded all the crumpled sweat-soaked cotton and elastic. Her hands were holding me at the waist, at the hips, at the shoulders—there was a moment to worry about birth control, of course; I had none because who could have known, but it was all right because Ellie had known, had planned, she produced the condom not with embarrassment but with a kind of pride that I had to admire, surprised and thinking that actually she might have been the most grown-up lover I had ever had—and we were moving together, bodies hooked tight, and she was breathing urgently in my ear and maybe we did lose ourselves then in the thing of our bodies, which were communicating something beyond all the things that we were thinking too hard. The differences between us, the barriers, and all the rest of what we might be feeling, what I was feeling, the shame and chagrin and uncertainty, were part of it, they were not transcended but translated, made part of the movement and rhythm, the way that sometimes in dancing, the music too loud for speaking, all the guilt and grief of daily living can be translated and made new in the speech of the body. All this, and yet. Because in the dimly lit room while we were pushing forward, she and I, against each other, pushing and feeling the rhythm changing and edging toward a swelling disorder, even then, without thinking it, I knew whose face I was seeing in the dark. I knew who I was possessing, defiling, her hands were holding me, so right, so wrong, and even if I didn't care, I knew that soon this moment would be past and gone and then I would be thinking about Charlotte West again.

16.

Maybe it was the tattoo that kept me opening the door, night after night.

She did not come around every evening, so I never knew if I would hear the knock. I forced myself not to wait for it, not to expect it. But most nights, over the weeks that followed that strange Fourth of July, she would come to the door late and we would spend an hour or two together on the odd little bed tucked under the eave in the room that smelled of mildew and old books.

I let it happen to me, this affair with Ellie West, and when she was not there it was hard to believe that it was happening at all. The days became more dreamlike, and I passed through them as if they were banks of fog that clung and dissipated as I moved forward. I was dazed each morning when, after a few brief hours of sleep, the old man would wake me to renew the day's routine. The day was a ritual and now the night had its own ritual, but the two did not, could not, touch, and I moved passively between them. Passively and often uncomfortably, because although it was a wonder to have this unlooked-for diversion, I knew that, really, it was not what I wanted.

It should have been. She was attractive, and, despite her sheltered upbringing and inexperience, she was perceptive and sharp-witted, with an unexpectedly sly sense of humor. She should have been what I wanted, if I had been able to see her, but I never could because for me—I can say it now, although I couldn't have then—she existed only as a pale shadow of her mother.

And I wondered what it was that Ellie wanted, from this, from me. Our meetings were romantic in a way, I suppose—they had the allure of their secrecy, because sex in secret always feels forbidden whether it is or not, so we must both have felt that thrill of doing something we were not supposed to.

I could tell that she had a romantic idea of me, one that I did not recognize at all. But it was a flattering image, this person I saw reflected in her eyes. There, I was coolly intellectual, an outsider who regarded the world in which she had grown up with devastating mockery and derision. I was the one who could give voice, without even speaking, to all the frustration she felt with the boundaries and conventions of her life in this small town full of old people and old history. And I think she found an image there that was flattering to her, too, the image of herself as the privileged one who would be admitted to the warm place behind the cool mockery that she imagined in me, the place from which we two might stage the drama of our difference from all the rest of the bland conventional world. But I did not recognize myself in that drama at all, and although it was flattering I lived in it uneasily. In truth, I had nothing to put in its place.

But I liked the tattoo, and eventually I asked her about it. I think I was surprised that she had it at all, and liked it for that surprise, because it unsettled my idea of who she was. It was drawn on the back of her left wrist, where the joint met the smooth white forearm, an image in blue-black ink of what looked like a pine tree or perhaps a small grove of them. It was a well-made picture, the lines finely drawn and the image stylized so that it looked like a woodcut print, the tree's several peaks winding upward and curling around her wrist slightly, following the natural curve there, the ink pattern like an extension of the blue veins beneath her pale skin.

At first I was surprised at the boldness of the placement, since it would be hard to conceal and most high school girls, I thought, would have chosen an ankle or a shoulder or some other discreet spot. The image itself was interesting, too, not drawn from any tattoo lexicon that was familiar to me.

So I asked about it, one of our nights together. By then I had lost count of how many, but it was late July by then, the fan humming in the window, me running a finger slowly along her wrist, the image catching a patch of moonlight among the shadows on the bed.

"Oh, that," Ellie said. "It's four trees, growing together. See?"

She sat up, holding her arm in the moonlight, and I could see them now, the four slender but distinct trunks at the bottom, rising and disappearing into a single body of lush pine foliage. "I had it done in New Haven last winter, right after I turned eighteen. I think the tattoo guy liked it that I brought my own picture. I drew it myself. Of course it was just a sketch and he changed it around and made it look good. It did hurt." She made a face. "But that wasn't the hardest part. The hardest part was telling my mother. I have never seen her so angry. Of course I knew that she would be. That's not why I did it," she said quickly, "but I knew it would drive her crazy, because she wouldn't like the tattoo, would think it was *low class* or something. I think the thing that really stung her was that I went out and did it and then it couldn't be undone. It was a thing she couldn't control. It was like she looked at me and for the first time she saw that she wasn't going to be able to make me be what she wanted me to be, whatever that is. Not always. Not forever."

Her face was turned away, looking out the window, and there was a confusion of feelings in her voice.

"She didn't speak to me for a week. And then there was Daddy. He didn't get angry or anything, he just seemed kind of disappointed or sad, and that was fine because it didn't mean anything, it was just Daddy being Daddy. I don't think he really minded at all. I bet that if it had been a little tattoo of a ship, he would even have liked it."

"So why did you want a tattoo of four trees growing together?" I asked, tracing the outline of the image with my hand. "I don't think I know that from anywhere."

She turned to lie on her back, her face thoughtful and a little dreamy, looking at the ceiling sloping upward into canted shadow. "When I was little," she said. "I mean, this is like my earliest memory. In the yard, near the house, there was this place where there were four pine trees growing together. It looked like just one big tree from the outside, but then I would crawl under the branches and underneath there was this crunchy bed of brown pine needles and you could see the four trunks there, thick, solid, and I would lie there like it was a little cave. If it was raining I could lie there on the fallen needles and not get wet, I would lie on my stomach and stick my hand out and feel the raindrops and I knew that I was safe in my little hideout where everything smelled of pine and the big branches were spread out above me. It felt comfortable. It was like this magical hidden place, this safe place, and it was mine. I still think of it whenever I'm inside and it's raining hard outside. That lost place."

The fan hummed at the window, stirring the thin curtains. For a moment I felt like that, there in the quiet of the darkened room with the world spreading wide outside, dangerous beyond knowing—felt as if I was in a space of safety, insulated from whatever storm might rise out there.

"It's lost?" I said. "Don't you go there anymore?"

She frowned. "I can't find it. I don't know where those trees are anymore. I've looked all over our property, but I can't find them."

"Sometimes we remember things differently from what they are—what they were. Things look different when we're older, taller. You've changed a lot since then. Everything has."

She turned to me again, looking puzzled, frustrated. "I know. I know. But I *looked*. I even looked at my grandparents' house, in case the trees might have been there."

"Your mother's parents?"

"No. Grandma and Grandpa West. They live near here. I never met my other grandparents."

"Not even when you were young?"

She shook her head. "Not ever. They died before I was born."

"Oh." I waited, really curious now, but trying to make the question sound idle. "Where did they live?"

"I don't know. My mother told me they were dead, but she doesn't talk about them at all. It's like she doesn't care."

"They must have died young. It's probably a painful memory for her."

There was a long pause. I lay back, trying to imagine what it could be, what murder or brutal accident Charlotte West might be trying to forget.

Ellie raised herself on an elbow and looked down at me. I had a guilty feeling that she could read my thoughts, but then she said, "All right. Now tell me something about you. Something important." She kissed me. "I want to know about you. Tell me about when you were growing up."

The words were like a trigger. All of a sudden, I felt lightheaded, off-balance. A trigger, and when the gun fired it tore a bright hole through a wall in my thinking. All my thoughts rushed like wind through the gap and I was dragged along with them. Maybe it was something about the question—*tell me something about you, something important*—or maybe it was something about Ellie West asking me about how I grew up, but at that moment I did understand something important about myself. And there was no way I could tell it to Ellie.

I had just realized, for the first time, that the way I felt about Charlotte West was the way I had been feeling all my life. And maybe I was my father's son after all.

When I was growing up, my father had seemed to live in a separate world—from me, my sisters, my mother, from his own life—a world made of the anger that he carried with him, an aura that obscured him, made him distant and unapproachable. It had always felt like an anger directed at us, directed at me, even when I was old enough to understand that really it was aimed backwards, at the past, and he was stuck there, trapped in a permanent state of outrage at the way that his own father had abandoned his inheritance.

So I grew up in a household that was demonstrably middle-class but that felt itself to be deprived, robbed of what it should have been. I don't mean my mother, an undemanding woman who seemed only baffled and concerned by all this. But for my father every weekend spent in house-repair drudgery was an insult, every coupon clipped and bargain made at the supermarket, every vacationless summer spent in the sweltering house, and on the train back and forth to work, was a reminder of what he had missed out on, what should have been his and his to pass on.

He took it out on himself, but that meant he took it out on us, too, in his ruthless managing of the household economies. Our little house, in a modest Maryland suburb, was supplied with only the cheapest, most generic products, and the furniture was secondhand, its upholstery worn to a shine. Every expense was a source of deep and permanent resentment, every dollar spent fed his anger. This was especially hard on my two teenaged sisters, because beauty products, even brand-name shampoos and soaps, had to be smuggled into the house, hidden like contraband. I was often shocked, visiting friends from school who lived in wealthier suburbs, in houses with luxurious rec rooms, bedrooms supplied with their own televisions and video-game systems, stereos and headphones and cameras. Shocked, like a virgin in a brothel. I was scared even to touch these treasures myself, because I could imagine, could almost feel, the silent fury that would uncoil in my father if he were to witness these displays of pointless expenditure.

He rarely raged or shouted, but his resentment was a constant threat, humming in the taut wire we walked all our days. The grim set of his mouth conveyed a frustrated desire, a sense that he would always be standing outside some kingdom of his imagining and wishing beyond all things to be inside, while the rest of us, if we could have put it into words, only wished that the kingdom had never been there in the first place. For him, this little corner of New England represented both promise and disaster, the best and the worst, and this summer job of mine must have had an almost mythic resonance for him: the son visiting the place from which the father felt that he had been disinherited, a return to the wound, the absence.

Now, for the first time, I recognized that same absence in myself, that same resentment. With surprise I recognized it. I must have believed that being so constantly aware of my father's anger, living with it and knowing it all these years, would inoculate me against it and keep me safe, free to be free like my grandfather.

But I was wrong, because how else to explain the way that Charlotte West lingered always at the back of my mind? If I could have seen myself clearly then, that summer, maybe I would have seen where the desire came from, and why it kept me burning.

But I didn't. I had always known, in some part of me, that I was using Ellie's body as the substitute for another. But what I didn't know was that the mother, too, was a substitute for something I could not get at even by having, possessing her. I was reaching through Ellie to get to Charlotte and reaching through Charlotte to get at something she had or was, something I had not even known that I lacked: that lost kingdom. And worst of all, even that desire was not mine, was secondhand, an inheritance.

I couldn't tell Ellie any of that. I couldn't even tell myself. Instead the knowledge surfaced, pouring for a moment through that imaginary bullet hole like a pinprick of bright daylight, and I quickly pushed it back out, sealed it away, thinking *Don't look. Don't let yourself look.* I actually squeezed my eyes closed, there on the bed in the nighttime shadows, as if there was a blinding light I needed to shut out.

I lay very still, my thoughts stuck there like a needle on a damaged record, with no idea what to say.

Finally I managed to shrug. I hoped there was no tremor in my voice. "There's nothing to tell. Just a boring suburban childhood. I'm afraid I'm not very interesting."

"There must be something." She had stopped smiling.

"Nothing I can think of."

"Nothing."

She smacked the mattress in frustration and pushed herself up and off, grabbing at her clothes and pulling them on roughly. When she was dressed, she frowned down at me, hissing, "You never give me anything. Nothing from you, nothing about you. What are we *doing* here anyway?"

I opened my mouth and closed it again, stupidly. She turned away in a fury.

At the door, she snatched up her flashlight and pointed it at me, unlit. She looked ready to cry and her voice shook. "I don't know if *you* even know who you are. Give me something!" Then she was gone, the screen banging behind her.

Three nights later, when Ellie knocked again, I let her in and neither of us said anything about that night. But before she left, I suggested that maybe she would like to come visit during the day sometime, spend a little time with me and the old man. I was backed into a corner, trying to find a way to offer her some access to my life outside of that room.

I thought it would be a way to move outside of the closed circle of our furtive nighttime rendezvous, to provide whatever it was that she needed from me, maybe. I honestly thought it would be a good thing for both of us.

17.

I was not particularly looking forward to my day at the beach, but you had to admit that the weather was doing its best.

The damp heat had receded and left a blinding sun that penetrated even through the gloom of the shaded winding roads that took me, after many slow swervings, to Alice Pickett's house. It was hidden by trees, but the driveway opened wide at the end. There, a sun-kissed grape arbor and a stone walk lined with bell-shaped flowers led to the front door. The house was large but unpretentious, made in one of the less austere variants of colonial style. It would fetch a small fortune if it was ever listed in the real estate pages, but there was ivy growing up one side of the house and the gray paint was peeling away from the wood in long strips. Under the bright jollying sun, though, any defects looked picturesque, some preservationist's platonic dream of Rustic New England Charm.

I stooped through the arbor and knocked at the door, where Alice, dressed to go out but not in what you would call beachwear, greeted me and led me inside.

"I thought that perhaps you would be interested in seeing my paintings," she said as she led me through the house to a sunroom that was serving now as an atelier. The walls were all many-paned windows and there was a faded couch littered with cushions, some embroidered, some with printed images of ducks swimming in cattail ponds. The floor was bare slate stones, with a sheet laid down beneath a stool and a half-painted canvas on an easel. Other canvases had been propped up against the low walls beneath the windows, and there were two other easels with finished paintings on them.

Alice surveyed the scene. "The light is much better here than those awful fluorescent things they have in the church basement," she said with some satisfaction.

I walked around the room, bending over and turning my head to look at the paintings. Most of them showed landscapes—a blue-green cove seen through a frame of leaves and blossoms, a grassy field swelling away into the distance on a cloudy day—and they were much better than I had expected. Not great works of art, but ideas thoughtfully and skillfully composed, with a flash here and there of something in nature truly captured.

"These are good," I said, relieved that I didn't have to lie. "Honestly." I moved over to one of the easels, which held an apparently finished painting of a man's head and shoulders. He was mostly bald, with a long face and a strong, handsome nose, and he appeared to be looking off to the left somewhere.

Alice came and stood next to me, a head shorter, and looked at the painting with her lips pursed critically. "That is Gregory, my late husband," she said. "Two years ago he passed away, but I still feel that he is here, somehow. The house is full of him. I hope I never have to leave this place, because then I will have to leave him behind." She smiled briefly. "I still curse him sometimes. It's a stupid thing, but not long after he died I was puttering around the house, taking out the garbage, which is something that Greg always did. The bag broke and spilled the garbage all over the kitchen floor. And I was so *angry* at him for not being here to do it, for going away and leaving me here alone with everything and this big mess on the kitchen floor. I sat down at the kitchen table and cried. Just cried. Dumb, isn't it? Stupid."

"Not stupid," I said. "Not at all."

"Well. Might as well get angry at the Red Sox for not winning the series." She turned back to the portrait. "It looks finished, but every week or so I find myself going back and working on it more, changing this or that, adding a detail, yet I still don't feel that I have got him quite right. I began with a photograph, but now I work from memory." She sighed, and a wry note crept into her voice. "I am fearful now to go back and look at that photograph. I have the feeling that he becomes younger and more handsome every time I go back and work on it. Memory is a dangerous thing, young man."

18.

As we approached the beach, the trees thinned and the sky grew broad around us in the full blaze of the late morning sun. The road ran through a grassy field now and the first wink of seawater beckoned from the opening horizon. We parked in a newly paved lot, the asphalt black and glossy, the white lines brightly ruled. Alice had brought a metal cane with her, and although she barely used it, crossing the lot with a brisk stiff gait as we moved toward a long low wood-shingled building, she glared at the cane resentfully and every now and then she whacked it hard against the asphalt.

We passed through the building and onto a wooden deck shaded by a broad overhang and lined with chairs and picnic tables. Below the deck there was a stretch of sand with a few sunbathers and parents watching their children build castles or bury each other under brown mounds like play-graves, and beyond that the sea, the Sound, wide and open and green under the bright sky, distant white lines of cloud hovering above the horizon. Long Island lurked out there in the distance, not so far away, with all its multitudes, hundreds of whom had surely come already this morning by bus and train and car, snaking along through heavy traffic and crowded railway lines, to make their way to the Indian casino.

Alice settled herself in a chair next to a picnic table, dropping the cane next to her with a clatter, and I sat down at the table, facing the water, to take off my shoes. The beach was lightly populated, a world away from the teeming public beaches of Maryland and Delaware, and the whole place struck me as oddly subdued.

Even in the shade I squinted against the glare on the sand,

counting the white bodies under umbrellas, in the water. "Alice, is this place—I think the word is *restricted?*"

She turned to me sharply. "It is a private club, members and guests only. But I think I understand very well what you are asking. The beach club was once restricted, yes, but it has not been for many years, I am glad to say. There are a number of members who are Jewish. There are no blacks who are members, but that is not a matter of club policy."

"How about Indians?"

She sighed and turned to look out at the water. "I take your point, I take it. I suppose that you are thinking that this is a town full of rich old white people. Well, it is. When I was young we would go to the drugstore in Saybrook that was run by old Mr. Lane and then by Miss James, and they were the only colored people I had ever met." She looked faraway for a moment. I thought, she remembers her youth, her girlhood, and it is sweet, as it is for all of us, like Ellie safe under her four trees. She remembers her parents when they were alive and strong to protect her and take her for an ice cream at the soda fountain, and the cherished reminiscence is also a memory of the time when there was colored and Jim Crow and no recourse to law and the two cannot be separated. "But that was a long time ago," she said, turning to me again. "And I am glad that we have a president at the moment who is not completely stupid when it comes to race politics, even if I could not vote for him myself."

"You couldn't vote? Why not?"

"Young man, I come from a Republican family." She spoke as if she were explaining to a dim student that Washington was our first president. "We do not vote for Democrats. My father would roll in his grave. But I think that rather than talking politics with an old woman, you might want to enjoy the beach. Please do. I have my book to read."

I went in, but stopped wading after just a few steps. The water was cold, painfully, bone-bruisingly cold, and I stopped there with the sea lapping frigidly at my knees, panting a little and staring at my pale legs disappearing down into the sand-pearled green.

I walked along the waterline, watching the waves shifting around my legs as I went. I stopped and looked up at the flat plain of the sea, wide and unknown. We stand always at one edge of it, stunned into meditation by the hugeness of it: the expanse, the depth, the darkness full of alien shapes and forms, all the bat-faced randomness of evolving life. Like the past, a place you could explore forever and never know it all.

I made my way back to the deck where Alice sat reading, her pinned hair coming loose in gray wisps in the sea breeze, and then went to get us some lunch. The window in the club where food was dispensed was indistinguishable from any low-rent beach food spot anywhere along the Atlantic coast: boiled hot dogs and cans of soda and bad soft-serve. No fine dining here.

I ate my hot dog from its white cardboard swaddle while Alice blew on her clam chowder and looked at the back cover of her book. "I never read mysteries when I was younger," she said. "But now I seem to be addicted to the things, and sometimes they can be rather well done. Like your Raymond Chandler. Why do you think they are so interesting to us, these mystery books?"

"I don't know," I said, pinning flyaway napkins under a bottle of mustard. "Maybe they remind us that nothing is what it seems to be."

She looked at me for a moment, thinking. "What makes you so certain that nothing is what it seems to be? It doesn't appear that way to me at all."

I laughed briefly at what I thought was a joke, but she ignored this, waiting for a response.

Feeling suddenly chilled by the breeze, I climbed down to stand on the sand at the edge of the deck, warming myself in the sun, looking out across the water. "There is a mystery I've been thinking about this summer," I began, not sure if I wanted to say this at all, but finding that I was saying it anyway. "Do you remember when we met the other day, by the church—do you remember I said that I had been thinking about one of Frederick's neighbors, Mrs. West?" I looked back at Alice. She pursed her lips in an expression I could not read. Disapproval, I guessed. But I was guessing wrong, and not for the last time.

"Yes, I remember. Charlotte West. She is mysterious?"

"I think so. At least, I don't understand her, but there seems to be something to understand. That's what a mystery is, right?"

She was still looking at me. Her expression did not change. "It is my understanding," she said, "that men who become acquainted with attractive women often consider those women as a species of mystery that requires their solution."

I opened my mouth to object but quickly closed it again. "All right. But still. I don't know how much you know about her." I paused. Alice said nothing, made no sign, sitting stone still and alert in her chair with her small feet barely reaching the deck floor. "But here is this woman, she shows up in town out of nowhere, with no past that anyone can see, and she seems to be determined, *is* determined, to make a place for herself in a small and tightly knit community that really doesn't want her to have a place there, that has its own rules and traditions. But she will do whatever it takes, it seems. And she succeeds. She takes her place there, and then doesn't do anything much except hold it. She doesn't try to make friends—I was watching her at a party at her place the other day and it seemed to me she had lots of admirers and acquaintances but no friends. She seems to want to succeed by force of will rather than by making herself welcome or ingratiating herself, and she does, and then the story just sort of ends. Do I have that all about right?"

She did not nod, did not move a muscle, just waited for me to go on. "So the mystery is, *why?* Because wouldn't there have to be a reason, a motive? An explanation. And *where* did she come from, anyway? Where would you have to come from to want to be here, since everyone here seems to have been here for generations and there doesn't seem to be any other reason to stay? I keep wondering if she could be from Europe somewhere. Or Quebec? She has that French maiden name and I can't place her accent from the one or two times I've heard her speak, but it doesn't sound like any American accent that I know, not like any accent at all. I just don't know." I stopped speaking, breathing deep in the salt air. Alice said nothing and her expression had not changed. At least I had said it aloud to someone, put my thoughts into words.

My eye was caught by a father and son passing, walking along the beach. The father was fit and tanned and in full preppy leisure uniform, pink polo, white shorts, boat shoes, no socks. His voice was carried up to us on the breeze, telling the boy something, authoritative, educational. I wondered, if I became a father someday, would that same tone creep into my voice, would I hold my head that way, cocked, lecturing but eager to know that my words were being absorbed, taken in, and if I did then who would I be, who would that person speaking to the child be? And that made me think of my own father, too. I tried to remember if he had ever walked with me on the beach that way, and then realized that this was precisely his wish, his dream of his life as it should have been, to be at this club, on this beach, in those clothes, far away from the sad suburbs and the need to worry about money, walking on the beach with me, the son, and telling me something interesting about lobsters or whatever it is that fathers who walk on beaches with their sons tell—

"Wait!" I turned around quickly, sharply, blinded by the sun, looking up into the shade of the deck. "Wait! What did you just say?"

Alice's eyes were keen behind her glasses. "I said she comes from right here. Grew up not five miles away."

PART TWO

July – August
1993

19.

The girl's eyes were something you could never forget.

What Alice couldn't remember was how it was that she had begun to do charity work in the first place. It had just seemed to happen to her, sometime in her thirties. The church, the Junior League—they were not, perhaps, the organizations she would have chosen, but they offered her opportunities to assist the old, the poor, the incapacitated, the victims of natural disasters or vicious husbands. If she was honest with herself, it was a way to remind herself that there were others who suffered in ways more dire than hers, than her ordinary, everyday pangs and disappointments, and to feel—no sense in denying it—the sense of superiority that inevitably followed.

Mostly her volunteer work was done in town, at the houses of other women or at the church. She found that she liked being in this community of women, even if often she did not like them individually; she liked the sense of bustle and purpose in their meetings, their activities, liked the occasional jokes and the times when they let down their guard and laughed about something together, some foolish thing that one or all of them had done. She had not had this in her life for years, not since she was young and unmarried and the war was on, and she remembered now how she had liked to collect metal and rubber, working alongside her mother and the other grown women and feeling the pleasure of that shared work, remembering even now with nostalgia the particular smell and light and sound of the public spaces, the gymnasiums or libraries, schoolrooms or church basements, where they had spent so much time.

But on this particular day she was out for a house visit, driving the big slow car that Greg usually drove and looking small behind the wheel, with June Chadburne in the passenger seat, talking about nothing, as usual. Alice thought that June was frivolous, and although she was friendly with her, she held June secretly in contempt and was not listening to the steady flow of chatter while she navigated the big car over narrow winding roads.

What had their errand at the Tilton place been? She remembered that the husband had been disabled in some kind of accident at his work, and that he was a drunk. Perhaps they had been delivering some food, though that would have been unusual. Maybe some clothes, some donated things. She had a vague memory of paper bags in the back seat, their contents shifting and clinking on the bumps.

She pulled the car over and stopped to peer at the mailbox, which read "Tilt" in black scrawl, the last two letters a smear, then she pulled into the gravel drive. The house was a sad thing, with paint peeling everywhere and the screen door askew. There was a rust-riddled truck with no tires propped up on cinder blocks on the front lawn, and two raggedy-looking children sitting beside it, looking up from an interrupted game.

Alice cut the engine and June sighed. "It looks like we've got our work cut out for us here," she said, drawing off her gloves, which Alice eyed, concealing her exasperation. See? Frivolous. Wearing white gloves and a bright summer dress as if she were Glinda the good fairy paying a visit to the little people. Alice was dressed more practically, in fact was daringly dressed down in clam diggers and a belted blouse, her hair held in a kerchief. But stepping out of the car, she, too, felt distinctly out of place and felt, too, suddenly, that her life had been terribly sheltered. She knew of course that houses like this existed, had seen the pictures in magazines, like those old photographs of Southern hovels and dust-bowl migration. But if this house was here, so close to where she lived, had always lived, then there must be plenty of others, too, and how could the two things exist side by side? There but for the grace of God, you had to think. Alice did not believe in God, but the words came to her then and she felt suddenly what a cruel and cunning sentiment it was, the apparent humility disguising a smug assurance that God chooses you and blights the other. But the feeling was still there in her; she could not look at the house or the dirty children without feeling a twinge of disapproval, without thinking, *How can you be living here if it is not your doing, your choice some way, how?* and she could not shake the thought even as she choked on it.

"Hush, June," she said. "That's enough. Let's bring these bags inside."

June hesitated. "Would it be all right if I stayed here, just this once, Alice? Would you be all right going by yourself?" She assumed a timid look.

Alice pulled out the bags and walked to the house, tight-lipped, energized by the annoyance she felt. She walked up the steps and at the top found that a woman was holding the screen open for her with an elbow, one hand busy with a cigarette, the other held loosely by a toddler.

The Tilton woman was wearing a shapeless housedress, its print long faded, but when Alice looked up into her face, she stopped still for a moment. The woman was long-limbed and olive-skinned, her dark hair hanging down around her face uncombed but somehow framing her features, even frowning as they were, just right. Despite the child, the door, and the cigarette with its long ash, she had a languid posture that made her look like she had deliberately struck a pose. Like a paper doll in the sets Alice had played with as a child. Just replace the clothes and setting with different ones, and a new picture would appear: this woman, standing now in the doorway of a mansion with a martini and an arm around a handsome man in a suit. It would look just right. They stood facing each other, two women probably about the same age, but Alice felt that they could have been from different species: the dark woman with the slow unconscious grace and the grim lines around her mouth, and Alice, a small woman in a kerchief and cat-eye glasses, with her practical clothes and bundled offerings, suddenly feeling intimidated and trying to hide it.

She stepped inside and put the bags down. "Mrs. Tilton?" she said. Inside it was dim and the floors needed sweeping. High small windows did little to cheer the place. The walls looked flimsy and she could see into a living room where a large chair leaned against the wall, stuffing showing at the seams, next to it a table with a large ashtray overflowing with bent cigarette ends. The rooms smelled of stale dust and smoke.

The woman nodded. Her face was hard to read, not because it had no expression but because so many different feelings were mingled there. She looked tired, but also resentful, wary, angry. Alice felt small and out of place, and her irritation with June buzzed away and left her. She tried to smile at the toddler, but the stunned look it gave her in return seemed more appropriate.

"How are you, Mrs. Tilton? I'm delivering these for the church. Is your husband at home?"

A flicker of apprehension in the woman's eyes. "He's sleeping," she said quickly. "What do you need him for?"

"Nothing. Nothing, I guess." She was not sure what else she should be saying, but felt that she should say something. "Is there anything we can do for you?"

The fear dimmed and a dull resentment, the woman's default look, returned. "Guess you've done it," she said.

"All right. Thank you, Mrs. Tilton." She felt foolish saying it, not the sort of foolish that she might laugh about later even, and the woman's lips curled in scorn. Alice fumbled with the broken door on the way out, banging her hip as she retreated and hurried down the steps, breathing hard.

One of the children, a girl, had come around from behind the rusted carcass of the truck and was standing in front of it, looking at Alice. Her dress was a long-faded hand-me-down that had once been gathered at the waist but the stitches on one side had come out, so it hung lopsided. Her dark hair was cropped above the shoulders and Alice would have guessed she was nine or ten, but the way the girl was looking at her, steadily and without embarrassment, made her seem older. They stood there, facing each other, for a long moment before the girl asked a question.

"Did you always have nice shoes?"

Alice looked down at her feet. She was wearing the white canvas flats that she wore for tennis or for working around the house.

Unable to help herself, she looked at the girl's bare feet, and then met her unblinking gaze. "Well," she said. "Yes. Yes, I suppose I have." She was thinking of the several pairs of shoes at home in her closet, her small clean closet. She had never been a clothes-horse, not by a mile, but of course you needed different shoes for different kinds of occasions. "I have nicer ones at home."

As soon as the words were out she wished she could have taken them back, but the girl was still looking at her with the dark steady eyes, not frowning but concentrating, and Alice felt that she could see or even hear the thinking behind the eyes, the mind taking in this information and working on it, working like fast-meshing gears on the problem it had set for itself.

"What kind of shoes do you wear when you go to school?" Alice asked gently, coaxingly.

The girl ignored the question, still gazing at Alice. "Where do you live?" she said.

"I live—not too far away," Alice said, a little unnerved.

The girl considered, the gears still working. "What's your name?"

"I—my name is Alice. You may call me Mrs. Pickett. What is your name?"

"Pickett," the girl said carefully, narrowing her eyes. "They call me Becky."

"Don't you—"

The question was cut short by a startling blast of noise, the car horn. Alice looked around and there was June, still inside the car, making an exasperated face and looking stupid there, Alice thought, trapped in the car like she was on a safari, windows rolled up against the beasts. Alice glared at her and then turned back. The other girl, this one younger, had come to investigate the noise and was peeking out from behind the old truck.

Alice was feeling self-conscious. "Well, Becky. It has been a pleasure to meet you."

"You came for the charity," Becky said.

Alice paused. "Yes, that's right."

"Do you live in a nice house?"

"Well. Yes, I suppose I do."

The girl nodded. It was something she had needed to make sure of.

"Goodbye, Becky."

The girl did not even nod this time. Her eyes had lost none of their uncanny intensity, and Alice felt the hair prickling her neck as she turned and walked back to the car. She found that she was thinking of Greg, of how much she was looking forward to seeing him sitting, reading a book probably, in their clean living room with its new television set, when she got home.

"What was that all about?" June asked when Alice had sat down and turned the key in the ignition. "You were having quite a little conversation with that girl." There was an edge to her voice, annoyance at being kept waiting in the hot car.

"She liked my shoes," Alice said.

June laughed, a malicious little scream. "Well, I guess you have to come out to the Tilton place to get a little appreciation for your fashion sense. Maybe you should pay a visit to those Swamp Yankees more often."

"That's enough, June," Alice said. She turned the car and paused at the entrance to the road. In the rearview mirror she could see the girl watching them with her dark eyes, still standing there, thinking and thinking.

20.

I didn't see her again for five years," Alice said. We had not moved from our places, she sitting on the deck, I standing on the cooling sand, while seagulls wheeled in high circles, hovered in the breeze, picked at scraps of garbage. "But I knew her when I saw her, standing in my doorway with that same serious look on her face. The dress she was wearing was old but very clean. I'm sure she had washed it carefully and thoroughly herself the night before, her hair, too, and even pressed or ironed it somehow, the dress I mean, and she had boys' shoes on her feet that must have been two sizes too big. But she still had that presence. Those black eyes, black as an Indian's. My little boy was four years old then and he hid behind my legs, peeking out at her, scared. Not because she looked angry or threatening, it was just the way she held herself very straight in the doorway, taller than I was by then, with that fierce desire and that dark, steady gaze.

"'I need to get a job,' she said. Just like that, no greeting or reminding me who she was. No hesitation or embarrassment. I asked her what kind of job she was looking for, and she said 'I guess whatever needs doing, I can do it.'

"I invited her inside, and that was the first time I saw her hesitate. So I said 'It's all right, Becky,' and she looked at me, and then she came in, slowly, looking around, like to make sure she wasn't walking into a trap. Then she just kept on looking around, taking it all in. Hungry. That's how she looked, though she wouldn't take any of the snacks that I offered. Not that kind of hungry. Maybe she was trying to satisfy herself that I hadn't lied to her five years before when I said that I lived in a nice house. I think I told myself I was embarrassed that the place was such a mess, with children's toys on the kitchen floor, but really the embarrassment was because I had seen her house that one time and I knew for sure that mine had to seem like it belonged to a whole different world.

"I talked to her a little bit, standing in the kitchen, not that it was much of a conversation on her side. She needed to get a job. That was why she was there and that was what she had to say. When I asked her if she wasn't in school most of the time, she just repeated that she could do whatever needed doing. Well, we had never had a maid, but after Daniel was born we had hired a cleaning service to come to the house once a week. I think it was a new service that had just started up, two girls would come in and clean, not always the same ones, and I knew a few other people that hired from the service, too. So I found their name and address in the yellow pages and I wrote that down for Becky. Maybe she said thank you, though it's hard to imagine those words coming out of her mouth, and then she went on her way. It never occurred to me until after she had gone to wonder how she had got to the house in the first place. Walked all that way, I guess."

Alice paused, looking out over the water. "She did take that job. I saw her once or twice with those girls. And I've thought a lot about her doing that work. Moving through the houses, scrubbing the toilets, washing the floors, invisible to the people who lived there, just another girl in white with a bucket or a broom. But she would have been taking it all in, the houses and the furniture and the books on the bookshelves, studying it all. She must have known, had an idea, even before then. She knew she wanted something, but she didn't know yet what all there was to want. So now she had the chance to learn, moving through the houses inch by inch, anonymous, touching every detail and memorizing it with her hands, coming home with the imprint of the floorboards on her knees.

"And what she must have learned there. Because, you know, the strange thing is that there is nothing nouveau riche about her, nothing flashy. Everything tasteful, understated. Once she set out to escape from her family, she could have determined to surround herself with luxurious things, things that boasted her wealth. That wouldn't have been surprising. But she chose differently.

"She worked at that job for a while, a year maybe, and then one day I guess she stopped being anonymous and invisible long enough for someone to see her. Not surprising, really. The surprising part is that she was ever able to be invisible in the first place, even in her cleaning-girl getup. Because she was always terribly striking. Even that first time I saw her, she was a bewitching child. She was hired as a maid or some such thing by the Brewsteads, they were a couple who lived out of town a ways." Alice pointed vaguely behind her, a gesture that told me nothing. "They had a large property, and they were a bit full of themselves for my taste, but an old family, what you might call a good one. They never mixed much, and certainly were not close friends of ours, so I only learned much later that she had found work there. All I knew at the time was that I no longer caught glimpses of her among the housecleaners, so I lost track of her. Eventually she left town, of course, gone for years. I have only spoken to her once since that day that I helped her to become a cleaning girl."

I stood still, waiting, while the sand shifted gently around my feet and distant children shrieked and splashed in the cold water. Alice said nothing. She was not looking at me anymore.

"You only spoke to her once since that day," I said, prompting gently.

Her eyes focused on me again, blinking behind the glasses. "Years later. It must have been seven or eight years. There was a party. At the house of a young woman named Mary Woodhouse."

"Wait," I said. "Hold on. You mean the party where no one showed up? That one?"

She was not smiling, but there was some satisfaction in her voice nonetheless. "So you have heard that story? Not surprising, I suppose. Well, it might as well be true, but it isn't, quite. There was one person who went to that party. I did.

"I was curious. Of course I knew that no one else would go, and that was just fine with me. I suppose I might not have gone either, but I was curious because I had seen this Lenoir person once in town and I thought I had recognized her. I knew that everyone disapproved of her, that no one wanted her to feel welcome, and maybe if I had not been curious I wouldn't have gone either. I'm sure I wouldn't have. But I was, and I did.

"It was a party—if that is the word for it—where all the things that mattered went unsaid. I went alone, and as soon as I got there I knew that I would be the only one. Mary opened the door and let me in and said my name, and there was Becky Tilton, all grown up and looking so beautiful it could scare you, wearing fine clothes and her hair done to a T and wearing a necklace that was probably Mary's. And beautiful heels. I took note of that. She came and took my hand and looked at me like a polite hostess and said 'So pleased to make your acquaintance, Mrs. Pickett. My name is Charlotte Lenoir, and I hope we will become fast friends' all in a distant, formal way, looking at me with those dark eyes, regal and serene and without any hint of fear or thought of being unmasked. They both made me at home, and we sat and had a drink, and we pretended that we had never expected anyone but we three to be there, and Becky and I pretended that we had never met before, and I pretended that I wasn't watching her keenly the whole time, and we made polite small talk and ate a tiny portion of the food that was laid out, and then after an hour I left.

"At the door, Mary took my hand and she looked at me with real feeling. She looked sad, terribly sad, and shining through the sadness was her gratitude, which I didn't deserve and I knew it. She said, 'It is such a pleasure to spend time with a lady who is truly well bred, Alice. Good night.' I knew that she was thinking bitterly of all the well-bred ladies who had deliberately chosen not to come. And Becky, Charlotte, she stood next to her and said to me, 'Yes, good breeding is so important, isn't it,' looking at me with something ironic, something cruel in her eyes and a movement of her lips that was not a smile.

"Maybe I am misremembering that look. But it did seem to me that she had changed, little as I knew her, then and now. It seemed to me that the hunger that I had seen in that little girl had curdled into something hard and sour, something more like a tyrannical will to take and conquer. Maybe something had happened to her, I don't know, or maybe it had been there all along. Maybe there is no such thing as innocence and it is only a trick of memory and nostalgia. But it was clear that she knew what she wanted and that she was going to do whatever she could to have it, to find a place inside the castle in whose shadow she had grown up. Because even if it was no castle, really, it would always look that way to her. It would always be the only one worth the effort of taking and having. If people have told you she was ruthless, then they told you right. Certainly she was cruel and opportunistic with Mary Woodhouse, and I believe that there is no one that she would not have used as a tool to get what she wanted. I guess she has it now, so maybe she is harmless now, but she looked dangerous then, even if I could not look at her then, or ever, without seeing in my mind's eye that barefoot girl standing in a gravel driveway watching me, all those years ago."

She stopped then. I stood for a moment, suddenly chilled in the shadow of the deck's roof. Abruptly, she said, "So, Kesey. It looks like we have been investigating the same mystery, such as it is. But I have been on the case for more than thirty years."

I hoisted myself up onto the weathered wood with its patina of sand and salt, got to my feet and sat on the picnic table. "You haven't ever spoken to her since that night?"

"We have nothing to say to each other. It's possible that she avoids me because she worries that I might expose her past. But if so she has never given me any sign of it, has never let on that she has ever known me. In any case, even if I were petty enough to do such a thing, which I am not, I hardly think it would make any real difference after all these years."

"And no one else knows any of this? You never told anyone?"

"No, no one," she said softly. "Not even Greg." She paused, seeming to think of something. I waited. "You know, Charlotte West has cleaned the toilets and bedrooms of half the women in this town, and as far as I know, not one of them has ever recognized her. Who am I to tamper with an ignorance as colossal as that?"

21.

As soon as Ellie knocked on the kitchen door the next day, I knew it was a mistake. Here she was, knocking on the wrong door at the wrong time of day, interrupting us in our lunchtime examination of the real-estate listings, and in that moment I knew for certain that no good could possibly come of it.

And of course I had completely forgotten that this was the day she was to visit us.

I had barely slept the night before, my mind buzzing, Alice's story repeating itself endlessly while I lay in bed and stared at the ceiling in the darkened room. It was a strange gift, this history that Alice had kept to herself for so long like a cherished treasure, and then had handed over all at once to a stranger in an act of pure faith, trusting that he would do the right thing with it.

But first I had to figure out what it meant, what it told me about Charlotte West, the woman who had spent her life hiding in plain sight. It seemed that she did have a secret, even if it was not the secret that I would have imagined or wanted, and she had been keeping it for decades, keeping it from just about everyone, including her husband.

And her daughter. Her daughter, whom she tried so vehemently to keep away from the local bars, whose tattoo enraged her. The daughter she needed to protect from the person that she had been before she remade herself. And now. How could I continue to see Ellie now, to see her and speak to her and not tell her any of this, because how in the world could I possibly be the one to tell her and how in the world could I possibly go on seeing her and not tell her?

But although I had been thinking hard about Ellie during the long night, I had forgotten that we had planned this visit, that I had proposed it as a way of forging a link between our nighttime trysts and the rest of our lives, a way of letting her into my life.

I had said nothing to Frederick. I thought it would be better to let the visit seem spontaneous, so that maybe we could avoid the awkwardness and the obligations of a planned meeting. Besides, I couldn't have told him that I had invited her over without explaining a great deal more—I shuddered at the thought. So we were both caught by surprise when the knock came.

I put down the newspaper and turned to open the door and let her in, trying to conceal my sudden anxiety.

"Hello," Ellie said, as nervous as I was and a little breathless, as she came in and stood by the kitchen table, her smile bright but forced. She was wearing a neat little summer dress, which threw the extreme casualness of our clothes into stark contrast, and carrying a plastic container. "I thought you two men might need a little break from your important work so I'm paying you a visit. I brought cookies."

She held out the container, which I took and opened, placing it on top of the papers on the table and murmuring thanks, forcing my own smile to match hers. Only the old man remained uncheered. He sat regarding Ellie as if from a distance, his head pulled back, lips pursed.

He turned to me, expressionless now, deadpan. "She brought cookies," he said.

I gave him a warning look, taking a bite of one.

Ellie looked even more nervous. "So what are you two reading these days?" she asked, a little too cheerfully.

"Right now we're going through the newspaper," I said. "In the evenings we're reading detective books. Raymond Chandler."

"You ever hear of him?" the old man said, watching her. He was sitting very still, not even smoking.

"Well, no. No, I haven't."

"Huh," he said. *As I suspected.*

"Daddy reads a lot, of course. He's always recommending things for me to read, but mostly I don't."

"You like those romance stories, I bet."

Frederick thought she was stupid, but she wasn't. I knew she could detect the harsh edge that was creeping closer to the surface of his voice, but she didn't know what to do about it. Neither did I. "No," she said. "I guess I read a few romance novels in junior high, but I don't care about them. And Daddy hates those Harlequin books."

I saw an opening to change the subject. "How is your father?"

She relaxed a little. "He's always fussing about something. Lately he's been fretting about whether he should sell a piece of land that he owns, north of Mystic, he said."

This was better. At the mention of real estate the old man became interested despite himself, I could tell. "Why is that something to fret over?" I asked.

"It's just the way Daddy is. He hates to part with any of the family property. I think this is some land that Grandpa West bought a long time ago when he thought he might need it for his business, but now nobody is using it. It's near that Indian land where the big casino is and Mr. Adams has been telling Daddy that he needs to sell it because he thinks that all that gambling is going to bring the Mafia"—she gave us a puzzled look—"or something like that to the area, and maybe they would want to force Daddy to sell the land to them. The whole thing has him really worried—Daddy, that is. He just can't believe that there could be *mobsters* out here. I mean, this isn't New York. But I guess—something about gambling attracts them?"

She took a nervous breath.

"Money," the old man said, his voice gravelly. "It attracts everybody."

"Especially real estate developers," I said, interrupting. "Mr. Adams. Is that Harrison Adams? Heritage Realty and Development?"

She nodded. "Yes, Harrison Adams. He and Daddy have known each other for a long time. But how did you—oh, at the party, the Fourth of July." We exchanged a look. It seemed like a long time ago.

"And why does Mr. Adams want to buy this very dangerous piece of land? Why isn't he scared to own it?" I said.

"Oh, well, I don't know if he actually said that it would be dangerous for Daddy personally. But you know, there might be things to worry about, maybe even legal issues. Daddy hates dealing with things like that, and Mr. Adams, this is his *business*, it's what he does for a living, so he would find a way to use the land or sell it to the right people or whatever. That's what he says, anyway." She raised a hand to tuck her hair behind one ear. "But I'm sure—"

She stopped abruptly. The old man had raised his dark glasses and his red eyes were fixed on her wrist. "Is that a tattoo mark?" he asked. It sounded like an accusation. His face was a lowering cloud of disapproval, changing the weather there in the kitchen in a heartbeat, and neither Ellie nor I was prepared for it.

"Yes," she said. She held herself awkwardly, looking like she wanted to hide her hand but could not find a place to put it.

The old man's voice was thick with contempt. "What're you, spending your time with sailors, hanging around by the docks? You riding around on the back of some guy's motorcycle?"

Ellie's face crumpled in shock and dismay, tears starting in her eyes.

"Frederick—!" I was leaning forward, as if trying to get between them. It had happened so quickly. I had missed the moment and there was no way back. I tried to think of something soothing to say but I was angry, too, angry at Frederick and twice as angry at myself.

He was talking to me now but still looking at her with disgust. "Who goes and does a thing like that? Some way for a kid to get back at the parents. It just shows you've got no self-respect—"

Ellie bolted out of her chair. She had been retreating into herself, coiling into a small defensive crouch, and now she choked out a sob, turned away quickly, uncoiling, and left the kitchen door banging behind her.

I had risen with her. I turned back, my heart beating fast, and glared at the old man, who had not moved from his seat. "What the hell was that?" I spat at him.

He stared back at me. "She's an idiot," he said flatly. "Coming over here. That tattoo mark. And now you think you're going to defend her. You're just thinking with your cock, that's all that is."

Maybe if there had been no hint of truth in it, I would have let it drop and run after her right away. But as it was I only got angrier, louder. "You dried-up son of a bitch. Who are you to decide whether she should have a tattoo or not?"

He put his hands on the table, glaring. "You want to take a swing at me? Go ahead. Take your best shot."

I was shouting now, standing over him while he sat there with his lip poked out. "Take a shot at you? Go to hell, old man. Maybe you can still swing your fists, but who cares? You're a cranky old bigot and you can't stand the thought that the world might be different than it was when you were twenty. Maybe you were just as fucking stupid then, for all I know. Maybe you were always a judgmental woman-hating prick. Maybe you always thought you always knew the truth and so it didn't matter who you insulted because you could never be wrong. Tough guy, picking on girls just out of high school. Fuck you. *You're* the asshole."

I was breathing hard, panting, angry but also hating myself as the words gushed out, sounding wrong and fast. I waited for him to yell back or to get up and come at me with his fists. But instead he leaned back away from the table slightly, raising his chin, paused there.

"Yeah. All right," he said, all the anger gone from his voice. "Maybe you've got a point, too. Okay, I guess you told me a thing or two, there." He sounded almost pleased, as if he had been waiting for me to finally put him in his place, give him what he deserved. Now I really did want to hit him.

I stood there, shaking, staring at him, my heart pounding, making me shake harder. I put a hand over my face in frustration, clenched my eyes shut until tears ran from them, and then I opened the door and went running down the driveway after Ellie.

She had a head start, but I was running, and she must have slowed down. I ran down the driveway, across the brief stretch of road, fallen twigs crunching under my sneakers, then up the West driveway, where I caught up with Ellie at the front door of her house. She was still crying, choking a little. I put an arm around her and she shoved me away, her face red, eyes streaming.

"I'm sorry," I began.

"Get away from me!" She turned the doorknob and pushed her way inside. I followed.

The house was dark inside. I didn't see anyone as I followed her into the large living room I had been in the day I arrived, long ages ago now. She moved swiftly through the room, past her father's neat, full bookcases and down a hall, hurling herself into a bathroom and slamming the door in my face. I hesitated there, hearing the sound of her crying through the door. I knocked softly and then tried the knob; it was locked. "Ellie, I'm so sorry," I said, but her crying was the only response.

I stood there for a quarter of an hour, uncertain, uneasy, knocking occasionally, provoking each time another muffled sob from the other side. Gradually my heart slowed its beating. I was breathing normally, the anger and anxiety fading, and all I felt was guilty and wrong.

There did not seem to be anyone else at home. No one had come to investigate the noises, and beyond our sad little corner at the back of the house there was no stirring of life. But I was uneasy. As my thinking calmed down I realized that I did not want to be caught there, trying to explain what I was doing in the house, alone except for Ellie locked in the bathroom and crying.

I walked back toward the front door, the floorboards creaking under my feet in the still house. The living room was dim and quiet, the windows shaded by thick trees growing close by, the air stuffy. I caught a smell of scotch—a trick of memory, surely—as I made my way past the bar and the sofa, the nautical lamp, the staircase.

My hand was on the front doorknob when I stopped, trying to

remember if there had been any information at all on the West family tree about Charlotte Lenoir, any parents or other relatives, anything that might tell me something more about her past.

So I went to the alcove where the family tree was enshrined, the apocryphal hunk of the old ship beneath it looking more than ever like an ordinary piece of weathered wood. There was not much light, so I stepped in close to read the names and dates. There was nothing more than I had remembered about her there, just the name and birthdate. But once I stopped to look, I couldn't help scanning the rest of the chart, wondering if I might run across some other name I had heard this summer. Following the looping pathways of inheritance among the squares and circles, I found that I could begin to see patterns in the weave, so that the genealogy was no longer just a confusion of lines. I noticed how the hand that had drawn up the lineage had made choices, how it preferred to follow the branches of the male line where it could, constructing a patriarchal lineage, but then when necessary it would fork off opportunistically along the female line in order to reach toward the desired origin, the *Mayflower* Man. It felt like learning how to read. Franklin West talked about how we in the present were the meek inheritors of an America made by great men of the past. But here that past was being made by people in the present, guided by their own claims and ambitions. Here was the keystone in the arch of American success, the inheritance that you build for yourself.

Looking at the lower reaches of the chart, I did notice a name I recognized: Brewstead. That was the name of the family that Alice had said Becky Tilton was working for after she stopped cleaning houses. *William 1912-1973*. He had been a distant cousin of Frank West's then. If he had lived longer he would have been a distant cousin-by-marriage to his former maid. William Brewstead's wife was *Sarah 1923-*. So she was still alive, or had been when the West family tree was made. Twenty years since her husband had died. A long time to be alone, growing old. Unless she had remarried. So many stories from the past, people from the past—

I stood up quickly, startled by the noise of two things happening simultaneously, the sounds coming from different directions. Ellie had opened the bathroom door and stepped out into the hallway, and at the same time the front door latch had clicked. As I turned to look, Charlotte West opened the door. She paused when she saw me, the daylight a bright frame behind her. I immediately wished myself somewhere else, anywhere else, but I knew too that I could not bear to be anywhere else, the two sensations pushing against each other, the friction between them prickling the hair on my scalp like a static charge.

She closed the door and walked in, hair and clothes and shoes perfect as always, no hint anywhere of the ragged little girl Alice had described. At that moment the whole story, the idea that such a girl had ever existed at all, seemed literally impossible. She looked at me for a moment as if I was a problem that might require a call to the local exterminator.

"Well?" she said.

Mouth open, mute, I gestured down the hall to where Ellie stood, just outside the door of the bathroom, looking disheveled and red-eyed. Seeing her mother, she gave a little cry, retreated inside the bathroom again, and slammed the door quickly.

Charlotte looked from the empty hallway back to me and I could see her beginning to guess, or to understand. To understand enough. Without any visible movement of her features, her face darkened.

She stepped forward, close to me, so close that I stepped backwards, a corner of the alcove stopping me with a sharp jab in the back. Her eyes, fixed on mine, were fathomlessly dark, the line between pupil and iris impossible to find, and her face was weirdly captivating in its anger, the face of an avenging angel. I could smell her perfume, her sweat, the outdoor scent the sun teases from cotton and leather, burnt and alive. She held my gaze pitilessly, and I think I really believed that she was going to slap me to the floor, or tear my beating heart from between my ribs.

Finally she said in a rough whisper, a hiss, "Get out. Don't come back. And don't ever come near my daughter again. Don't ever come near anything that belongs to me."

Then she was gone, moving toward Ellie in the locked bathroom, and I walked out the front door and closed it behind me, my fingers shaking on the knob.

22.

They were still shaking when I turned the knob to open the kitchen door. I don't know what I meant to say to Frederick just then, but whatever it was it stayed unsaid, because Duke was sitting there at the table with the old man. Duke nodded hello and watched me curiously. I must have looked ashen. I was feeling battered, jittery, emptied out like a poisoned belly.

The old man, however, was obnoxiously cheerful. "Jesus, Duke, you should have seen this guy earlier. He gave me a real talking to. Boy, did he chew me out. It was a goddamn thing to see." He seemed genuinely pleased, energized, while all I felt was shame and exposure. He had goaded me into yelling at him and now that I had done it I felt foolish and betrayed, as if I had been lured out into the open and then left there stripped naked. I glowered, but Frederick was paying no attention, absorbed in lighting a smoke.

Duke took a thoughtful sip from his battered thermos and regarded the old man. "Well, I'm sure you had it coming, Frederick."

He turned to me. I think he could feel the tension in the room and decided that a change of subject was needed. "Kese, before you came in, we were just talking over a funny coincidence. Frederick was telling me that you've been hearing from your friend next door"—I think I winced—"that her dad's been getting the strong-arm from Mr. Harrison Adams, wanting him to sell some land he owns."

He paused. I nodded, sighing, and decided to pull myself together for Duke's sake. "That's what she said. More or less."

"Well, the reason I say it's a coincidence is because I hear—confidentially, sort of—that Heritage Realty has been up to its elbows in that kind of business lately. You remember Clinton? Of course you would. Well, Clint's the one who mentioned it to me. Heritage has been buying up as much land around the reservation as they possibly can. Trying to get it as cheap as they can, too. People—politicians, tribal leaders, too—have been nervous ever since the casino opened, even before it opened, nervous that organized crime would step in and get involved, maybe even take over the casino some way or other, work it from the shadows, break some legs, take a nice share of the profits and run the Pequots like puppet bosses. Something like that, I guess, is how the boogeyman story goes."

I was trying to remember what exactly Adams had said to me during our conversation. "Is that a real concern? I mean, is there really even a mob in Connecticut? A shadowy organization that confiscates your gin and tonic water if you don't mow the lawn on Saturday?"

The old man stirred and pointed a thick finger at me. "Sure there is. Just a couple of years ago there was a big bust, huge. Patriarcha family. Big network all over New England. Don't fool yourself. But that doesn't mean Adams isn't full of shit."

Duke toyed with his thermos, turning it on its bottom edge in a wobbly circle. "It's not a *completely* unrealistic concern," he said, thoughtfully. "There have been other tribes that have had trouble with local mobsters, sure."

"Of course. Because they're a bunch of fucking amateurs. Any mob boss with a brain could see that here's a bunch of guys who don't have a goddamn clue what they're doing. They're like fucking Mickey Rooney playing around in the backyard with Judy Garland. 'Gee fellows, let's put on a show!' It's an invitation for someone who *does* know how to run an operation like that to step in and make a buck."

"But," said Duke, "like you say, that still doesn't mean Adams isn't full of shit. And he is. He's trying to take advantage of the situation to make some money. There's all this confusion around the casino, lots of unhappy local homeowners. Then everybody, the politicians and the lawyers too, gets nervous about what might happen if the mob gets involved. So if you're a certain kind of savvy real estate developer, you figure, hey, this is perfect. You do what you can to keep those rumors about the mob alive, and while everyone's nervous, you try to convince people who own land near the reservation that they should be selling to you. Why should they stick around and wait for crime to come to the front door? Then you can wait and sell the land at sky-high prices to the very rich tribe next door that is looking to expand its boundaries, or maybe you can develop it yourself and take advantage of this remarkably well-placed spot, very convenient for businesses that might want to cater to all those people who come to the casino. Easy money."

The old man leaned back, thoughtful, chin in the air. "I wouldn't put it past the son of a bitch."

"So what happens now?" I asked.

Duke shrugged. "Got me. Nothing? Isn't that what usually happens? I'm not even sure if there's any crime being committed here, strictly speaking."

We sat in silence for a moment, meditating on that. Then Duke stood and stretched and picked up his thermos.

"Well, I'm going to get out there. The lawn's got to be mowed, Saturday or not."

"All right," the old man said. "But Jesus, Duke, you should have been here. This guy really told me off."

23.

I stayed awake late that night, staring at the ceiling into the early hours of the morning, wondering if Ellie would come. Not waiting, I told myself, but awake nonetheless.

The knock on the screen never did come, though I jumped and watched the door every time a branch creaked or an animal wandered past outside.

I wondered if she stayed away by choice or because she had been forbidden, wondered what had happened after I left. Would she have confessed everything, or kept silent and left her mother to guess what she would? If she stayed away by choice, if she had decided never to come again, I couldn't blame her. Although I had been furious at the old man, I knew that it was my fault and my doing, and I knew too, guiltily, that a part of me was glad to think that this might be the end of the affair.

She did not come that night, nor would she come the next night, or the one after that. I didn't know it then, but it really was over.

The day passed sluggishly. I was still not done being angry at Frederick and his mood was even more dour than usual, so we did not speak to each other if we could avoid it. The sky was overcast and everything looked dull, so dull it was painful to have to keep your eyes open and all familiar things looked ugly and there was nothing new at all. We read the papers as usual, but neither of us could stay interested, so we gave them only a desultory skim before turning on the television and looking for a movie to watch, but of course there was none.

Finally the old man grew weary of having someone in the house who was even more sullen and taciturn than he was, and sent me on an errand. He wanted to buy some stocks in the portfolio that he was forever tweaking, so he gave me directions to his stockbroker's office and an envelope with his instructions in it. The day was cool and I had few clean clothes, so I left the house still in a foul mood but perversely well dressed in slacks and a button-down.

I parked in town and walked past the church, its spire pricking at the low-hanging gray of the sky. The address I was looking for was a white-sided colonial, with a modest black sign outside the door that read OWEN PAYNE: LEGAL AND FINANCIAL SERVICES. I walked in expecting a lobby or waiting area and found that I was already in the main part of the office, a dim carpeted room with a low ceiling and one small window. There was a desk with a lamp, a desktop computer, and several neat stacks of papers on it. The wall behind the desk was decorated with frames containing a law degree and a couple of official certifications. Beyond the desk there were two open doors, one revealing a storeroom and the other containing a photocopy machine, one bulky gray side of which was visible as I walked in.

At the sound of my entrance a man appeared in the doorway of the copy room, peered out at me, and then came into the office. He was short and thick around the middle, with thinning gray hair, and everything about him seemed pinched. He was wearing a shirt with vertical stripes and a contrasting all-white collar that was noose-tight around his neck, so that the flesh gathered at his throat above the pinch of the collar fastening. The shirt bulged out from there around his torso before being tied off again at the waist by a tight black belt. "Can I help you?" he asked, his voice pinched too, high and drawling, like a Yankee Truman Capote. He gazed at me from behind the rounded silver frames of his glasses.

"Are you Owen Payne? I'm here to deliver something from Frederick Hardt." I held out the envelope for him to take. "Some stocks he wants to buy."

"Ah, Frederick," he said thinly, taking the envelope. He put it on his desk and then put his hands in his pockets, leaning back to regard me. "Are you a new employee of his?" He looked me up and down with a sort of unpleasant amusement in his face.

"You could say that, yes. Well, thank you. Goodbye."

But as I turned to go I caught sight of the law degree on the wall and swiveled back. "Excuse me, Mr. Payne?" He raised a skeptical eyebrow. "I wonder if I could ask you a question. I see that you're a lawyer as well as a stockbroker?"

He gazed steadily at me. There was something sinister about the high sharp voice emerging from that bound and doughy body, but he clearly enjoyed hearing himself speak, and once he began he was prepared to go on for a while. "I am indeed, young man. The law is my first calling, my preferred profession, and I perform whatever legal services I can for my clients. I draw up many wills, as you may imagine, wills and other contracts, provide legal advice when it is desired and requested. But this being a small town, with many people who wish to invest their considerable funds, my services have expanded over the years in the direction of financial advisement and portfolio management. A small-town lawyer has many duties. He is like the scribe of antique times, the mind of the village, its intellectual crossroads, the interpreter of specialized knowledge that is obscure to the ordinary citizens. If he does his job right, he comes to know, sooner or later, where all the bodies are buried. If he does it well, he never lets his knowledge become public."

I tried to look appreciative. "I wouldn't want you to betray any trusts. I just wondered if you were familiar with a company called Heritage Realty and Development?"

He continued to look at me, bluff but unblinking, hands in his pockets, rocking on his heels. "What, exactly, did you say you were doing for Mr. Frederick Hardt?"

"I'm helping Frederick out temporarily, just this summer," I said vaguely, and then I took a plunge. "But I work as a freelance writer, and right now I'm researching an investigative piece about land transactions in the area around the Pequot reservation." Once the lie was spoken, I became interested in it. I was not generally very good at lying or at fooling people, and I was approaching this ploy with an experimental curiosity. It was a stroke of luck that I wasn't wearing my usual shorts and T-shirt, so that I looked at least marginally professional, and I had enough reporting experience from college to bluff my way through any questions Payne might ask. You never know, I told myself in the moment. Maybe there really was a story here, yet another mystery to unravel. Maybe I really could write it.

His words were deliberate now, a performance of caution, and he was eyeing me closely. "I am of course familiar with Heritage Realty and Development; it is a major business in the area. Do I understand that your *investigation* of this topic and your interest in Heritage, in combination, suggest that you believe that there is some element of malfeasance in their conduct—this presumably being the reason for your interest, or for your belief in the public's potential interest in whatever story you might write or publish in whatever venue?"

The question sounded like a trap, but maybe it was just the way he talked. "I don't believe anything," I said. "But, yes, I am wondering if there might be some dishonest dealing."

He nodded, but not as if he agreed with me. When he spoke his tone was one of dismissal. "Let me be frank with—what was your name?"

"Kese."

"*Kese.* Let me be frank with you. Harrison Adams, who is the driving force behind Heritage and all its doings, is an acquaintance of long standing and a man whom I trust and respect. I advise you to end your ill-conceived pursuit of this inquiry, because although I know nothing concerning any land transactions that have been conducted in that area lately, any accusation of wrongdoing or dishonesty on the part of Mr. Adams or his team is surely baseless. Put your journalistic skills—which I am sure are formidable—to work on a project that is worthy of them."

I forced a smile. "No bodies buried there, then."

"Indeed, no. May I ask how you came to be concerned about this question in the first place?"

I hesitated, trying to decide what I could and could not say.

"I heard—I heard from one of the neighbors, Franklin West, that Heritage wanted to buy some land that he owns near the reservation."

He dropped his shoulders, letting go of a tension that I had not noticed there before. "Well, Frank West," he said. "I am sure that there is nothing wrong in that. Frank is apt to have an overly sentimental attachment to his family's holdings. I am sure that any misgivings he feels about selling it come from that source, nothing more. Do you have much contact with the West family? I would not have thought that Frederick would socialize much with them, or with anyone, for that matter."

I was beginning to regret my improvised fishing expedition for information about Heritage, which had got me nowhere, and kept me here longer. The air was stuffy and both the office and Owen Payne's conversation were claustrophobic. "I've seen a little of them. Frank was very friendly to me. And his wife is—a very remarkable person."

Payne's gaze was on the floor, his voice squeezed through the tourniquet of his collar. "Never trust a woman," he said, a cold little smile playing over his lips. "My mother always told me that."

Just then there was a stirring in the back room that Payne had emerged from, a rustle and a jingling. A moment later, a small dog trotted out and stood in the doorway. It was compact and lithe, its fur white and tawny brown, with large alert ears and a tail that curled forward, its head cocked slightly to give it an expression of lively attention, as if curious to hear what we had to say.

"This is Buck," Payne said, looking down at the dog. "An elegant specimen, is he not? Do you know anything about dog breeding?"

"Nothing," I said, truthfully.

"A very interesting subject. I often think that it has a great deal to teach us. We like to think that in human affairs we can rid ourselves of the instrumentality that we practice when we breed animals, that the pragmatic and aesthetic goals of the breeding enterprise can be put aside in favor of some well-meaning principle of respect for the dignity of the individual human. An absurdity. We are all made by our genealogies, ones that are no more or less dignified than those of the great dog lineages, and that deserve to be treated with the same utilitarian care. But we cloud everything in human affairs over with sentiment."

We were both still standing, Payne with his hands still in his pockets. I did not want to mimic him, but all of a sudden I didn't know what to do with my hands. "I'm not sure I follow you," I said weakly. He seemed to be pursuing a train of thought, as if the conversation had been going in this direction already.

"Our laws reflect this absurdity," he said. "They are an irrational patchwork, constructed and amended over time to try to accommodate our sentimental feelings about families and children, which of course are themselves whimsical, changing as decades pass but never progressing. Take an example. Some years ago now I had a case," he was gazing at the floor again now, something amused and almost sly in his expression. "One that required me to research a few things about our adoption laws. Did you know that it is possible, common even, to legally rewrite the history of an adopted child, to alter the past so that the record will show that the child was born in a different state, a different city, to different parents? The idea is to counteract what we might see as the stigma of being adopted. In the name of what we consider to be the child's best interests—as if such thing could exist, and of course we know that there are only adult interests and agendas, masking themselves behind this conventional piety—the child's history is erased. Not completely, of course. There are ways to get the information, but you have to know that you are looking for it, and how could you know that, if you do not know there is anything to look for?"

The room seemed to have no source of fresh air at all, and I had begun to smell the cloying perfume of an air freshener. I licked my lips and cleared my throat. "I didn't know that," I said hoarsely. "Were we talking about adoption? I thought you were saying something about dog breeding."

He smiled in his pinched way. "Perhaps I was. I had more than one thing on my mind."

He turned to regard the dog, still standing there watching us with its intelligent expression, its air of alert and patient waiting, ears and tail at the ready. "Buck is a Basenji. Are you familiar with the breed?" I shook my head, wishing the conversation over and done with, but he went on. "Hunting dogs, from the Congo originally. Decades ago a small number of the dogs were brought to England to serve as breeding stock. This is how breeding works. Centuries of mixture and mongrelization produce a dog which is then taken up by professionals and institutionalized as pure. The problem was that because of the small gene pool from which all Western Basenji had been produced, the dogs were prone to liver disease. Western breeders had to go back to Africa, back to the source, for more pure foundation stock, a new infusion of good strong African blood." He looked indulgently at the little dog, which looked back at him. "So whatever else you might say about diversity in our little corner of Connecticut, at least I can claim to have the only nigger dog in town."

The casual way he said the word, the intimate gaze of the dog, the looming stuffiness of the room: it was if he had lured me in close and then slapped me in the face. The Basenji dog was looking at me curiously with its small patient eyes, as if it was prepared to answer a question that I had forgotten to ask. Suddenly I was suffocating, almost panicky. I just wanted to get out, to be outside where there was air and light, where I could breathe again, where I could breathe the air and never, ever see Payne again. "I have to go," I said. My voice sounded thick and far away.

Owen Payne was grinning at me as I backed toward the door. "The pleasure has been all mine," he said, his smile small and mocking. "And give my best to Frederick Hardt—" His voice was fading as I opened the door, stepped out, too fast, almost slamming it behind me, and then finally I was outside, in the same cool gray overcast day I had left behind, and I was squinting, amazed to find that it was still daylight and that the world still existed as before, moving fast toward the street and taking great gulps of air as if I had been trapped long underwater with no hope of ever seeing the surface again.

24.

Evening came as a relief. While we were eating ham sandwiches in silence for dinner, a wind blew in and pushed the dull sky away, and by the time we stepped outside to read, stars had emerged behind a smudged gibbous moon. Invisible clouds moved by in gusts of dark, and a breeze pulled at the pages of *The Long Goodbye* as I read.

For a while the old man worked silently at his barbells, grunting occasionally as he hoisted the weight. Then he sat down, an unlit cigarette dangling from his lip, listening closely to the story. At one point he barked out a laugh at a particularly harsh put-down delivered by the narrator.

"That Marlowe's got a hell of a mouth, doesn't he?"

I lowered the book. "It's awfully convenient that he always has a devastating comeback on the tip of his tongue," I said. "Plus the hoods and stiffs keep setting him up. He's a comedian in a world full of straight men."

"You've got the whole thing backwards," he said. "He's surrounded by assholes and he's the only one who's shooting straight. He's the only one who sees what a fucking pile of shit the world is and isn't afraid to say so."

"And so that's brave? Just complaining about everything all the time?"

"Goddamn right it's brave. It's always brave to tell the truth."

For a moment right then I felt that I understood something about the old man, maybe even understood clearly what his wife, my grandfather's sister, had seen in him. It was not just that his background was a rebuke to her family. It was him, too, his belief that he was debunking the false world, that must have appealed to her. The role he had chosen for himself was to say all the things he felt that others were too polite to say, or what they would never even think but were somehow gratified to hear him say, even if they shook their heads in disapproval. How could he step outside of that role, even if he wanted to, with all the rest of us depending on him to speak out so that we could pretend to be scandalized, so that we could be kept safe behind the screen of his obscenity?

It was a thought that I was to have again, years later. The old man was dead by then, found cold on the floor of his bathroom by one of the cleaning women, a heart attack. I made the drive up for the funeral and took a room at a motel in Saybrook. The room was quiet, anonymous, with its bedspread roughened by countless launderings, a view of the parking lot, and a television whose channels I browsed idly through the evening hours while the world outside grew dark.

In the morning I put on a dark suit jacket, wrapped a scarf around my neck, and stepped out into the chilly morning, the cars in the lot still glazed with a fine sheen of dew.

It was October, the peak of the season, and as I made my way down the familiar narrow winding roads I drove in a slow constant rain of brightly colored leaves, drifting down ahead and behind as far as I could see, falling silently, covering the grass and the mossy boulders and the low stone walls in drifts of gold and fuchsia. Autumn sunlight slanted across the road and illuminated the leaves, dry and bright, finely veined, browns and reds and lambent oranges, falling and falling while I drove, pasted to the asphalt where other wheels had driven over them, covering over my tracks behind me.

Then I was in the graveyard, listening to the minister and thinking how much the old man would have hated to hear him. It was a burial service, so at least there was no church ceremony for his spirit to rebel against, and it was sparsely attended. I did not know any of the three other mourners in attendance, two old men and the minister's wife, but after a few minutes I felt a hand on my shoulder and turned to see Duke standing behind me, wearing a dark knit hat and with his perpetual red stubble looking especially bristly in the cold sunlight. So we stood and went through the ritual, all of us in our dark clothes, our breath rising in clouds and disappearing while the rain of autumn leaves continued unabated around us, rustle and hush, slowly filling in the open grave.

When the service was over and all the hands had been shaken, Duke and I stood apart from the others. Later there would be time to have a drink and talk and learn the news, but for now we were silent. After a few moments, he gestured behind me. "Say. What do you think old Frederick would have said about these people over here?"

I turned to look. A small family group had entered the cemetery and were standing near a gravestone nearby. Even mourning their dead, they had a look of entitlement about them, and they were conducting their business with an air of propriety. The middle-aged father, in particular, held himself stiff with a kind of self-satisfaction. All this was good and right, his posture seemed to say; we lay the flowers just so and we stand unsmiling in our handsome clothes and the ritual has been observed.

I looked back at Duke. He raised his eyebrows.

"Assholes," I said.

He did not smile, but nodded, slowly, solemnly, as if with a deep sense of satisfaction. Frederick was still saying for us the things we were too polite to say for ourselves. A leaf fell on Duke's shoulder and hung there on his worn wool coat, fragile and persistent, the insignia of an unknown order. Then we walked back toward the parking lot.

But that was all to come. It was out there, waiting for us.

Frederick didn't seem to be in a hurry to continue with the reading, so I put the paperback aside. "All right," I said. "Fine. Tell me some truth. How did you lose that finger?"

It was hard to tell, in the uneven glare of the porch light, but I think I may have caught him off guard for once. He did not look at me, but stared ahead, sitting on the stone edge of the terrace. Then he picked up his pack of cigarettes, took one out, tapped it on the stones, and put it in the corner of his mouth.

"That was a long time ago," he said. The lighter flared against the glasses, dark depthless mirrors. "I mean, Jesus, ever since I can remember I've been addicted to some goddamn thing or other. Smokes, sure, there's always been them. These days I take my Prozac in the morning, then I chew on Xanax all day just to keep things quiet, but back in those days it was beer. I was pretty tough then. Pretty fucking stupid, too, if you want to know the truth. I used to walk around with my chest puffed out in a white T-shirt with a pack of smokes rolled up in the sleeve, my hair slicked back, trying to look like some kind of tough guy I'd seen in the movies." He laughed at the memory, a bark that turned into a deep-down guttural cough.

"I had this job back then, working at a factory outside Hartford, running a machine tool. Work my shifts all week, then Friday night would come, I'd head down to the store and buy twelve beers, bring them home. I was living with my ma—we'd been in this shithole country fifteen years and she still could barely speak the language. So Fridays I'd sit myself down at the kitchen table, too exhausted to think straight, and drink them all, one after another, *bam, bam, bam*. Christ, it's good to be that young.

"Then Saturday afternoon I'd drive over to this bar where all the characters from the university used to go. They'd sit at their tables in their overcoats with their scarves hanging down and they'd argue, and I'd be sitting at the bar nursing a beer and reading the papers. Eventually those guys got interested in me, and some of them used to come over where I was sitting and we'd talk and I'd tell them a thing or two. In another lifetime I would've liked to sit there like they did, like there wasn't anything else to do in the goddamn world but sit and talk about books and philosophers, drinking, with their scarves hanging down. Must be quite a fucking life.

"So I was working at the end of a shift on a Friday, and I was tired out and thinking about the beer I was going to be drinking later on, not keeping my mind on the job, and that machine caught hold of my hand. I went to yank it away but the bastard had my finger. Jesus, it hurt. Mangled it. Tore it apart. I finally pulled my hand away, the finger just tore off, and all of a sudden there was blood everywhere, blood on my clothes and the floor and the machinery, and I was yelling and then everyone came running over. Some guy wrapped a rag around my hand and said we'd better go to the doctor, and then I really started yelling. They all gathered around, strong guys, big wops most of them, and they were trying to hold me, get me calmed down, and I started bucking and fighting, telling them I wasn't going to any goddamn doctor. But they wrestled me down and dragged me across the floor and out into the street, screaming and fighting, and I was still shouting that there was no way they were getting me near any Yalie son of a bitch in a white coat with a license to slice me up, and they didn't know what to do, so finally they dragged me out, got me in the back of a truck and drove to my house. I was berserk by then, just in an animal rage, kicking and yelling at them, so they get me in the door and there we are in the kitchen, me screaming and them screaming back, all of us covered in blood and grease and sweat, they're knocking over the chairs and trying to hold me down on the kitchen table, shoes slipping in the blood on the floor, and then Ma's there, pulling at her hair and screaming in German and I start yelling back at her in German too.

"And then, Jesus, there's this one fucking guy, Eddie. He's come in with them, but he's not fighting or trying to hold me down. He's just standing there, leaning against the kitchen sink, he's got a cigarette lit and he's smoking, just standing there watching. And somehow while I'm gasping for air so I can start yelling and fighting some more, he shakes his head and says, 'For Christ's sake, Fred, what's the big idea? All you lost was a finger and you're carrying on like it was your goddamn cock.' Everything went still for a couple seconds, everyone just froze where they were. And then I opened my mouth to yell again, but that guy was still standing there, looking at me like I was just a dumb fool, and I don't know what happened but my mouth was still open and when I listened to hear what I was yelling at him, instead I heard myself laughing, lying there pinned down on the table with some spilled flowers lying by my ear, laughing hard, harder than I ever laughed in my life. Then everybody started laughing, all the guys, even Ma was laughing, and it's just lucky that she didn't understand enough English to know what he had said, but we were all just helpless, laughing and laughing while Eddie stood there shaking his head like we were all nuts.

"So then they patched me up, stopped the bleeding, and we all had a few beers to celebrate. The hand healed up, didn't even take too long." He held his hand up, splaying out the fingers and the smooth stump.

Then he seemed to grow meditative, taking a long last silent drag. He flicked his cigarette away and it rolled and skipped in the wind, a small thing whose only life was fire and burning, carried away into the dark.

"Funny thing," he said. "I hadn't given a thought to Eddie Slope in years, now his name comes up twice this summer."

I tried to remember where I had heard the name before. "Wait. You mean that he's the one—"

"Yeah, that guy at breakfast the other day. Asking for him, like he hadn't been dead for years."

"You said he died in a car accident?"

"Out on the Post Road. Twenty years ago, almost. I left that factory job not too long after I lost the finger, went and worked up in Hartford for a while. By the time I came down here, working as a contractor, Eddie had left that job and he was hiring himself out as a lawn man around here. This was before Duke, you understand. So I was out working on these old houses, and I used to see Eddie around. Sometimes I'd stop and bullshit with him a little. Funny guy."

He paused and shook another cigarette out of the pack, did not light it yet, playing with it absently while he spoke. "I never did get all the details on that car crash. Eddie was driving, I heard it was a big mess. Wrapped the thing around a telephone pole going around a sharp curve late at night. Could've happened to anyone, I guess. Christ, you never know."

I had been watching the cigarette, but now I looked up. "He

was driving, you said. You mean there were other people in the car?"

"One, sure. Guy named Brewstead. I never could figure that. Not that I ever asked, but Brewstead was a big-time asshole. You know, big house, thought he was some kind of anointed character because of his goddamn family history. I never could figure what a regular guy like Eddie was doing driving him around, but who knows. He must have done some work out on the Brewstead place sometime or other, maybe the guy needed a ride or something. Mister goddamn big man."

"William Brewstead?" I asked, turning the coincidence over idly in my mind, like the cigarette in the old man's fingers.

He looked at me sharply. "What, you heard of him?"

"I think the name came up," I said. "Do you want me to read some more?"

He puffed out a sigh. "Okay, sure."

I picked up the book and looked down at the page, scanning for the place I had left off. But I couldn't focus. The strangeness of the coincidence, of William Brewstead turning up again here, had set me thinking, but the thinking had nowhere to go. These stories from the past were crowding around me, demanding attention, acting like if they could be put together they might mean something, but there was no way for me to tell if they did or not, no way to even make the connections make sense, because I just didn't know enough.

There were some things I had been careful not to look at too closely since my trip to the beach with Alice Pickett, but I knew I could not avoid them forever, because there was still Charlotte West. I don't know if I had realized until Alice told me her story just how much I had invested in my idea of Charlotte. And the strange thing was that now, even knowing that she was not a displaced European countess or the dark flower of the New England aristocracy, even though she hated me for messing with her household, I wanted more than ever to know how she had come to be where and who she was. Maybe the urgent desire I had felt for her was receding now, but I still owed it to that betrayed part of myself to explain how it had been seduced in the first place. And there was still the mystery, the pieces of the puzzle: my fingers were itching to pick them up and see where they fit.

I had mostly just allowed the bits of information to come to me, so far. I had asked a few questions here and there, but I hadn't really done anything. I had been pretending that I wasn't really looking for answers, afraid of being pulled too far into an obsession, finding connections where there weren't any. Well, it was time to start looking.

Beyond the dim illumination of the porch light, it was dark and clear and breezy, the stars bright above. The night was a sea of information, full of constellations I did not know.

"Frederick."

He looked up, frowning.

"I'm going to need to take some time tomorrow afternoon. There's an errand I need to run."

Then I went back to the book.

25.

The woman in the yard watched me as I drove up and parked, squinting into the sun with a hand shading her eyes.

It hadn't been hard to find her. There were three Tiltons in the local phone directory, but their addresses all seemed to be next to one another, and now I could see why. The driveway ended in a patch of gravel where a couple of dusty cars were parked. On the grass beyond, there was a kind of compound made up of three trailer homes clustered together, stuck in a clearing surrounded on the left and right by tall evergreens. The ones on the sides looked old and faded, but the one in the middle was well cared for. A narrow deck had been built onto the front of it, and two plastic flowerpots hung from the railing. A gray rope was strung between two of the trailers, with wooden clothespins clinging to their perches along it. Behind the trailers were two or three weathered wooden shacks with tall dry grasses behind them receding out of sight over a hill, and the weedy front lawn contained a trash barrel and an old picnic table. Next to them a woman in jeans and a T-shirt was sitting on a metal chair webbed with a fraying plaid, bent over a metal bowl, peeling potatoes.

She continued to watch me as I got out of the car and walked toward her. I threw out a tentative wave that she did not return. The day was still and quiet, and she sat unmoving, holding the peeler paused in its work.

I tried a smile. "I'm looking for Jerry Tilton?" I said, my voice rising more in uncertainty than in a question. It had been one of the names in the phone book.

A pause. "That's me." She looked wary, as if there was no news that could come to her from the outside world that could possibly be worth the hearing. She was fortyish, I would have guessed, although the years had not been gentle with her. In truth, it looked as if the years were having a good laugh at her expense and she both knew and resented it. She had light brown hair with a few wiry gray strands in it, and a slight frown was creased into the lines around her mouth. Her dark eyes had a curiously blank expression, or maybe that was part of the wariness, too: they were waiting without much hope to learn what they would have to express.

I introduced myself, but there was no sense in trying to put her at ease since I knew I had to plunge ahead and make a stab in the dark that would be not be easy for either of us. I took a breath. "Do you have a sister named Becky?"

Now the eyes came to life, looking at me sharply. She was silent for what seemed like a long time, but when she answered her voice was steady. "Used to. I haven't seen her since I was a girl. Who's asking?"

Good question, although *why* would have been an even better one. But I was here, and there was no sense in stopping now. No sense in lying, either. "She's a neighbor of mine. At least I think she is, but she goes by a different name now. Did you know that?"

"Did I know what."

"That she—that she had changed her name?" It sounded foolish, but I wanted to find out how much she knew. Did she know that her sister had deliberately planned a kind of escape, that her career to date had been a gambit whose apparent aim was to reinvent herself in the image of everything Jerry Tilton was not?

She looked straight at me, the lines around her mouth pressing down, deepening. "I don't care what she does. Why do you?"

"Maybe it doesn't matter." I hesitated, then took another step out on the thin ice I was walking. "She has money."

The eyes were fierce now, contemptuous. "She has money. Who needs her money? I don't know her and I wouldn't ask her for anything. Damn right it doesn't matter. Come around here asking questions about a sister I haven't seen in thirty years. A neighbor, you say. Who is she to me, and who the hell are you?"

"I'm sorry. I didn't mean to upset you."

She stood up from the lawn chair and put the peeler down, wiped her hands on her jeans. "It's time for you to get going. I've got things to do." She began to gather her things together to take them inside.

I turned away, feeling stupid and ashamed. I rested a hand on the splintered wood of the picnic table. Just beyond it, at the edge of the clearing, was a huge pine tree, a wide thick expanse of prickly foliage drying in the summer sun with that sharp clean smell of evergreen surrounding it. An image of the West family tree flashed across my mind, that lifeless spindly thing of lines and boxes, absurdly juxtaposed with this lush architecture of branch and root, more like a house than a tree, something you could take comfort and shelter from, something you could look at every day out your window and come to depend on, something real.

Something real.

And then the world seemed to tilt away from me, blood rushing in my ears with the shock of sudden, certain knowing. I whirled, fast, to look at Jerry Tilton walking toward one of the trailers, her back to me, the bowl balanced under one arm.

"You're her mother."

I did not say it loud, but my voice seemed to echo in the dry clearing.

The way she stopped. The way she stopped still, I knew immediately that it was true. She did not move for a moment, standing straight and quiet, and then something in her collapsed visibly, her shoulders falling and all the stiffness going out of her back, the arm holding the bowl sagging at her side. She turned to look at me, stricken, the frowning mouth unmoving. I walked toward her without taking my eyes off her face, seeing the resemblance clearly now, the eyes, the forehead, the curve of the chin. A different resemblance than the one I had been looking for.

"You're Ellie's mother," I said, wondering. "Ellie West. Or whatever her real name is."

She looked back, something in the hard face cracking below the surface.

"Ellie," she said. "Yes, that's her name. Eleanor Tilton. I always called her Ellie. I gave her my last name. Her father was gone by the time she was born so I gave her my name."

"How?" I said. "How did it happen?"

She started walking straight ahead. I thought she must be in a trance state, but then she sat down at the picnic table, dropping the bowl with the peeled white potatoes and the peeler in it. I came and sat across from her, still watching her in wonder. I didn't have to explain; she knew exactly what I meant.

"She was just thirteen months old when Becky came back. Thirteen months and walking. Used to walk around with apples. I'd slice up an apple and she'd walk around the yard with two handfuls of slices. Couldn't stand to let them go till she had eaten them all so when she'd fall down she didn't have any way to stop herself. Fall flat on her face if I wasn't there to catch her. Or on her elbows. Her arms were all bruised up because she never could let go of those apples, but she liked walking around so much." She stopped, looking off into the distance, looking rueful, as if she still could not believe her baby daughter's stubbornness, like it was all still in the present and she was sitting telling a neighbor about it and shaking her head in fond exasperation.

"I wasn't any teenage mother or nothing like that, but I was on my own. Working as a waitress, but it got hard once she was born, 'cause I could barely pay for the day care and didn't have any relations I could trust with my baby girl.

"Then Becky came back. Becky, or whatever she calls herself. Came back different, too. I hadn't seen her for years, ever since she left. She was just a teenager when she went, and I must have been getting to be one too. I never knew why she left, exactly. She had been working around town, making pretty good money. I always admired her 'cause she was so much braver than me, she was never afraid of anything at all. Walk right up to a big house in town and ask for a job and get it. I admired her, but I was always a little bit scared of her, too. I grew up with her, shared a bedroom all those years, but I still never felt like I knew her, not really. She never told any of her secrets, not to me or anyone else.

So it wasn't any kind of surprise when she didn't tell me anything about why she was leaving or where she was going. Just came home one day, packed a few things, gave me a look, and said she'd be back someday.

"When she came back she never said where she'd been for all those years, and that was just like Becky. Gone all the time I was growing up, leaving me doing my best to figure out how to be a grown woman, doing my best to help out Mom and to keep my little brother safe from our father. She missed all that. Hell, she didn't want to try to fix anything, she just wanted to get out, get away. And she did. Came to see me wearing these beautiful clothes, wearing them like she'd never worn anything else, sitting right in my little place over there wearing her beautiful clothes and talking different, and with a different name, too. Told me she'd changed her name and that she was going to come back and live right around here, not far away, but with her new name, and nobody was going to know where she came from. And then she told me she was going to be married.

"I'm no fool, or not always anyway. I said, 'Wait. You're saying that you've been here for a while and you're just coming to see us now?' And she says, 'Coming to see you, Jerry, just you.' Not like she wants me to feel good about it, but just like she wants to tell me she doesn't want anyone else to know she's here, and she isn't going to go talk to anyone else, especially not our parents, who she doesn't ask about and they're dead anyway. She probably knows that already, too, because she says, 'But I knew that you were living here, and I know that you have a daughter, too.'

"That was why she had come to see me. She wanted my Ellie. Wanted to take her. Didn't even try to persuade me. Becky never tried to persuade anyone about anything she wanted to do or have, and less now than ever. She just does it, just takes what she wants. All she said was something like, 'Jerry, I am not going to see you again. But I want to take Eleanor, to live with me and be raised as my daughter. You understand what that will mean.' And she took her. The persuading part she left me to do for myself. And I did it. It was hard, but it wasn't complicated."

"She meant that you wouldn't see your daughter. Not ever again?"

"I took what she was offering. I knew she wouldn't be any kind of loving mother to her. Maybe I even took some comfort in that, knowing that though my baby was away from me, didn't even know me, I'd still be the one who loved her the best. I *am* the one who loves her best.

"I kept my part of the bargain, and I knew Becky would keep hers. She might not love her, but she would never harm my Ellie, I knew that for sure, absolutely for sure. And the important thing was, I knew she'd raise her with all kinds of things that I'd never be able to give her. Money. Nice clothes. Never having to worry. Not even knowing that she didn't have to worry, you understand? Not even knowing that there was such a thing as having to worry about money and everything else. So, yeah, I took what she offered.

"Sure, I've driven by that house. Sometimes I've spent a whole afternoon just driving around, driving by slow, hoping to catch a glimpse. It's a comfort just to do that, just to be near to where she is, knowing she's there and she's better off, not having to worry about anything."

What can it be like, I was thinking, what can it be like to be a mother, a father even? How can you look at your child without thinking, *Once she was impossibly fragile and only I kept her alive; once she was mine absolutely and now she belongs to a world I cannot control or buffer, in which we are all abandoned and unable to protect even the ones we would die to protect, and now I long only for that past in which keeping her alive was the best thing I could do or be?*

"There are always things to worry about," I said softly.

She was staring off into the deep shadows of the evergreens, her eyes shining, ready with tears. Suddenly she looked at me, her gaze intense, hungry. "You. You must have seen her, maybe even talked to her. Have you talked to her? Is she all right?"

I hesitated for a moment, looking back into the hungry eyes. "She has grown up into a very fine young woman," I said finally, the words feeling stiff and dry in my mouth. "She's going away to college this fall. I don't know where." I did know, of course, but I didn't want to give the impression that I knew very much about Ellie, because I did not want to answer more questions about her, did not want to lie, or tell a truth that was too complicated to convey.

She didn't seem to notice my hesitations. She smiled, the tears starting now from her bright eyes, nodded. "I'll find out where. I won't go there, nothing like that, but I'll want to know. I'm so proud of her." The frowning look of resentment faded when she spoke about Ellie, and in those moments the resemblance was even more vivid.

I waited a moment. "Did she—did Becky help you out at all?"

She looked up sharply, eyes narrowing. "You mean did she offer me any *money* for taking my *daughter*?"

"No, no," I said quickly. "I didn't mean that, not exactly. It's just that—she's your sister, after all."

"Nothing like that. You must have figured out by now that Becky's got her own set of rules. Her own damn game, comes to that. No, she's never given me a penny since she got back, since she married that man and changed her name to West. And I haven't asked for one, neither. I had to meet with them both once, to make all the arrangements for them to legally adopt my baby, sign all the papers and things like that. He seemed like a nice enough man, seemed like he would make a good father to her. I said that to him honestly enough."

"Wait," I said. "So Frank West never knew that you were his wife's sister?"

She shook her head. "Course not. Becky couldn't have had that."

"So no one else knows?"

"No one, probably. Except you, now. Becky would definitely not be happy to know that anyone else was in on it. Ellie doesn't know she's adopted. Some people know that part, of course—the husband and the lawyer." The lawyer. What was it that Owen Payne had said? Something about a case where they had legally changed an adopted child's history—was I remembering that right? But Jerry was still speaking and I had to pay attention. "And of course everyone I know knows that I gave my little girl up. But about us being sisters, no. Becky's careful. The only person I thought might have known was a cousin of my mother's, drove in here with her husband to drop off a couple things that one time that Becky was here. But she didn't recognize Becky, she had changed so much and was dressed so different, and I made up some little story about who she was and why she was here. Jean did look at us a little funny, but she never said anything about it afterwards."

"Jean—that was the cousin?"

"Jean Slope, yes. Once removed."

I knew the answer before I asked the question. "Jean Slope. What was her husband's name?"

She looked at me blankly. "Her husband. Eddie was his name. Why?"

It was something I couldn't take the time to think about just then. "Just a coincidence," I said. "Did Becky ever tell you anything about where she was all those years that she was gone?"

Jerry Tilton looked at me wryly, shaking her head. "I told you. Becky keeps her cards close. Never told me a thing about where she was going, never talked about it when she came back. But like I said, she came back different. Not just the clothes and the way of walking and talking. She came back harder. Maybe it was just the years, happens to all of us. And she was always, well, she always pushed herself real hard, but after she came back it was like there was no pity to her anymore, like she was going to take whatever she wanted and no one was going to stop her. You know what I mean?"

"I think I do." I felt like I should embrace her or give her some farewell touch, some gesture of acknowledgement, but instead I reached out awkwardly to shake her hand and said, in a strangely formal voice, "Thank you for talking to me."

She ignored the hand. That hungry look was in her eyes again, now that I was about to go. As far as she knew, I had it in my power to see her daughter any time I wanted to, talk to her, touch her, even. Then she waved a limp hand, and I let mine drop.

I left her sitting at the picnic table. But before I went back to my car, I had to know for sure.

Pausing next to the wide expanse of pine tree behind the table, I knelt down to peer into the shadows. Underneath was a carpet of dry needles and broken ends of twigs, and, rising from it, four sturdy trunks disappearing into the mesh of branches spreading above, like a low roof to keep out the rain, a shelter and a solace, a place lost forever.

26.

Over the next few days I spent whatever free time I had at the library. I had only the vaguest ideas about what I might be hoping to find, but I didn't know where else to find it.

What I still couldn't figure out was why. Every new thing I learned seemed to come trailing its own distinct and troublesome *why*, giving each fact, if they were facts, a distorting aura of unlikelihood.

So Becky Tilton had come back to town and appropriated her sister's child to raise as her own. I could say it in my head now, as flat and bald as that. It even made a kind of sense. It fit with what I had learned about her return, her determination to become the thing she wanted to be and her disregard for how that desire might affect other people, whose own desires were weeds to be brushed aside as she cut her path forward.

Yes, she would not have hesitated to take the child, the Ellie I knew, the Ellie I now knew far too much about. But why did she want the child, and why choose to take someone else's child at all? I couldn't remember if she was married yet to Frank West when she first came to see her sister, couldn't remember if Jerry Tilton had said or even known, but surely they had not been married long enough to know for sure that they could not have children, if that was the reason. The reason was buried somewhere else, outside of what I knew or could guess.

The library in town was small, but the inside of the old building was neatly kept and newly painted, the pale walls shining under fluorescent lights. There was a lone librarian at the desk, a tall dry man with stern glasses and three or four hairs lying flat across a bald head. I kicked off our acquaintance by asking if I could use the library without a card.

He looked at me coldly. "You may use the library's resources," he said, pronouncing each syllable distinctly. "Although you may not check out books from the collection. Let me take down your name."

"Kesey Jones," I said, spelling out the first part. Like Ken Kesey, my mother had grown up in western Oregon, and she had named me after him. She liked his books and his wildness, she said, and I wondered if naming me had been her last attempt to claim some part of me, to protect at least that one part from my father. Maybe there really was some wildness in the name, because people always heard it as Casey Jones, the engineer, who died in a legendary train crash. Because of the Grateful Dead song and its mention of cocaine, rather than any memory of poor old Cayce Jones, the name had been a running joke of my high school years.

The librarian did not look as if he spent a great deal of time laughing at jokes about what people's names sounded like. Without a word, he handed me a laminated slip of paper labeled "guest pass" and turned away.

The library's book collection, like the building, was small, and seemed to be evenly split between yellowed old books that might never have seen the light of day and bestsellers of recent years, mostly mystery and romance novels. But as I had hoped, the place did have collections of several local newspapers that dated back decades, so over the next few days while Frederick took his afternoon nap I would spend my time at the microfilm machines, squinting at the scratchy backlit images. Time crawled by like a wounded thing, just me and the stoical librarian there in the building, the lights humming subliminally in the stale hush of the room, the microfilm whirring past, stopping, moving on.

I found a wedding announcement for the marriage of Franklin West to Charlotte Lenoir, interesting only for its brevity—apparently no one had wanted to make it a big society event—and in later years there was some occasional mention of one or the other of them, usually an article containing a reference to the West family business. There was one feature about local families with *Mayflower* connections that had a photo of West smiling stiffly at the camera. But nothing that told me anything I didn't know already.

Casting about for something else that might lead me somewhere, I started looking for coverage of the car crash that had killed Eddie Slope. I was not sure about the exact date but I found the article in the *Day* easily because the accident had happened just a month or so after the announcement I had found for the West wedding. But again, there was little that was new there. The car had run off the road after dark on a treacherous curve, striking a telephone pole and killing both passengers. The article was concerned almost entirely with the death of the passenger, prominent citizen William Brewstead—of whom there was an obituary in the same issue—and mentioned the driver, Edwin Slope, only in passing.

Two strikes, and I didn't even know what a hit would look like. I looked over at the librarian, standing tall and forbidding at the front desk, apparently immune to any desire for human contact. He never made small talk with the patrons who came in, mostly women in their seventies or eighties. They came in, conducted their business with him in a few quiet words, and were gone again, leaving the faintest tantalizing trace of summer breeze and heat behind as the door swung closed.

I started moving backwards, through the seventies, into the sixties. When would Becky Tilton have left on the mystery trip from which she returned as Charlotte Lenoir? Headlines skimmed by in a blur, endless lines of meaningless writing broken up by photographs so blotted by reproduction that they looked like black windows.

Eventually I gave up on the larger papers and started going through microfilms of the local community weekly, the kind that has gardening tips, stories about bake sales, and op-eds about which intersection needs a stop sign. There I happened across a photograph of Alice Pickett, thirty years younger and smiling politely, holding a young boy's hand at a Fourth of July parade. He was holding a tiny American flag and looking seriously at the camera. I looked back, staring into his blurred eyes as if I might find reflected there the answer to a question I did not know how to ask, something deeper than desire for a piece of candy thrown by a Shriner.

After that I gave up on looking for anything in particular and let my eyes wander over the photographs as they went by, all those images from decades ago, pictures of old people who were now surely dead, pictures of laughing children who by now had grown up and lost their sense of humor, pictures of impressive snowfalls long melted and forgotten by everyone except me, now, here in my small cell of memory, bringing the unremembered past into view again for a bright passing moment, the historical record of trivial events illuminated from behind by the humming machine.

I had been leaning back in the chair, balancing it on two legs, but suddenly I sat forward, the two front legs of the chair thumping down hard on the floor. The librarian looked over sharply, but I ignored him, leaning forward to stare into the screen, because I was sure I had glimpsed the face of Charlotte West.

The photograph had been taken in the summer, at an ice-cream stand, which was visible in the background. But the focus of the picture was a big old clunker of a car with three teenaged girls standing around it. The two girls standing on either side of the car, next to the front doors, were both posing for the camera, one with a hand on her hip, the other leaning with exaggerated nonchalance on the car. The photograph was grainy and dark, but the girls looked as if they could be related, and with their long straight dark hair, high cheekbones, and serious eyes they could have been the younger sisters of Joan Baez, making the Harvard Square scene on a sunny day, mugging for the camera in their cutoff shorts and V-neck blouses.

Standing behind them, against one of the back doors, was someone who looked like a young Becky Tilton, though with her dark looks she could have passed for a third sister. She seemed less eager to have her image captured, and she was looking straight at the camera with a solemn and intent gaze, one that was at odds with the summer-fun theme of the picture. If you were not looking for or at her, the face would be easy to miss in the busy scene, with other people and other cars in the background around the ice-cream stand. But for me it was the center of the photograph, the still point around which the scene arranged itself.

Was it her? I squinted to read the caption.

"Summer on the Sound." Local high school graduates Miriam Beauclaire and Aline Dale beat the heat at popular meeting place Bud's Cones.

That was all. There was no accompanying article and no photographer's credit. I wrote down the names of the two girls, double-checking the spelling, and the date of the issue, June 1966. But it had to be her. I pushed my face closer to the screen looking for some detail, but the closer I got the less I could see, the image dissolving into abstraction, a scatter of black blotches.

I stretched my arms, leaning back away from the reader. I gathered up my things and put away the spools of microfilm in their boxes, feeling a weight lift at the thought of escape from the silent, chilled room.

On my way to the door I waved to the librarian at his post behind the circulation desk and called out, "Thank you." He looked up skeptically over his glasses and watched me go without a word.

27.

The Emmett Service Station was just south of Essex on a quiet two-lane highway, a little white building with a peaked roof that made it look like a house. The outside of the place was surprisingly trim, with no peeling paint or accumulations of grime—Duke was clearly not the only one in the family who believed in neat and thorough work—a little roadside cottage that happened to dispense gas and repair engines. There were the usual parked and double-parked cars waiting to be serviced or picked up, and a couple of customers filling up, mopping their brows in the heat as they watched the dollars and gallons spin by.

Before leaving the library I had quickly gone through the collection of local telephone books, but without finding anything useful. There were a number of Dales, and one Beauclair, although the spelling was wrong, but no exact matches for the names. I could not see myself cold-calling all the Dales in southeastern Connecticut, especially since I had no idea what exactly I was going to say to all those strangers. *Hello, ma'am. Did you maybe have some ice cream twenty-seven years ago?* Instead I decided to ask Duke. He had lived here all his life, and he navigated enough varied social circles that he might have heard the names, or might at least have some idea where I could start looking.

But when I went home to ask the old man if he was going to be working the lawn anytime soon, he told me that Duke wouldn't be around at all for a week or so; he was needed at the garage that his family owned. I considered letting the week go by and discovered that just the thought of waiting that long made me feel desperate and exhausted. It was August already. The summer was melting away and I knew now that, like it or not, I was determined to learn as much as I could about Charlotte West's story. So I asked the old man for the address and took another afternoon off.

Inside the building I walked to an office in the back, a small room where a bikini calendar shared wall space uneasily with stern scripture, printed out in bold on sheets of computer paper and taped up at eye level, with a word here and there in capital letters for emphasis. *He that believeth not is CONDEMNED already. Every TREE that bringeth not forth good fruit is HEWN DOWN, and cast into the fire.* Sets of car keys hung on a row of hooks on the wall, and a small fan kept the dust circulating. The desk was a mess of invoices, one large stack held down by a grease-stained calculator. The woman behind the desk looked to be forty or so, with blonde hair, dark roots, and a harassed appearance. She turned away from a small black-and-white television as I came in and asked what she could do for me.

"I'm looking for Duke Emmett. Is he around?"

She gave me a doubtful once-over and then nodded toward a door on the left. "He's in the shop. Go on ahead and take a look."

The garage was busy with activity. Two cars were inside, one up on the lift, and three men were working on them, unspeaking, a radio talking sports in the background. Duke looked up when I came in, his face damp with sweat and a smear of grease across one cheek, and came over to me. Like the other two men he was wearing a dark blue jumpsuit, but while theirs had badges with their names sewn on, his had a sticker reading "Hi! My Name Is" on which he had written his name in broad neat capitals.

He seemed unfazed by my appearance at the garage. "Kese," he said, wiping his forehead. "What brings you here? Everything all right with Frederick?"

"Everything's fine. I just had a question I thought you might be able to help with."

"Do what I can."

The other two men were still working, but one raised his head from behind an open hood and said, "Duke."

He sounded uneasy, but Duke turned, unhurried, to look at

the man. "Kese, these are my brothers, Cal and Ethan." With his head of reddish stubble and his mild demeanor, he was definitely the odd man out here. The brothers were both dark-haired and dogged, shooting brief unhappy glances in my direction and then lowering their eyes again. I nodded at them. "Sometimes when things get busy here they can use an extra set of hands, so I come over and help out."

I nodded, anxious to get to what I had to ask him. "So I've been down at the library looking through old newspapers, and I found a photograph from the sixties that shows someone who looks like Charlotte West with two other girls. Their names were"—I pulled a piece of the library's scrap paper from my pocket, unfolded it and showed it to him—"Miriam Beauclaire and Aline Dale. I was wondering if you might have heard those names anywhere?"

Instead of looking at the paper, he was looking at me, curiously. "You were—looking through old newspapers trying to find pictures of Charlotte West?" he said. I realized that I had blurted all this a little breathlessly, and that maybe it sounded strange without an explanation. Then I thought it might sound strange even with one. I could feel myself turning red, but I pushed forward anyway.

"That story you told me about her, I guess it got me interested. I wanted to know more about where she came from, and—all right, I don't think I can explain everything right now, so let me do that some other time. But here's the thing I didn't think to say. This picture I found, it was taken right around here, at some ice cream stand down by the water called Bud's Cones. It was from a local paper. That's why I thought you might know these names."

Duke still wore a look of uncertainty, looking at the names on the paper, but before he could make a reply there was a sound from the front of the garage and a man stepped in out of the sunlight, talking to himself under his breath. He too was wearing a blue uniform, but he was older, in his sixties maybe, with iron-gray hair cut short, a florid face and small quick eyes that fastened on me and Duke as soon as he looked up, held us balefully for a moment, then flicked back to the brother standing by the open hood. "Ethan, that Volvo should've been done half an hour ago." His voice was quick and harsh. "Get it finished. That faggot lawyer who was in here last week just brought his BMW back in. Claims he can still hear *noises*. You're gonna need to take it out again."

Duke was shaking his head, frowning, like someone who had an unpleasant job to do. "Pop," he said. "Language. None of this faggot stuff."

His father looked like he was breathing hard. "Call it whatever you want, it's a sin and a shame, boy. You can get back to work, too, instead of worrying about my *language*." He paused, his angry eyes boring a hole in Duke's forehead. "They already took the word *gay* away from us. Used to be you could talk about having a gay time, but now you try to say that, someone's gonna be smirking and laughing up his sleeve like you said something dirty. Their dirt. It gets into everything like a poison."

"Maybe if people have been calling you a faggot or whatever else for long enough you don't really care what words you take away from them," I said.

There was a moment's hush. Ethan was staring at me, and Cal slowly pulled his head out from under the car on the lift. The sports show on the radio was the only sound in the garage. The father's face turned red and his jaw muscles bulged. Then he walked through the stillness to where Duke and I were standing, staring steadily at us. Duke stepped very slightly forward, his face a blank. He knew what was coming, even if I didn't.

Then his father hit him, hard, on the side of the head, knocking him sideways. I flinched in shock, looking on in amazement while Duke straightened back up, still unhurried but squinting against the pain. His father stood there, shorter and thicker than Duke, one hand still clenched in a solid red fist. "Get back to work," he said. "And get him out of here." He gave me one quick furious look, then turned and walked out, slamming the door that led to the office behind him.

The brother on the far side of the garage ducked under the car he had been working on and came toward us, wiping his hands on a rag. His name badge said *Cal*. Duke was rubbing his stubbly jaw and opening his mouth experimentally, blinking his eyes, but Cal was staring at me with a kind of amazement, as if he could not believe that anyone could be as stupid as I clearly was.

"You've got a mouth on you, kid," he said.

"Oh my God. Duke, I'm so sorry," I said. "I didn't mean to—"

He waved away whatever I was going to say. "Wasn't your fault," he said. "Every once in a while someone has got to tell Jack Emmett something he doesn't like." He rubbed at the reddening side of his face. "Cal, Pop hasn't lost a thing off his right since back when we were kids."

Cal nodded but did not smile. From under the Volvo's hood, Ethan said, "Pop's right, though. Come the flood, that ark won't be picking up any Adam and Steve." It seemed to me that he was mixing his Bible stories, but this time I kept my mouth shut.

Duke dropped his hand from his face, gazing over at the raised car hood. "Depends on who's in charge. If it's me steering the ship, I'll be picking up anyone that needs a ride."

Ethan's head emerged into view, his dark face tight and angry. "Duke, you *know* who's in *charge*. Now just because you can waltz in and out of here as you please doesn't give you the right to talk sacrilege."

Duke just looked at him, and there was another moment during which no one moved or spoke, while an advertisement blared on the radio, the tinny voice echoing in the garage.

"You," said Cal. He was looking at me, sort of. He had the kind of eyes that never meet yours directly, that stay mostly on the ground and only occasionally flick up just long enough to hold your gaze for a furtive moment. He looked older than Duke, but seemed less at home in the world. "Those names you said, the ones you were asking Duke about. One of them was Miriam Beauclaire?"

I nodded, relieved at the change of subject. "Yes, that's right. And Aline Dale."

He shook his head, eyes resting on the paper that I still held in my hand. "I don't know that one. But I used to know Miriam. We were in school at the same time, just about. Maybe she was a year or two older than me. Indian girl?"

"Could be," I said.

"Uh-huh. Miriam. I remember her from school. Pretty girl. I didn't know her very well or anything like that. Probably wouldn't remember her at all except that she was the only Indian girl I knew back then."

"Wait," I said. "So she was a Pequot? And you all are too, right?"

Cal stiffened. Duke said, gently, "Cal and Ethan, they spend a lot more time with Pop than I do, working here at the shop and all. And Pop definitely doesn't approve of anyone in the family calling themselves an Indian, no matter how much money's involved."

"Heathens," said Ethan flatly. He was leaning on the car and watching us now, watching with that same wary half-averted gaze that Cal had.

"Heathens," Duke said, looking absently at Ethan. "Never mind how many of the tribal members are Christians. Now, with me it's different. Pop has given me up as a lost cause and a lost soul. It might be different if Mom was still alive, but as it is, the whole Pequot business just reminds him of something about her that he'd rather not remember."

"She wasn't a Pequot," Cal said.

Duke looked at him quizzically. "Mom? Not exactly, but her great-grandmother—"

Cal shook his head. "Miriam. She was Indian, I mean she *is* Indian, but something else. I never saw any Pequots around here that looked anything but white, but she looks like a real Indian."

Something in the way he shifted the tense. "Have you seen her—I mean, more recently than high school?" I asked.

Cal glanced up at the office door for a moment. He lowered his voice, looking briefly at Duke as he spoke. "Look, Pop doesn't know anything about this, okay? But sometimes Mandy and me, we go over to that Indian casino and play a little bit. She likes the slots. I play a little poker or blackjack. He wouldn't approve. You know. But it's a way to relax a little bit on a Friday night. I don't see what's so wrong."

Duke was looking keenly at his brother, like he was finding something interesting there that he had never suspected before. Then he looked over at Ethan and seemed to catch something in his expression.

"Ethan," he said. "Have you been over to that casino?"

Ethan was looking at the grease-streaked floor. There was a long pause. Then he said, "Yeah, okay. I've been there once or twice, maybe. Just curious, you know." He looked up defiantly. "Won fifty dollars one time."

Duke chuckled. "You know, I've been over there gambling with Uncle Noah a few times myself. Looks like we've all been sneaking around behind each other's backs. Pop's going to have to kill all of us. It'll be a bloodbath." He was shaking his head, laughing quietly, and Cal and Ethan almost looked like they might be smiling, though they were both still watching the office door closely.

I was worried that Jack Emmett might come back, too. I turned quickly to Cal. "So you've seen this Miriam down at the casino? Do you know where she lives?"

He shook his head. "No. I might have said hello, that's about it. But she's there—" He paused, embarrassed again. "She's there every weekend night. Far as I can figure. Mostly playing slots. Every Friday and Saturday night, and always by herself, seems like."

"Thanks," I said. Cal and Ethan were already resuming their work in silence.

Duke was looking at me in that curious way again. "Seems like you got what you came for," he said.

28.

I arrived back at the house in the early evening, the old man at his usual station under the light at the kitchen table, dark glasses raised, peering closely at the label of a prescription bottle.

"Want me to read that?"

He looked up, dropping the glasses into place. "Nah. Who cares what the side effects are if I'm going to take the goddamn things anyway. Hey, how about a sandwich, huh?"

I opened the refrigerator and started pulling things out. Bread, ham, pickles, mustard. I took out two plates and two glasses. The old man popped a couple of pills in his mouth and swallowed.

"Your buddy Adams was here this afternoon," he said.

I stopped. Looked up from the plates. "Adams? You mean Harrison Adams?"

"He was over at Frank West's place for some goddamn thing or other, probably still after him about that land deal. Then he came over here. I couldn't figure out what he wanted, to tell the truth. Probably hoping he'd find me keeled over or something so he could start making plans to buy the place." He tapped a cigarette on the table and lit it, inhaling deeply. "Huge man with the bullshit. He ought to have a business, blowing smoke up people's assholes for them."

"Is there much of a market for that service, do you think?"

He raised his eyebrows as if he was interested in the question. "You'd be surprised. He asked about you, too. Had some idea about you working for a newspaper or something. 'Investigative reporter,' he said. Jesus. Any idea where he got that from?"

I kept spreading mustard. "No idea at all," I said. "What did you tell him?"

"I told him he was talking nonsense, then I told him to go fuck himself, just on general principle. Probably the most fun I'll have all day, you want to know the truth. Hey, how's that sandwich coming?"

After we had finished reading for the night and I was lying in bed in my darkened room, I tried to figure out what would have brought Adams out here. Could he have come on purpose looking for me? It sounded like the story I had told Owen Payne about working on an investigative piece about Heritage had come around to him, somehow. I did not want to think about what it meant that Harrison Adams had apparently been talking to the lawyer, or that there was some intermediate link between them.

I didn't really care whether Adams thought that I was a real reporter looking into his business dealings, and it was even pleasant to think that the idea made him uneasy enough to try to pay me a visit. The part I didn't like was the implication that the lawyer had somehow gone out of his way to relay the rumor to Adams. Was Adams worried enough about whatever business he was up to around the Pequot reservation that he didn't like the idea of it coming to public attention? If so, then good riddance. But I wondered what I would have said if he had actually confronted me with the story. How long would it be before that lie came back to me? I would have to confess it, and I squirmed just thinking about doing that.

I turned it over in my head for a while, but there were more interesting things to think about, and eventually I came back to the question of Miriam Beauclaire. Even if I had not quite admitted it to myself, there was no doubt that I would be going to the casino to look for her. It wasn't even a choice I was making. I just knew it was going to happen.

I was lying stretched out on my back staring at the ceiling, my head resting on my hands, wishing Friday night would come more quickly, when I heard a sound at the door, light, quick. I turned my head, listening to see if it came again. Ellie? I had not seen her since that last disastrous day. I listened, intent, but there was no sound. I sat up and stepped quietly into my shoes, then went across the room to the door and listened again, hearing nothing but the usual sounds of the night, cicadas buzzing in the trees.

Finally I opened the door. Nothing was there.

I stepped outside and closed the screen door carefully behind me, making as little noise as possible.

Outside all the sounds were louder, no longer muffled, and the cicadas seemed raucous and close. It was a windless night with no visible moon, and the darkness loomed around me. Unable even to see where I was walking, I felt my way along, trying to be quiet, although the fallen pine needles crunched lightly under each slow step. I maneuvered my way around to the far side of the garage, where my groping hands found a large boulder.

I clung to the rock with both hands, touching the thin layer of moss that coated it, and stared out into the impenetrable dark, my heart pounding irrationally, full of that deep-down fear of the unseen, the darkness, the old instinctive terror of things that come out at night. I held to the stone as if the night's secrets, hidden from sight, might somehow be transmitted through it.

There was a noise out on the lawn, a shifting of leaves or branches, and there—down where in my memory the driveway turned a corner, was there was a deeper patch of darkness standing out from the wider dark, a shadow where no shadow should be? I strained my eyes, staring until I could not be sure what I was looking at, listening furiously, breathing hard and shallow, every hair on my scalp alive. I had wild thoughts of bears and mountain lions and other animals not native to New England attacking and tearing me to pieces, of thieves or intruders murdering me and the old man together, tying us to chairs and slitting our throats.

Out of nowhere there was a sharp sound, a crack, just to my left. I jumped, then turned to run back into the woods, away from the sound. But I had only taken two quick steps before I tripped and fell headlong, hitting the ground hard.

I lay still, blood pounding, listening desperately. But in the aftermath of my own crashing fall, the night was still. All I could hear was the faint rustling of something small moving away, a possum or raccoon, whatever had made the noise.

Feeling more stupid than scared now, I picked myself up, starting to feel the scrapes and bruises. I sought with my hands and found what I had tripped on: the remnant of another one of those low walls of stacked stones, one that I hadn't noticed before. I remembered something Duke had told me, that these walls were not just lining the roads, that they crisscrossed the woods everywhere in this part of New England. When white farmers had begun to clear the land for planting they had found the fields full of stones, had spent backbreaking days and weeks toiling to dig them out and stack them, the earth seeming to push up more and more of them with each new plowing season, as if the land itself was cursed. The farmers said that the devil himself had put the stones there to thwart them.

Brushing pine needles and leaves from my aching knees, I thought I knew how they felt. I was too shaken and annoyed now to feel the terror of hidden intruders that had brought me outside in the first place. I felt my way back along the outside wall until my hand touched the rough mesh of the screen, caught the door latch, and then I was back in my room, not even bothering to lock the door behind me.

I climbed into bed again, my breathing still shallow, heart beating in the dark, and I lay there awake for a long time, listening intently to the sounds of insects in the trees and small animal shufflings, feeling uneasy and unmoored from humanity, haunted into the hours of early morning by the lurking wrongness of the world.

29.

The tower rose out of the wooded hills, coming into view as the car rode over the crest of a swell and began to descend. The traffic was heavy on the winding road I had been following, with occasional cows and horses looking up with bland eyes at the cars and buses that made their way toward the casino.

Dorothy and the Scarecrow must have felt this way, watching the emerald spires of the city rising out of the unassuming landscape. Strange enough to have left Kansas behind, but who could have guessed that there would be a metropolis right there at the edge of the poppy field, plunked down in the middle of all that nothing?

Oz for sure. A fairy castle, a cluster of towers layered against each other, the decorated pediments rising and receding like liveried footmen flanking the stately central structure. August's evening sun was caught and held in the columns of windows and on the turquoise roofs above, beacons to attract the pilgrims who were teeming in from all over to pack the highways and country roads, pushing on toward the bright oasis where they could take part in the great drama of money's gain and loss, where they could pay to watch the dice roll, the cards turn, the wheels spin and the bright bunches of cherries line up in perfect duplicate.

On the roads leading into the reservation, I had surveyed the houses, so different from the ones I had been living among all summer. There were farms with tumbledown barns and silos, and then interspersed with these were modest houses of one or two slight stories, with finicky, aspirational yards, the grass trimmed a little too neatly, perhaps with some flowers in window boxes or a decorative well in the front. Then occasionally a suburban mansion would appear, hidden back among the trees, sprawling over two or three residential plots, either under construction or recently completed. There was no old money here, only old farmland, and the rest was all petit bourgeois and nouveau riche—the foreign words we use in order to keep telling ourselves that class distinctions don't really exist in America. Traffic had been moving swiftly, then, as if hustling us past the odd contradictions of the local real estate, but it slowed now so that we could contemplate the grand towers for which we were bound.

I found a space at the far end of one of the parking lots and walked up through the parked cars toward an entrance to the casino. It was a long walk, and I passed the time by tallying license plates. The vast majority were from Connecticut and states nearby—Massachusetts, New Jersey, New York—but there were many others, too. Visitors from across the nation were here tonight.

I went inside with the idea of walking through the building quickly, to get a sense of the layout, and within minutes I was lost. After the austere New England atmosphere I had been breathing all that summer, the sudden blaze of commerce came as a shock to the system, and I found myself wandering, followed everywhere by the constant stale smell of cigarette smoke, through an array of stores and corridors and attractions, all bright with Vegas glitz and alive with flashing lights and waves of swirling, sourceless sound: voices, echoes, synthesized beeps and whooshes, a simulated ringing of bells and cha-ching cash register noises and the jackpot sound of change pouring forth in dazzling Scrooge McDuck quantities. I tried to imagine my stingy father here, taking all this in, but it was impossible. He would have had a heart attack and died on the spot.

The broad hallways were full of people, all looking more purposeful than I did. The groups of senior citizens in their sweatpants and white sneakers moved along briskly, off the bus and ready for action, like everyone else, the teenagers posing self-consciously and not looking at their parents, the younger kids eating ice-cream cones, all of us moving down the concourse. Windows on one side looked out to the impossible outdoors. On the other side were rows of stores and then, out of nowhere, a sort of old-fashioned Main Street America, tall housefronts, store facades, with lights behind curtains on the upper floors, even. The American dream itself. But how strange to find it here, the old dream replicated for gambling tourists on an Indian reservation. If not a city on the hill, then how about instead a palace in the swamp?

The swampland itself was invisible now. Through the great windows of one of the gambling rooms—where cocktail waitresses circulated with trays of drinks, lipsticked and smiling, wearing short skirts and headbands, each with a single bright feather rising from the back—you could look out on the darkening land itself, evergreens, rock formations, and forested hills, all picturesque in the orange glow of sunset. You would never guess that this was reservation land, useless for farming, a bog strewn with great immobile rocks. The Pequots had been pushed and legislated away from their seaside grounds, exiled to this landlocked and unarable patch of earth, good for nothing except, it turns out, building a great machine for the extraction of money. It had turned out to be fertile after all.

Sculptures and other artworks by American Indians had been placed here and there along the corridor, and at one point I came upon several glass cases containing historical artifacts, one of them an ancient, weathered piece of wood from a Pequot palisade fortress of the kind that had finally failed to protect them when the English had burned down an entire village, not far from here, more than three hundred years ago. I stood in front of that case for a long time, trying to imagine the horror of that massacre, and thinking, too, of another glass case, the one in Franklin West's living room with its piece of *Mayflower* wood inside.

Then the main corridor that I was wandering down opened outward, and I walked into a vast atrium where a crowd of people were gathered around one side of a large fountain, cameras flashing and a muddle of voices, oddly hushed, dissolving in the sound of water. Set above the fountain, on a mound of stone, was a translucent statue of an Indian man down on one knee, pointing a bow with an arrow notched in it up toward the sky. I had seen images of this statue already, everywhere, as I wandered the casino, on postcards and advertising brochures. It seemed to be the icon of the place. Around it the trunks of artificial trees rose into the air, their branches reaching up over us like a shelter.

As I stood there, the room began to darken, while a manufactured fog rolled in, the statue glowing pale. A red light shot upward from the tip of the raised arrow, piercing the fog. The sky responded with a sound of thunder, and then it began to rain, the statue man magnificently unmoved as the water ran down his face and splashed lightly on the surface of the pool below, casino chips and coins littering its bottom, thrown for wishes, thrown by people forever looking to change their luck. The coins winked in the light as the indoor thunderstorm faded, Washington and Jefferson and Lincoln, all staring at the sky through watery refractions.

As the show ended, the background noise of bells and beeps washed into the room again, and I was reminded of my purpose in coming to the casino. Miriam Beauclaire. Cal Emmett had said that she played the slots, so I headed in the direction of the ringing bells.

The slot machines were everywhere, though. They occupied acres of the casino rooms, so I now found myself navigating through an even more dizzying landscape as I walked through the maze of machines in rows, in clusters, lining the walls. Engulfed in color and flash, I walked, trying to keep my attention focused on the players rather than the machines. The sound in the room was less cacophonous than I had expected—it was more like an atmosphere, a thickening of the air, discordant, ambient, forever shifting as I moved through it. The rooms were huge, the lighting low, long strands of smoke hanging high in the air like the ghosts of rock formations, with slot machines side by side, hundreds of them. Each had a name and a theme to differentiate it, but the game was always the game. Boxcar Bonus, Dream Catcher, Aztec Gold, Cool Cat Cash, All That Glitters, Hard Boiled, American

Original, High Noon, Ring Quest, Knockout!, Super Money Grab.

The players went on working the machines, each with a slightly different rhythm, some intent, some bored, sipping drinks, chewing lips, holding neglected cigarettes turned to long skeleton fingers of ash. I walked through the rows feeling lightheaded and lost, squinting at the players, trying to find the face of a woman that I had only seen in a bad grainy photograph taken when she was almost thirty years younger.

I felt conspicuous, walking slowly and trying to get a view of the faces of the players, and I tried to look purposeful—Kesey Jones, boy reporter—but it hardly mattered. No one looked up or took any notice of me.

Row after row, room after room, my shoes padding along the carpeted floor, the faces becoming indistinguishable after a while, so that sometimes I would find that I had walked down half a row without really paying attention, and I would have to retrace my steps, looking carefully at the faces I had missed. It was possible, of course, that she was not there on this particular night at all. I had no idea who she was. Maybe she had children to attend to, a date to keep, an aging mother in the hospital, or something on television had caught her attention on the way out the door and now she was sitting on the arm of her couch, the ring of the car keys hooked over one finger and forgotten, the lights in the house already turned off, the blue-gray glow of an old movie illuminating the mystery face that I was hunting for at this very moment, miles away.

But no.

Cal had said she was Indian, and I had slowed to examine any woman whose skin looked darker or whose features might have been right, scanning noses and cheekbones. Her hair was dark in the photograph I had seen, but that meant nothing. In the last half hour I had already seen far too many older women with deep unnatural tans and hair bleached blonde to trust a detail like that. But in the end, when I saw her, I knew.

She still had the long black hair, streaked now with gray lines that could have been drawn on for decoration, the stiff hairs creating a frizzed halo around her head. Her face was handsome, nose prominent and eyes large and brown, but she was wearing too much blue eye makeup and a lipstick that was the wrong color for her skin, making her face look ashen. There was a drink beside her in which most of the ice had already melted. She was sitting in front of a game called Big Combo and its colored lights played across her face in changing patterns and reflected in her eyes.

This was the girl in the picture, grown into a woman too old for her age. But it was hard to know how to approach her, with the two games on either side occupied and the seats bolted and pointed forward so that the only intimacy the room encouraged was the one between player and machine. I lingered awkwardly for a moment, watching as she slapped a lighted button, pulled a lever, the wheels spinning in a blur just long enough to create some suspense, and then the play was over. Then another: slap, pull, spin, end. The briefest of stories.

I cleared my throat. She did not look up or pause in her routine.

Feeling foolish and exposed, the only one in the room who did not belong there, I stepped forward into her peripheral vision, looking at the side of her face. "Excuse me, ma'am?" I said.

She pulled the lever, watched the spin. "Yeah?" No jackpot.

"Are you Miriam Beauclaire?"

She continued not looking at me. "Who wants to know?" Her voice was rough. She still looked a bit like Joan Baez and it was disconcerting to hear the gravelly undertones when she spoke.

"I was wondering if I could ask you a few questions. About Charlotte West."

She paused for a moment, hand on the lever, before pulling it. "Never heard of her," she said, and then pulled hard.

I waited until the pictures stopped spinning, a horseshoe, a pot of gold, a bar.

"Maybe you knew her by another name, because she used to be called—"

Now she did turn to look at me, her face hard and the sharpness of her eyes made more alarming by the way they had gone rheumy from staring close at the machine, cutting me off quick and harsh. "*Becky*. All right, little man. I said who wants to know."

I met her gaze the best I could. All at once we seemed to be alone in the room, the ringing bells and bongs and clinks receding, a line of electronic waves breaking on a distant shore.

"I do."

Her eyes widened in annoyance. "Yeah. So who are you?"

I fell back on the lie I had offered to Owen Payne. "I'm a freelance writer, working on an article about—about her life."

She did not even pause before dismissing this idea with a monosyllable of contempt. "The hell you are. You don't look old enough to be much of anything. For a second I thought you might at least be a cop, but look at you."

"All right," I said, feeling the heat in my face. "I'm sorry. I thought you might be more likely to talk to me if—all right, okay. But I have been investigating, really. I met her this summer, her—and her family, too. Maybe I was a little bored. I started asking questions, and the questions have all led to more questions. Eventually they led to you."

Her eyes moved quickly, looking around the room, then came back to me, flashing anger. "Who did? How did you find me?" she demanded.

I didn't want to name Cal, or Duke, or anyone, but I didn't want to seem evasive, either. "I—found an old photograph in a newspaper. She was in it, and you were too, and I started looking for you, and this is where I found you. I'm sorry if I'm disturbing you, Ms. Beauclaire."

But a change had come over her face, a new expression, as if she had suddenly understood something and now everything was explained. Her lip curled in a hard smile, and she leaned back a little, as if to see me more fully.

"You," she said. "You've got the hots for her. Shit. I should've known."

I started to protest, but she was shaking her head and turning back to the machine. She pulled the lever again.

With a kind of desperate resolve, I went on. "All right," I said. "Will you tell me how you knew Becky?"

She kept playing, ignoring me. She was good at it.

I stood there for a few spins, feeling hopeless but unwilling to leave.

"I'll pay you for your time." I could not believe that I was hearing myself say this. But she was listening. "Twenty dollars." It came out almost as a question.

"He's got it bad," she said to the electronic face of Big Combo. She paused for a moment. "Fifty."

I dug into my pocket. I had brought more money than I usually carried with me tonight, vaguely feeling that when you go to a casino you should bring cash, even if you didn't come to gamble. "I only have forty-five," I said.

She waited a beat, then, without looking up, she tapped the horizontal shelf below the display, where her hand rested beside the lighted buttons.

I put the money there and then knelt down on one knee beside the machine, still feeling awkwardly exposed. "How did you know Becky Tilton?" I asked, keeping my voice low. No one could have heard me and surely no one would have been interested either, but the bribe seemed to make our conversation illicit.

She was still looking straight ahead, into the machine, through it, while I watched her profile, the strong straight nose and the slightly sunken cheeks, the lips wearing the wrong color and dark eyes reflecting the many lights of the slot game. She ran a hand through her hair, a rough, uneven movement that seemed to reflect the agitation, the difficulty and resolution required to break the surface of memory.

"I knew her from when we were both cleaning houses. My sister Aline and me, we worked for a maid service during the summer, there were a bunch of us local girls who did. We worked there in the summertime because the rest of the year we were in school, but Becky had dropped out as soon as she possibly could, maybe sooner, and she was working there year round even though she was maybe a year or two younger than I was."

"Aline," I said. "She was your sister?" The other girl in the photograph had been named Aline, but her surname had been identified as Dale.

She made an irritated gesture with her hand, brushing the question away. "She was my cousin, but we were both raised by my mother. We were the same age, grew up together, lived our whole lives together." Something sad crept into her eyes, but then she brushed that away, too.

"We didn't know Becky real well when we were on the cleaning crew. Kids like us, we worked as slowly as we could, took as many breaks as we could, goofed off if we thought we could get away with it. But Becky worked real hard all the time, young as she was. Like, driven, you know? I understood that later on, when I got to know a little bit more about how she grew up. We weren't rich or anything, me and Aline, but we grew up with a mother who loved us. She worked hard and she didn't take any shit from us, but we got by okay. For us, having a summer job was nice and it gave us spending money for movies and all. But for Becky, she was seriously poor and her old man was a drunk and her mom was a trip, too, and that job was her way out. Like, a matter of life or death, and there was no way she was going to lose it, or let anyone persuade her to slip out back of whatever house we were in for a quick smoke or just to goof around. So she wasn't real popular with the other girls. Aline and me, we weren't exactly popular, either, 'cause of being half Indian, and the white girls mostly looked down on us like they did the Spanish girls, there were a couple of them too. I think that's why we didn't mind Becky's holding herself apart from us. Like, she didn't seem to notice that we were Indian, or that the Spanish girls were from wherever they were from. She just held herself apart from everyone the same. You couldn't really like her, because she didn't like you, but Aline and me, we thought she was okay."

Once she started talking, the words came flowing out, so fast that I had trouble keeping up sometimes, thinking somewhere in the back of my mind, *She wants this. She has been waiting for the chance to tell it. The money was just a form, an excuse, so that she could tell herself later that that was the reason she talked to me, told me the things that she has maybe never had the chance to tell.* I said, "You and Aline, are you Pequots, then?"

She looked up then, not at me but up and around, at the casino, the long lines of slots, the smiling girls with the feathers in their headbands, carrying drinks. "No," she said, sitting up straighter in the chair. "Not Pequot. Both my parents were Mohegan. Well, both were half. Aline's mother was my mother's sister, but her father was part Cherokee. Came up here from down south to work on some construction project, stuck around long enough to be Aline's father but not long enough to ever see her first birthday, moved on to the next job when this one was done. Full-blooded, he claimed, but I doubt it."

I was afraid of losing the thread of the story she was telling. "So the maid service," I prompted her. "You and Aline and Becky."

She shook her head. There was something mocking in her eyes, the faded echo, maybe, of an old flirtatiousness. "Little man with a big plan. Keeps his eye on the girl. Can't say I blame you, 'cause she was always something to look at. Always had something about her that was—interesting. Especially to men. Blessing and a curse, for sure."

She sighed, shook her head. "The year we graduated, Aline and me decided we weren't going to work cleaning houses anymore. We'd had eighteen years to look around us, long enough to figure that there wasn't anything for us around here except to work some dead-end job like Mom did, keep on cleaning rich people's houses or tend bar somewhere. Maybe if we were lucky we'd get married, clean house and change diapers and cook meals for some deadbeat until the day he decided he wasn't coming home anymore. So we decided to get out of town, start our lives somewhere else, see a little bit of the country while we were at it. I had an old car that an uncle of ours had fixed up, and Aline had a cousin down south, her dad's side, so we figured we could start by going down there, maybe find something interesting to do, and if we didn't then we could just move on to the next place." She smiled a little, her face lit by the neon glare of the slot machine.

"We made the plan to go one night that spring, while school was still on, decided that we'd go right after school ended. Made the plan sitting at this bar out in the boonies somewhere, and we laughed a lot and drank a lot, and then we got in the car and headed home, feeling fine, driving down the road in the dark listening to that Dylan song about How does it *feel?* real loud with the windows down and the wind blowing our hair around.

"We passed a bus stop on the side of the road, and standing there waiting, dressed up all neat, was Becky. We hadn't seen her in almost a year, I guess, and we came screeching over to the side of the road and made her get in for a ride home. She'd quit the cleaning crew and was working for some rich old people, some kind of regular maid work, probably paid better. She was living out there, I don't remember why she was taking the bus that night. Visiting someone maybe. So we told her all about how we were going to take our big road trip that June, and we were feeling so drunk and happy about everything that we asked her did she want to come with us. I think we were pretty sure she wouldn't want to, and she didn't. Just said no, she couldn't do that, in her serious way, and we dropped her off at her house and that was that.

"Or so we thought. Then come the beginning of June, she shows up at our house one night out of nowhere. I swear I don't know how she even knew where we lived, but there she was, looking even more serious than usual. It was always hard to tell anything about how she was feeling, but I'd say she looked bad, miserable. Maybe angry, who knows. Standing at the front door not smiling and asking would it still be all right if she came with us when we left town? I said sure. I wasn't too pleased about the idea of it right then, but it was us that asked in the first place so how could we say no? She didn't even come in the house, just nodded and asked where she should be and when, left us a phone number and nodded again and went back off into the night.

"So she came on that trip with us. Three girls on a road trip, and Becky was so dark we looked like we could've been three sisters. We ended up in North Carolina where Aline's cousin was staying, where her father's Cherokee people are from. We were in high spirits the whole way, but most of the time Becky was real serious, and faraway, looking out the window like she barely knew we were there. Like she was thinking hard about something. She stayed with us for a few weeks, but Aline's cousin wasn't too thrilled to have the three of us all there in her little place. So one day she left. And that was that."

Miriam stopped. She looked agitated, staring ahead and chewing her lip as if she was still playing the game and was settling in for a long losing streak. I waited, not sure if this was the end of the story, not happy with it. Something was missing, something left out. It was as if she had turned a radio dial and her story had flowed out like a song, and then halfway through she had gradually turned the volume down, event and detail fading out, as if the tapering off might fool me into thinking that this was the song's natural end.

Finally I said, "But you came back home. And you knew that she had come back. Did you ever see her again?"

She frowned. It was as if she was holding her mouth shut. Then she said, "Little man, you should take what you think you know and walk out of here. Go back to your life and forget about that woman. Some things you're better off not knowing."

"Do you know where I could find Aline? Maybe she would be willing to talk to me."

She looked up slowly at me, then lowered her eyes. "Aline killed herself ten years ago."

"Oh," I said. "I'm sorry."

"She had her reasons."

There was a long pause. Then she sighed. "All right. Yes. I saw her, once. We thought there was a bright future out there for us, and then we found out that there wasn't. Found out that there isn't anywhere to go in this damn country, and that you're not young for very long. So we came back. A few years later Becky came back too. *Charlotte*. Huh. Maybe she learned the same thing we did, but you wouldn't ever know it from the way she acted afterwards. I saw her when she first came back, talked to her. I haven't talked to her or heard anything about her since she got married, since she got rich. I think she just wanted to make sure that I wouldn't ever blow her cover. Not that I ever would, even knowing what I know about her."

My lips were dry. I cleared my throat and said, "What do you know?"

"I know that she killed a man."

She spoke without emphasis, did not even lower her voice. I steadied myself, putting a hand on the cool metal of the machine. I felt the pieces falling all together, dominoes falling too fast for me to follow, the knowing too swift and immediate to be knowledge. "Who?" I said.

She continued, head down, ignoring me, or maybe I had spoken too softly and she misheard the question. "Right here," she said. "She didn't kill him herself, of course. She had it done. Had it made to look like a car accident. I figured out why, too."

A car accident on the Post Road. An accident. I said, quickly, interrupting, "Yes. It had to be. Because of her daughter."

Her head snapped up and for the first time she looked straight into my eyes, hers wide with a gaze that was so fierce and strange I would have backed away if I possibly could have. "Daughter? *Daughter?*"

Her voice was pitched high, she was almost shouting. I was confused and put my hands up, trying to calm her down. It occurred to me suddenly that she could have a daughter, that maybe she had misheard, again, in the swirling jangle of the windowless room, and thought I had said something about her child. "Ms. Beauclaire," I said, enunciating. "I'm sorry, I didn't mean your daughter. Not your daughter."

Bad to worse. She let out a wild screech of laughter, meant to be contemptuous, maybe, but it came out high and hysterical, rising above the din of the room. Several of the players turned to look at us with startled red-rimmed eyes, then went back to their games.

Miriam was glaring at me with that same dangerous intensity, breathing hard. She put her hand to her chest, the stones on her necklace rising and falling in shallow waves while she worked to calm herself.

"No," she said finally, grimly. "No. We went south, like I said. And when we got there, Becky told me—"

She stopped, gazing past me, looking back and down into the deep well of memory, I thought, until memory answered back. A deep voice that seemed to be somewhere high above my head said, "Excuse me, sir."

I turned, awkwardly, from my position down on one knee. Two men were standing behind me. Casino security, unmistakably, in their matching dark suits and attitudes of impassive authority. I stood up to face them, and though I was as tall as they were I could not help feeling impossibly scrawny. Both men were broad and muscular, their shoulders and arms straining the seams of their suit jackets, one with dark hair slicked back and the other in a flat blond buzz cut. Both had hard thick hands and hard thick faces. Bouncers dressed up in casino formal.

"I hope you're not bothering the lady," said the dark one, "but either way you don't seem to have any business to transact here. This might be a good time to cash out your chips for the evening, sir."

"I don't have any chips," I said stupidly.

"Then I'm afraid we will have to ask you to leave. Right now."

"But—I was just having a conversation with *the lady*—" I turned, gesturing toward Miriam, but the seat was empty, the cash gone from the slot machine's console. I looked around wildly, but she had disappeared. It was just me and Big Combo and the vast noisy room.

I turned back to the two men. The dark one raised his eyebrows as if he had just put me in checkmate and gestured the way out with one arm, polite but adamant. Neither of them took their eyes off me until I started walking. The three of us went back through the casino, past the stores and games, past the artifacts, the fountains, the recorded voices, the Indian who makes the rain fall. The crowds parted for us and stared at the unexpected entertainment, almost as good as a perp walk, parents whispering to their kids, the corridors buzzing as we passed, alive with the thrill of witnessing someone else's misfortune. The bouncers played their part, staring straight ahead, their expressions carved in stone. I tried not to look furtive and criminal, but I knew that my face was red and that my jeans and sneakers contrasted badly with the dark suits.

They left me at an exit that led out toward the parking lots. The blond one held the glass door open for me and said, "Good evening, sir." I clenched my jaw, said nothing, and did not look back.

I paused on the curb and found that my legs were shaking. I was angry and humiliated that my body would react in such a craven way to a confrontation with authority, and took a deep breath to calm myself. The blue light of the moon was visible in the shadows behind streetlights, but the air was damp and spiked with the promise of rain.

Walking back through the parked cars, I began to shake off the adrenaline and managed to start thinking about what Miriam had told me. *She killed a man.* I needed time to think that through, but right now I wanted to try to remember as much as I could of what she had said, the words already slipping away, rearranging themselves, my mind starting to tell its own version of the story, emphasizing the details that I was drawn to instead, maybe, of the ones that were truly important. *Mohegan. Bus stop. Road trip. Especially to men. She had her reasons. How does it feel.* I was annoyed to find that I was running through the song in my head, words and melody and music, the song running on a parallel track in my mind like a radio playing in the next room that you do not even know is distracting you until you find that you are not paying attention to the work you thought you were doing all along. *With no direction home. A complete unknown.* And was it really possible that she was capable of murder? I was so busy matching up the pieces and snapping them together that I had not yet had time to pause and think about whether the picture the assembled puzzle would show made any sense or not. But maybe that didn't matter, maybe you just had to put together the puzzle and then look at the picture, and you couldn't worry about whether you liked the picture or not or whether it made sense to you or not, because it is so easy to lie to yourself when you want to and you never know that the lie is what you want until you have talked yourself into it and accepted and acted on it already. But she said she did. Miriam said she killed someone.

"Excuse me, friend."

I was nearly at the end of one of the parking lots. In fact I saw now that I had almost walked past my own car. Standing next to it was a tall man wearing a gray suit jacket. I was beginning to feel distinctly underdressed tonight. His hair was neatly combed and parted, his face mostly lost in shadow, but I could see that his eyes were unusually pale for his dark complexion. The contrast was appealing, and his voice was pleasant, friendly but not familiar.

"Looks like rain this evening. Got a light?" I started to reply, but as I did I saw that he was holding a lit cigarette already. He followed my eyes and seemed to smile at my confusion. Before I could say anything, I was grabbed roughly from behind, my arms pinned behind my back, and another man, compact and muscular in a black T-shirt, stepped directly in front of me.

I opened my mouth to shout and he hit me quickly, hard, wrenching my head to the side, and all that came out was a broken yowl. *That doesn't sound like me*, I thought, the pain like a blinding light against which I could not close my eyes. He moved like a boxer, hitting me in the gut once, twice, three times, steady and rhythmic. The iron taste of blood was in my mouth and I bent forward, wheezing, held up by strong hands behind me.

"That's enough," said the pleasant voice of the man in the gray suit. He seemed to have moved behind me and the voice was disembodied, directionless, coming from all around and everywhere. Dizzy with pain and unable to catch my breath, the world was floating and agitated and I was the raw wound at its center. The man in front of me stood alert and waiting, his head shaved and darkened by a permanent shadow of stubble, watching me with bright eyes.

"What do you want?" I croaked. The pain seemed to circulate

through my body, all its normal functioning, breath and the senses and the movement of blood, co-opted into the service of spreading hurt. "I don't have any money."

"We don't want your money," said the voice. The bald man cocked a keen eyebrow, as if to say he wouldn't say no to a dollar or two. The hands holding me from behind seemed to tighten.

There was a pause. I breathed with difficulty, casting about wildly for an explanation. All I could think was: this only happens in movies, not in real life. "What is this," I said, hoarsely. "Some kind of message?"

The voice laughed softly, close behind my right ear. "Sure. It's a message," it said. "See if you can figure out what it means."

Then came a smash, an explosion loud without sound.

There was a moment between consciousness and the other thing where time was absolutely compressed, before it blasted forward and the dark asphalt seemed to rush at me in a wave that never ended, and then there was nothing.

PART THREE

Summer's End

30.

Aflick in the dark, a flicker.
Thunder.
The smack, the blow, the smash.
It is threatening rain in Los Angeles.

A man walks out of a store, out from under the awnings, squinting up at the sky when he hears the thunder. Once on a certain day a man walked across a street in Los Angeles. He is already dead, long decades dead, but he is still and always walking across a street in Los Angeles in the first sprinkling of a rainstorm to come, turning up his collar and dodging cars as he makes his way.

It is always happening and I can see it but I am not there.

The streets are gray and the cars are gray. The white shirts are light gray and the shadows are dark gray, infinite variation and gradation of gray with the bulbous heavy old cars passing in the rain on an overcast evening, bug-eyed headlights, tires hissing on the darkened street surfaces.

The sidewalks are alive with shoppers, young women in skirts with stylish hats and headbands in many shades of gray, sailors, military men, browsing, passing briskly on their way to their many somewheres. The man takes his place in the scene, enlivened by it, belonging to it, jaunty, slapping his hand on a fire hydrant as he walks. Making his way past cars and strangers in his dark suit, dark gray. Across the street there is a bookstore. Acme Book Shop. The kind of name you might give a bookstore on a movie set.

Then he is stepping inside, walking with purpose, and a woman is walking the other way toward him, as if these two strangers had made an appointment to meet at this exact spot, or were destined to meet here, and they stop when there is just a foot between them, the books arrayed behind in rows and columns.

Novels. Engineering. Literature. History. The gorgeous clutter of the bookstore, the order and disorder, an invitation to search and investigate and lose yourself. They stand facing each other, the same height if not for his hat, pushed back casually on his head so that it rises like a cocked eyebrow. She wears a polka-dotted dress, tied at the neck, with a dark sleeveless something over it, belted at the waist, hair tied back, glasses, someone's fantasy of a sexy librarian. She fondles her pencil idly.

You begin to interest me, vaguely.

I'm a private dick, working on a case.

Thunder. He is dead and if she is living she must be an old woman. But they are here now, young and alive, looking each other up and down in the shelter of the bookstore with the dusty books around them on the shelves and the delicious rain outside keeping them there and making them feel the shelter and the closeness. But where am I. Am I inside the frame, am I Marlowe or even Bogart settling into an easy enjoyment of my own desire for her, or am I her, the young actress stealing her one scene, the young woman intrigued, or am I lurking just outside, not myself somehow but instead some disembodied principle of looking that has no fulfillment but only the unending suspension of fascination and want. I want to know what color her gray dress is, what color the polka dots, how easily the knotted bow at her throat might slip undone with a pulling finger.

You'd make a good cop.

Thanks.

The sound of rain and the occasional thunder like tympani provide the music for the scene now. They move to the window where the rain is dripping from the awnings, umbrellas are popping open, bodies huddle against shop windows to stay dry.

He is looking out the window at the bookstore across the street, the one that keeps a secret lending library of pornography in the back, the one whose proprietor, the man with the Charlie Chan moustache and the devoted young male lover, will soon be found dead and the only witness a drugged giggling naked girl with clothes on, nothing unusual, all in a day's work when trouble is your business. He has his mind on the case, and she has made up her mind to seduce him, watching him out of the corners of her eyes while Franklin Roosevelt smiles his approval from the wall, practically winking at her, the old reprobate, as she gives the detective that sly open-mouthed leer. She teases the pencil without mercy. He looks at her and recognition dawns, they both feel it, a compact signed and sealed between them then and there. Lucky he has a bottle of rye in his pocket.

I'd a lot rather get wet in here.

Well. Looks like we're closed for the rest of the afternoon.

The way she pulls the blind down on the shop door, smiling at him while she shows off her curves. Joseph Breen must have been asleep and drooling on his Bible that day. They drink their rye from paper cups.

What's the matter?

Just wondering if you have to—

He makes a gesture with two fingers as if he is putting out his eyes, or hers. Men seldom make passes. Obliging, she takes off the glasses and lets her hair down, licking her lips and looking sidelong at him while he is looking away. Does her face look just a little bit like Charlotte West's just then or am I dreaming it. And who is she looking at, Marlowe or me. Where am I. Outside the rain is coming down, dripping from the awnings and splashing on the sidewalks, and inside it is warm and dry and it smells of old books and her perfume and strong liquor in paper cups.

They make a toast and then everything dissolves because it is time to look away, a moment's sheer vertigo, and in the ellipsis, timeless time, they are fucking. Impossible forties sex, pornography in black and white, glamorous faces unimaginable without their clothes, unimaginable the fumbling with zippers and the foreplay and the genitals.

And where am I and what am I when the lights go out. Is this my fantasy or someone else's and I only the voyeur, the eye that cannot look away and cannot break the frame but can only linger outside, longing for a place of safety, a shelter in which to curl warmly while the rain falls and falls outside and cannot touch me, a place where everything is dusky gray and the shadows enfold us all in our shared dream of shelter. A lost and gone place already, lost and gone forever.

Because when the world dissolves it does not come back, it should come back but instead I am dissolving too and in dissolving the particles of my body seem to return, taking form, weighing me down and making me heavy and clumsy and blind. I am blind or else there is nothing to see because all the gray shapes and surfaces have broken down.

I walk through ash. Thick shifting eddies of ash, as if I were a spent match at the bottom of an ashtray in a forties movie, but I am walking through it, the ash a constant thickness and never any more or less of it or any change in volume or texture no matter how far I walk, so maybe I am walking in place while the world moves and drifts around me. It moves and drifts and the ash changes. It has sound, a white noise, a low constant electrical fuzz of sound, and now the ash is moving, a jumble of black and white motes like television static. I am still walking through it, walking through static, my body invisible to me but there somehow, hidden in the shifting and immobile storm of grainy black and white. I walk on and on, walking without a body, until finally it begins to change again, the static begins to thin out and take solid form and I realize that I am not walking anymore but that the motes are plucking at my skin, that I can feel them, that they prick at my nerves and trickle on my face and make me wince and blink when I open my eyes at last.

Rain.

A light rain was falling on my face. It was dark where I was but there was a light somewhere nearby and it illuminated the drops, isolating them for a moment as they fell, caught in midair, sparkling like sequins before falling into the dark.

I lay groggily and watched them fall, slowly becoming aware of my body again. At first it felt like one big bruise, aching and swollen, and then the pain resolved itself slowly, flowing and concentrating. My head, my face, my side, my stomach. I was lying on my back under an open sky, outstretched tree branches visible above, and the surface under me was uneven, lumpy. The damp air carried a rank smell.

I moved experimentally and there was a rustling sound beneath me. Pain shot through my side and back, sudden and intense. I squeezed my eyes shut and hissed out a breath between my teeth, but kept moving, trying to get some purchase with my hands on the plastic lumps underneath me.

I sat up and looked around, blinking in the dark. I was sitting on a low pile of ancient trash bags, half-filled and dirty and slightly decayed, with occasional holes where corners of the discarded objects within had poked through or animals had gnawed the plastic. *Thrown out with the trash.* I wondered if it was a choice made in the name of symbolism or just one of convenience. Next to me the side of a dumpster rose, rusted where the green paint had peeled away. Rainwater dripped from it onto the garbage and the asphalt below, which was pitted and cracked, lines of green shoots growing up where the hard surface had split apart. A few yards away was a building, the back side of a building, a blank windowless wall of bricks painted yellow. Off to the right there was a short metal staircase leading to a rusted back door with a light burning dimly above it.

I lifted myself off the garbage bags carefully, my movements jerky and painful. *Roughed up.* The phrase floated through my head and it was exactly how I felt. A rat waddled out from among the garbage bags and hurried into the shadows near the building. I brushed myself off, feeling how wet my clothes were, noticing a few latticed patches of small scrapes and bruises on my arms and hands, tender and swollen. Behind the dumpster were dark shapes of trees, the soft sound of the rain falling. Maybe somewhere beyond were houses, streets, lights, but I could not see any. I straightened up, groaning like an old man, and took my first shaky steps.

Who would have wanted to beat me up, frighten me, and why? With a shiver I remembered Miriam in the casino. *She killed a man, she had it done, had it made to look like an accident.* Charlotte West. Could it be? Her face, close to mine, her dark eyes lit up with anger, and no pity in them, none at all. *Don't ever come near anything that belongs to me.* She could have had me followed, she certainly could have wanted to prevent me from finding out anything about her past, the past she had worked so hard to hide away and keep under lock and key. She could have had it done, she could have—

But I was not dead. The connections were hard to make, and it was hard to imagine that she could have known that I was pursuing information about her life at all. Could she have been having someone follow Miriam? That seemed impossible. The whole thing seemed impossible and I could not make any of it add up in a way that made sense. At the same time it was hard to feel that I was being paranoid when I had just been deliberately beaten and dumped.

I crept cautiously around the building, listening for voices or other signs of life, but my assailants appeared to be gone, and surely if they had wanted to keep me close they would have tied or locked me up.

I reached the front of the building and found that it was an abandoned convenience store, windows boarded, lighted signs gone dead along with the high curving lights that stretched above the parking lot, more weeds growing up through the pavement of the disused parking spaces, nothing for sale. Everything must go.

But I was still here. Standing in the dark lot with the light steady rain coming down and no idea where I was or what direction I needed to take, I felt strangely euphoric. They had beaten me up, but I was still alive, and if the point of the beating had been to warn me away from my investigation, then I was not persuaded. I was still alive, and I was ready to start making sense of Charlotte West's story, ready if necessary to force it to make sense, to give up its meaning. I was ready.

The two-lane road that the store was on stretched away into indecipherable tree-lined darkness in both directions. No houses or other signs of life were visible, and no cars had passed during the minutes I had been standing there. One direction looked as good as another. Soaked already, limping a bit, holding my side where the pain was sharpest, but electric and amazed in the knowledge that I was not dead, I started walking.

31.

Freedom.

That's what it felt like. It must have. The air clean and sharp, the sun shining on everything, pulling heat out of the dusty old upholstery and rising reflected in bright unending glare from the road and the hood so that the world seen through the windshield was all a yellow dazzle.

It was like a weight slowly lifting, starting the moment they left the foliage-tunneled surface streets behind and got out on the highway, the sun beginning the slow process of burning off a lifetime of damp and cool, as if their skin, even, was coated by moss or mildew from long years of what they hadn't even known was confinement. Until now, when the weight began to lift and they could gulp in deep breaths, lungs freed from long constriction and blood beating harder, veins rising to the surface of the skin to feel the warming sun and the chafing cleansing wind—all of it possible not because any of this was new but because they knew that this was not just another trip to the beach or the store, one from which they would return to the same stifling atmosphere they had lived in all their days, because this time they were leaving, getting out, beating it for good, saying so long, suckers, hitting the road, Jack, and don't you come back no more.

They could feel it, these three girls who were now on their way, buoyed by the belief that this was the beginning of everything and that they were all glowing with possibility, that they were made entirely of future. Even Becky, younger and more serious than her companions, more prone to turn inward, even she was caught up in the spirit of the trip, the windy romance of the open road and the getting out, the escape. So maybe she wasn't quite as lone and dour as Miriam remembered it later.

They talked and joked, giddy, drunk on it all, luxuriating in the big old car, a Dodge in a shade of blue that was maybe supposed to evoke the sky or a robin's egg but that looked more like something to coat your stomach after a greasy meal and was rusted at the edges after too many New England winters—and wasn't that what they were getting away from, after all, weren't they headed for someplace where cars never rusted and nothing else did, either?—with a dusty dashboard, and the upholstery inside was some kind of vinyl that soaked up the heat and seared your bare legs when you sat down on it. But they stretched out on the big seats and slipped their shoes off and took possession of that car, remade it from something meant to molder in a family driveway somewhere into a dream machine, destined to cruise the highways endlessly with its three hip sirens, luring square and unwary truckers to their doom. They held their hands out the windows in the streaming wind and laughed. They sang along with the radio and the highway sang back. They were unmoored in America, which is what America is for.

Yes. I can see them, the three of them, out on the road, but I could not have seen them this clearly until now.

And I have to take care. I have to try to get it right, because that summer when I was trying to understand Charlotte West I got so many things wrong. So many things I didn't see clearly or well, not Charlotte, or the others, or myself either. So maybe by telling it now I can get it right, maybe they will no longer be trapped in my telling. I'd like that, to set them free of me at least, free to be who they are, who they were, even if I can't change any of the things that happened to them or the things they did.

So I need to try to tell them right, these three young women, and the quiet one in the back seat for sure, I need to see them clear and tell what happened that summer, that trip.

I have to imagine things the way they had to be.

Becky was too young and had no license, so the two older girls took turns driving, theoretically, but most of the time the arrangement was the same: Becky in the back seat, watching out the window, studying the passing landscape; Miriam driving, looking chic in her Wayfarer knockoffs with her long black hair blowing around her face, watching the road, while she smoked and let the vent window carry the ashes away; and Aline in the passenger seat with her bare feet propped up on the dash, reading. They could never understand how she did it without getting nauseous, reading newspapers or her books on radical politics and reading out quotations for the other two or making her deadpan unfunny jokes. Becky was mostly silent, searching the blurred world of trees and billboards for clues to her future, joining in the conversation only to laugh at a joke or to answer a question. The cousins in the front seat were a team, Miri and Ali, together again and always, out on the road, ready to give Neal and Jack a run for their money.

Aline read out a newspaper article about an Indian in upstate New York who had gone to prison for protesting against the appropriation of tribal land for another white development project.

Hey, Miri.

Yeah?

What's black and white and red all over?

You got me. A newspaper?

No, dummy. An Indian in his prison clothes.

An hour later Aline was reading aloud from a paperback that chronicled the history of American Indians since the arrival of the *Mayflower*. She stopped and splayed the book over her bare leg to keep her place, looking out the window. After a few minutes she said:

Hey, Miri.

Yeah?

What's black and white and red all over?

An axe-murdering zebra.

C'mon, Miri.

All right. What?

A goddamn shamefaced Pilgrim.

That's real funny, Ali. I'm really enjoying the jokes.

They stopped early on the first day because they wanted to

see New York City and Miriam had a friend, a couple of years older, who lived there. The city looked good as they came up to it, scaled to their aspirations for the trip, all those tall buildings of shiny metal and glass and solid stone, packed together right up to the waterline so that there didn't seem to be any island at all there, just a city made by a pagan god to rise straight up out of the flowing rivers.

But when they got down onto the city streets they did not like it. Here too the streets were tunnels, even if it was buildings instead of trees that cast the shadows, and they began to feel confined again, cut off from the sun and the open promise of the highway. When they had finally crawled downtown and parked, the air felt close, it was hot, there was garbage out on the curbs and the smell of putrefaction everywhere.

Miriam's friend Joan cleared out of her apartment and gave them a tarnished key, packing a bag and heading out to play house with her boyfriend, so that they saw her only twice in the next two days. Nice of her, sure, but to tell the truth the country mice felt abandoned in this big rushing alien place. Somewhere out in the city there was excitement and energy, they could feel it like a tiny constant vibration, a jitter whose source they couldn't trace. Somewhere there was a scene where they could be having a ball, doing whatever it was the hip kids were doing in places where people were real, not like home. Somewhere it was all going on, but they never got close to it. Or maybe it was all over for New York already, the beatnik scene done and the folk scene splintered and everyone smoking pot nowadays so it didn't feel like anything special anymore. The zeitgeist had packed up and headed west to California and everyone was out there now soaking up the sun and waiting for the next thing to happen.

Maybe it was in the grip of that feeling that Miriam, browsing the racks at a record store down the street one day, bought the latest Beach Boys album and brought it straight back to the apartment, climbing the three flights of stairs that smelled so strongly of urine that it stung her eyes, and put it on the record player.

She played it constantly while they were there, and they stayed inside the stuffy apartment with its meager sunlight and its single fan running rough and constant in a back window, Miriam smoking and Aline reading, and they listened to the record while the great city outside went mostly unexplored. Miriam associated the California boys with good times, simple pleasures, the magical western seacoast, but the songs were strangely dense, mournful, heavy with longing, and they sounded just fine there in the dark rooms of their idling New York days.

Some square shit, Joan said when she saw the record, wrinkling her nose and advising Miriam to get a copy of the new Dylan, but Becky liked it. While she lay awake at night, unable to sleep with the sound of cars and the sudden piercing voices and laughter from the street that always came loud through the window just as she was drifting off, the lyrics would repeat in mantra-like loops in her head.

I once had a dream so I packed up and split for the city
I soon found out that my lonely life wasn't so pretty

She wondered at the alchemy by which the words, so banal on the face of it, could become wise and strange when they made contact with the music, the eerie high sliding harmonies and the layers underneath, sometimes as spare as echoes in an empty room, sometimes swollen thick in a mass of sound, with obscure noises creeping in around the edges. The songs were oceanic, full of green wavering depths, waves on the surface and shifting tidal currents and eddies swirling below.

Maybe a life could be like that, she would have thought, like those songs: however dull and ordinary the basic material might be, however tainted, maybe the form of it could still be manipulated, crafted, grandly imagined, and so you could still give beauty and meaning both to the whole.

These were strange days for her. She had never been happier, however little it might show, and a part of her dared to hope that there might be a future out there, wherever, however—a life that she might inhabit and make her own.

It was a relief to pack and leave the apartment, and they greeted the old Dodge waiting patiently at the curb where they had

left it as a long-lost friend. They were impatient, delayed in their
going because they had been waiting for Joan to return to take
her key, and it was early evening by the time they crossed over
to New Jersey. Aline looked back through the windows at the
high Manhattan buildings, their promise restored once you were
leaving and could feel a pang of loss inside the pleasure of being
in motion again, the low sun spreading a sheen of orange and
crimson over the skyscrapers and everything else, too.

Hey, hey, Miri.

What?

What's black and white and red all over?

All right. What?

This.

They avoided cities after that, bypassing or skirting around
Philadelphia and Baltimore and Washington, heading west and
south with the roads, crossing the Mason-Dixon line along the
way and keeping an eye on the temperature gauge as the weather
went from warm to hot. They had a destination but weren't in a
hurry to go there right away and have the trip over so soon. So
they kept on, west and south, aimless and yet in motion fast and
straight. Miriam and Aline wanted to see the country, and Becky
was willing to go along for the ride, sitting in the back seat with
her thoughts while the road signs passed her by.

They stopped at campgrounds in the evenings, sleeping in
the car or sometimes in a cabin if they could get one for cheap.
The nights were warm and they left the car windows halfway
down when the mosquitoes weren't too bad. When they woke
they would find a pump or a pond or once in a while even a real
shower, and wash up the best they could. Then the day was on,
and no telling where it might take them.

Underneath the seats of the car and crinkling underfoot when
they shifted their feet, the fast-food detritus collected—dented
paper cups with plastic lids, paper straws, waxy wrappers with
mottled patterns of greased translucence. One time they stopped
at a McDonald's and all three girls spontaneously and without
conference ordered chocolate shakes, and it seemed an auspicious

sign, which they honored by breaking down in laughter, even Becky joining in, under the cool bland gaze of the woman at the register, before taking to the road for an hour of slow-sipping meditation while the miles ticked by on the dashboard.

The world passed, its details uncertain under the flat glare of the sun. There were gas stations with cardboard signs in the window advertising bait or produce for sale in the back, with old men and women behind the counters with courtly drawling accents like something out of a movie about the South, and sometimes younger men and boys working the pumps who would smile through the windshield while they cleaned it when they saw that there were three young women inside, the sort of thing you wait for all week and then tell your friends about when you get off work, making it sound like they were three movie stars.

But often people did not smile when they saw the three girls, the sour-faced old women at cash registers at the gas stations, the men sitting out in chairs in front of the main street diners where they stopped to eat, who eyed them with desire and disapproval, the waitresses inside with hair teased and curled, dyed blonde and worn in some elaborate Eisenhower-era do. They looked at the girls with their straight black hair and light brown skin, their cutoff shorts and loose casual shirts and couldn't decide if they were Mexicans, Indians, hippies, or something worse.

So the girls preferred to be out on the road, in the car, where they only had to cope with those truck drivers who slowed to ogle and maybe even call out, or make obscene gestures to which Aline would respond either with a display of ironic pouting or, if she was in a less generous mood, a weary middle finger. Miriam grumbled about them, but Becky ignored these exchanges completely. She read the signs. Monongahela, Chattanooga, Tuscaloosa. Billboards with advertisements for hair tonic, automobiles, cigarettes, Standard Oil, Kountry Kitchen, Doublemint Gum. There were roadside churches, shacks with crosses and hand-lettered signs, and there were stands selling fruits and vegetables, houses built up close to the road, weeds growing tall, farms with horses, cows with their large slow eyes, never pausing in their chewing, tractors standing immobile like agrarian-propaganda statuary, men in straw hats, riding mules or walking along the side of the road, wooden fences running swift and uneven alongside the car for miles, hawks floating dangerously in the thin blue sky, an occasional large house in the distance with tall white pillars, treed hills, hay bales, schools, stores, drive-ins, diners, and Coca-Cola everywhere like a religion.

It all got mixed up in her head with Aline's voice from the front seat, like a movie that had the wrong voice-over dubbed in. One day Aline read a whole chapter of *One-Dimensional Man* aloud, but more often it was stories from the newspaper, Bobby Kennedy and Richard Nixon, Johnson, Vietnam, the draft. The news of the world and the nation drifted into the back seat, softened and blurred by the humming of the engine and the rushing of the wheels, and Becky could not match it up with the roadside moving so vividly past her window. It did not seem possible that the news could matter to anyone or anything out there, or in here either. That must be another world, another country.

The Dodge broke down finally somewhere in Mississippi. Maybe they felt then that this was what they had been waiting for, that the plan all along had been to drive until the car stopped or else go on driving straight into the Gulf of Mexico and disappear forever beneath an oily rainbow dissipating on the still water. They walked until they found a house and got a tow to the nearest garage, where the proprietor eyed them with distaste and said they could come back for it the next afternoon.

There was no town there, so they hitchhiked to a motel six miles away and spent their first night in real beds, Miri and Ali sharing one, since they had left home. But none of them could sleep, because they knew that this was the end of the trip, the beginning of the end, that after this they would have to get on with whatever it was that they thought they were doing, and the days and years stretching ahead looked the way Monday always looks on Sunday night.

So they were bleary-eyed and sober when they retrieved the car the following day and pointed it back the way they had come, taking a different route to make of their trip a kind of unclosed loop, crossing into Alabama, where they spent their last night sleeping in the car.

When they got to North Carolina and began to near their destination, Miriam and Aline perked up and began looking around and talking, began to pay attention to their surroundings and take stock of this new place they were arriving at. Becky watched the signs passing. Greensboro, Charlotte, Asheville, Cherokee, Lenoir. The landscape here was different from New England, more open, the trees by the roadside less dense, tall thin unclimbable trees in woods interspersed with rolling open farmland. Maybe it would be different enough.

Becky watched the signs, and by the time they arrived and parked the car and stretched their wobbly legs, she had given herself a new name.

32.

I t was late, but a light was still on at the back of the house. I could not see it directly, but as I passed under a tangle of darkness that must have been the grape arbor, part of the back lawn was visible, grass streaked by a dim patch of light like a shadow in reverse.

The rain had stopped now, and the night was full of that green musty smell, almost rotten, the smell of life and growth, with water dripping from trees and gathering in pools, insects starting to buzz around again. There was no doorbell, so I knocked loudly and waited, hoping I did not look completely unrecognizable when Alice came to the door.

It had taken some time to find my way back to the casino. I had walked a couple of winding miles down back roads, passing an occasional house but not daring to knock on any doors. I must have been a sorry spectacle, and I felt ragged, putting one foot in front of the other again and again, keeping my eyes on the wet gravel at the side of the road where I walked.

Finally I made my way to a busier road, and I did not even have to stick out a thumb. A bearded man in a pickup truck pulled over and motioned me to get in. I asked if he was going to the casino and he raised his eyebrows, looking at me solicitously and asking if I hadn't better be getting home. But he took me. It was the high point of the night when I discovered that my car was still there where I had parked it.

I had spent a few moments looking at myself in the rearview mirror, sitting under the lights in the casino parking lot, trying to make myself presentable. My face was scraped and bruised, my hair and clothes soaked with the rain, my ribs ached, and at the back of my head I could feel a large swollen tenderness, but I knew it could have been much worse. I was lucky to have escaped without any more serious injury, lucky to be walking and talking. I said it to myself one more time, mouthing the words in the mirror's reflection: I am still alive.

Now, standing at the front door, I heard noises from inside the house. Moments later a porch light came on directly in front of me. I blinked and squinted as the door opened and Alice Pickett appeared, looking up at me. I had been afraid that she would be in bed already, but she looked wide awake, with a baseball cap perched incongruously on top of her gray head and a pad of paper in one hand, a pen thrust through the wire spiral that held the pages together.

"Alice," I said. My voice was rusty. "I'm sorry if this is a bad time."

She looked me up and down, taking in the damage and the soaked condition of my clothes, and then held the door wide for me to come in.

In the kitchen she looked at my bruised head and seemed to decide that she did not need to call for an ambulance. Then she gave me some aspirin, poured a tall glass of water, and led me back through the house to the atelier where I had been before, turning on lights and turning them off again as she went, leaving all other rooms dark, the imperative to avoid waste not a necessity here but rather an ideology, a weight-bearing pillar in life as she knew it.

The room was transformed at night. The many windows, which opened the space of the room outward into the surrounding lawn when the sun was shining, were now opaque, darkness a solid wall behind the glass. If you did not look directly at the windows, if you absorbed yourself in the contents of the room, the night simply became wallpaper, but if you looked out, it pressed in, engulfing and unknowable. Having been assaulted by figures hidden in darkness once already tonight, I was keenly, uncomfortably aware of how exposed we were to the outside world, of how easily we could be seen, an old woman and an injured boy, and I could not help thinking how night reveals what a fragile and absurd act of faith it is to build a house and live in it, to keep our possessions in it, to have possessions and lives at all, with that darkness pressing in at the windows.

The room was lit by table lamps, Alice's landscapes dimly visible on their easels, throwing shadows, the dead husband regarding us from a corner. A small television stood to one side, ballplayers moving on the green field. There was a comfortable-looking chair pulled up in front of it, a table with a lamp nearby, and thrifty Alice had turned over a plastic bucket for a makeshift hassock. She placed her pad of paper on the table.

"What's the notebook for?" I asked.

"For notes, of course," she said briskly. "Notes, statistics, scores. When you get to be my age it becomes difficult to keep all the relevant information in your head." She frowned at the television. "My Red Sox are down three runs in the eighth and there's no chance at all for them to win the division, but it looks as if your night has been much worse." Then she turned off the game and sat down, propping her feet up on the bucket, while I hesitated in my wet clothes.

She made a dismissive gesture. "Sit. It's an old davenport, there is no possible way you could harm it. What on earth happened to you?"

I sat on the edge of the couch, wincing at my bruises, and took a drink of the water. "Some men beat me up in the parking lot of the casino. It wasn't a mugging, they didn't take anything. They were waiting for me by my car."

She was a hard woman to shock, but she adjusted her glasses and gave me her full attention. "Why on earth would anyone do that?"

I ignored the question. "Listen, Alice. Something close to twenty years ago, two men named Eddie Slope and William Brewstead were killed in a car accident not far from here. Slope was, as far as I know, a factory worker. Brewstead was a wealthy man with a fancy Wasp lineage. What were they doing driving around together?"

She leaned back in the chair and frowned. "You get badly beaten and, apparently, drenched in the rain, and instead of seeking medical attention or going home to rest, you come to see me at eleven o'clock at night, to ask me this."

"I'm trying to tell a story. I'm hoping that you can help me tell it. Please, Alice."

I was still a little dizzy, and the lamps were bright blurs at the edge of my vision, but I tried my best to show that I was determined.

She sighed. "All right," she said. "It's a simple question with a simple answer. I don't know anything about Eddie Slope working at a factory. In fact I never truly knew him at all. But at the time you're talking about, he was doing yard work for a number of people I knew, yard work and other odd jobs, and I know that he often worked for Mr. and Mrs. Brewstead. It would not have been surprising for Eddie to give him a ride somewhere for any number of reasons. In fact." She paused, eyes narrowed. "I seem to recall, when I read about the accident in the paper, that they were on their way to look at some lumber that Eddie was going to use for some small construction project out at the Brewstead house. They were particular about the materials they used—to preserve the architectural integrity of their house, you understand. It's a very old house and William Brewstead, like a number of other people around here, could trace his family back to some of the very first settlers of New England. This is the *fancy Wasp lineage* you mention."

I thought for a moment. "Whose car were they driving?"

"I have no idea. Is that important for your story?"

"I don't know. Probably not. But all right. You already know what this story is about." She knew as soon as she saw me at the door, I thought. And she wants me to tell it, but I still don't know what it is. I will have to tell it to know for myself even; I will have to listen to myself tell it in order to know what I know.

I took a deep breath, feeling it in my battered body. "When she was sixteen or so, Becky Tilton left home. She went away with two other girls and they drove south a ways, but she didn't stay with them very long, a few weeks or a month at most, they were just a way for her to get out of town. She needed to get out of the place she was born in because she wanted to make something of herself, she wanted to be a whole new person and as long as she stayed here she would always be the poor child of poor parents. She would be known and understood that way all her life and even after she was dead, but not long after, because no one would remember her for long. She was ambitious, but to realize her ambitions she had to get away and the two girls with the car got her away and then she got away from them, too.

"And after that, who knows? Who would even want to guess what she did or had to do over the next few years while she was busy remaking herself, making herself into something new?"

It would be crazy to guess, I was thinking, speaking steadily, pausing to drink water and clear my throat while thought ran quick and disorderly underneath the story I was telling. It would be crazy to guess because the truth is always stranger than anything we could have imagined anyway. To find out, you would have to ask her, and she is the last person who would ever tell the truth about it, because the whole point of making yourself into someone new is that you have to disguise absolutely the fact that you were ever anything other than what and who you are now. So she would have had to efface her past entirely. She would have had to become *good* at the effacement, it would have had to become second nature to her, a second nature with the appearance of first and undeniable nature, a fiction more real and believable than the fictional self that was thrust upon her by unlikely parents and unconvincing circumstances. To Becky, all those poorly scripted details of her upbringing and coming of age were like the set at an amateur theatrical performance. All she had to do was push a little to discover that the houses were all facades and the trees were cardboard and the people were cutouts propped up from behind. She had realized that a long time ago. But it would have taken time and effort to make something more real and true to put in place once the stage effects had been torn down and swept away, starting from nothing.

"Whatever she did, it took several years for her to remake herself and to decide that coming back here was what she was remaking herself for, and then she came back. She was in her twenties, her beauty deepened now, with just enough mystery and upper-class reserve in her speech and manner. Although she seems never to have been able to completely disguise the hardness underneath, the determination to take and have all the things that Becky Tilton did not, and to have them in the place where Becky had never been meant to have anything. She could not hide entirely the fact that she didn't care what she had to do or who she had to hurt or even marry in order to get what she wanted. It took at least one false start, but she managed it. She married Franklin West."

I had been staring at my hands, concentrating on the words as I spoke them, but now I looked up at Alice. I was beginning to get to the part of the story that, I was guessing, she didn't know about.

"She married him and in doing so she acquired access to money, a position in a class and a community, and one thing more, a daughter. But not her daughter or his, either. She had a sister with a small child, a little girl named Eleanor Tilton. Not long before she got married, Charlotte Lenoir went to see this sister after her years away, and she—*appropriated* the little girl. Took her, adopted her, changed her future and her history, and gave her the name that she, Charlotte, had taken for herself at such a cost of effort and time. West. Ellie West."

I wanted it to be a shock, and I could see the reaction in her face like a sudden recoiling, but I kept going because this was just the first shock, just the light slap that wakes the sleeper enough to listen to what comes next. "She adopted Ellie and raised her, kept her side of the bargain she had made with her sister. God knows why she couldn't have just provided money to the sister, enough to help her out, maybe just put something in trust for the daughter, the niece, for when she came to the age that she is now. I don't understand it. But mostly I don't understand why she didn't want to just have a child of her own. I know that this is what she did, but I don't know why. Do you?"

Alice stirred, looked uncertain. "No." She hesitated. "But." A longer pause. "I'm thinking back to those days. It seems to me that she and Frank did leave town for quite a while, a long honeymoon or what have you, after they were married. And it was after they came back that they had the child—I don't remember ever seeing the girl as a baby. I probably never saw her before she was school age. But I remember there was some gossip, some whispering, people speculating that she had trapped Franklin, had seduced him and got herself pregnant and then he had had to marry her. I never put any stock in that sort of talk, myself. People would have said anything about Becky in those days."

"Charlotte."

"All right. Charlotte."

"Would they have said that she was a murderer?"

She just stared at me, stern and apprehensive. I met her gaze. "She killed Eddie Slope and William Brewstead," I said.

She drew back from me, eyes wide. "It was a car accident. How." She stopped. "Why on earth would she have even wanted to—to *kill* those two men?"

"She took the daughter and raised her as her own, her sister's child. But on the day that she goes out to talk to her sister, to strike the bargain, just by happenstance, an older cousin of theirs drops in with her husband in tow: Eddie Slope. Maybe they aren't there for long. Probably they don't even recognize this Charlotte Lenoir. Of course she wouldn't have said anything to identify herself as Becky Tilton. Instead she passes herself off as something, a charity worker, say. Remembering, maybe, a visit from a charity worker years ago, some deep part of her resonating with the repetition and the irony. And they drive off, none the wiser.

"But what if that wasn't the end of it. Suppose later this Eddie starts thinking, or maybe his wife says something or someone else says something and it starts him thinking. However it happens, he figures out who Charlotte is, who she was. Maybe if he pursues it hard enough and thinks about it enough and asks the right questions, he even figures out about the daughter who isn't really hers. But either way, he has more information than is good for him."

"Are you sure it's Eddie Slope you're talking about?" Alice asked.

I ignored this. "And add to it the fact that this is a woman who has just married a wealthy man, a man with a position in the community, a man who in fact has a deep investment in the idea of his illustrious forebears. So she has good reason to want him not to know about her own forebears. The husband is always the last to know, but even better if he doesn't know at all. She has a secret newly minted, and speaking of mints, she now has money, too. So I think that Eddie decided to leverage the secret in order to earn some money for himself.

"That's why she had him killed. She couldn't have known for sure, of course, that Eddie had kept the secret to himself, no matter what assurances he might have offered. So for certainty she substituted swift action, because it was not long after she and Franklin West were married that Eddie died, before that honeymoon trip, even, if that's possible. Or better: during the trip. To be off in Niagara Falls or Paris or Mexico when the actual deed was performed and only to hear of it later, not to have to react to the news, but to return from a long trip so that it would not even have been news anymore but just a fading memory, a misfortune of months ago. That would have been ideal. No need to wonder, when someone relates the story, whether her face betrayed knowledge or guilt, because no one would bother to relate the story at all.

"And no, I don't know how she did it. She must have hired someone, but I can't imagine who or how. It's all shadowy to me and all I can see is scenes from movies. Meetings in dark rooms, dangerous men, cash in thick bundles on a table, none of that seems real, but some kind of transaction must have taken place, because even if we can't quite believe it, someone was paid a sum of money and two men died. Maybe the car was sabotaged, fixed in some way to explode or to malfunction, the brakes gone and a sharp turn approaching fast, or they were just killed outright and then the car deliberately crashed, left in gasoline flames to burn away evidence and curiosity. I know it all sounds unlikely, it all sounds like a movie again. It seems like a plan that could go wrong a hundred ways, and she's not a woman to take chances, but who could have linked her to the accident anyway?"

I stopped, breathing hard, sitting on the old faded couch among the duck pillows with the blood thumping at the back of my head. Alice was sitting back in her chair as if she had been thrust there. She looked older, more frail. *At least I said it*, I thought. *At least now it won't just be my responsibility. Now someone else will have to think it too.*

"But surely he knew that he was adopting a child," she said.

"Frank West? Sure, he knew that he was adopting her. He just didn't know that the child was his bride's sister's daughter. Because then he would have had to know that she was his bride's sister in the first place. But, yes, they all had to meet face to face one time, at least. In a lawyer's office or in front of a judge or an adoption official. I still think it's strange that she would take the risk of it."

"Yes, why do that?" The question was rhetorical, but also pointed. She paused, then said, slowly and still skeptically, "I will not ask you how you know any of this, or even how much you know and how much is—invention. But am I to understand that you believe that the men who attacked you tonight were also hired by Charlotte West, since you have developed the theory that she has a history of hiring violent men?"

"I don't know. But I was at the casino tonight in order to talk to a woman who knew her in the past. It doesn't seem likely, but none of it does."

"No," she agreed. "None of it does. And why did you come here to tell me this?"

I looked down at my hands. A long scratch ran along the curve of my thumb, a raw dotted line of half-dried blood, the skin raised and red. Then I looked up again, quickly.

"You already know, don't you, Alice? The same reason you had for talking to me down at the beach. I wanted to talk to someone else who was interested, who cared, someone who could help me put the pieces together."

She was still drawn back in her chair. "I can't help you put these pieces together. I don't like the picture. I don't agree with it."

"Fine. You don't agree with it. I won't ask you to agree, or to like it. Then can you just tell me one thing? What did she say when she came to see you, when she first came back?"

She opened her mouth quickly to object, then said nothing. She looked at me for what seemed like a long time. I could hear her breathing, and mine. Then she sighed and with a little struggle she got up from her chair and walked out of the room. I could hear her moving through the house, her footsteps and the flick of the light switches, and then I couldn't hear her anymore.

I took a breath. I had felt that the story had to be true, mostly anyway, but nonetheless I was relieved to have any small conjecture proved right. Because at least that meant that the others might be right, too; at least I might not be hopelessly trapped in a web of my own devising, inventing explanations for the past and then believing them, like a lunatic who doesn't know that he is insane and that all his paranoid interpretations lead back into the closed maze of his malfunctioning mind. It was tricky, this following of hunches, but what else was there to follow?

I sat on the couch under the illumination of the table lamp with darkness pressing in at the windows, flat and looming. So much not to know out there. So much not to know that you don't know, and how to begin, just to begin, to imagine it when you cannot even feel it as an absence?

Alice came back into the room, the last light flicking off behind her as she walked in, and sat down again in her chair without looking at me. She had an envelope in her hand and she fidgeted with it as she talked, beginning as if she were picking up my unspoken thoughts and following their thread, as if our thoughts had converged and become one thread, its twining strands indistinguishable for long enough at least to tell the story that we were, willingly or not, telling together.

"Nothing means anything, but we keep going anyway. That's what you do when you are raised as I was raised. That's what we do, we keep going. But of course we have our lapses. On some odd night when the wind is from the wrong direction and everything gets stirred up we have a few drinks and dig the artifacts out of the closet. Or maybe one day while cleaning out a drawer we spend an hour reading the old letters and for a while we are distracted, lost in the fruitless contemplation of time gone by, for a while memory takes over and has its way with us, and dream and waking blot together. And then we wake up. The sun is shining, there are things to be done, so we put it away again. We keep going.

"None of this is natural for me, young man, this groping around in the past with no light to see by, and this making it up as you go along. And it *is* natural to me to be circumspect and to keep things to myself. But I started this. I let you get under my defenses, I still don't know how, or why. I started the whole business and I have only myself to blame.

"Yes. She did come to see me. Just once. And not for long. It was months after the business with Mary Woodhouse, after the party.

"She came to see me at my house. I was the only one home, and I suppose it is possible that she was careful to arrive when she knew that I would be alone, because I do think—I know— that she wanted to speak to me privately. I don't believe that she could have had more than two or three outfits at that time, but she would have kept them in best condition and carefully ironed, and in any case she always looked better than anyone else you saw outside of the movies. So she stood there on my front step again in her skirt and blouse with a scarf tied at her neck like a dark-haired Faye Dunaway, looking nothing like the little girl who had stood there years before. I took her into the kitchen and invited her to sit down, but she did not sit. She told me what I already knew, because everybody knew it already: that she was engaged to be married to Franklin West. She didn't sound like a breathless bride-to-be, of course, you will not be surprised to hear that. She just told me, the way you might tell someone that you had bought a new hat. Then she took out a piece of paper and handed it to me. She said, 'This is for you, Alice. You can do what you like with it. It is the death certificate of Becky Tilton, the last time I put that name on a piece of paper, and I never will again. She doesn't exist anymore.' Something to that effect. I was confused by the gesture, confused by everything. Why me? Why this? But she just said, 'Goodbye, Alice,' and left. No *thank you* and I didn't expect that, but not even an explanation. Maybe I didn't want that either. I think I was just sad, the way you are always sad when you say goodbye to someone, sad to reach an ending. And sad like the way you feel when you love something that does not, cannot, love you back. When you offer up everything that you have to the indifferent world, knowing that there can be no return and feeling the emptiness of it, having nothing to fill the emptiness with but your temporary and insufficient sadness."

She stopped then and opened the envelope, carefully removing a sheet of paper, unfolding it, and not looking at it herself before leaning forward and handing it to me. It occurred to me that when she had gone to get the paper she had been out of the room for less than ten minutes, maybe closer to five. *She knew exactly where it was*, I thought. She did not have to think about it at all, where to find the old envelope in a house filled, surely, with the accumulations of seventy years, all the old shoeboxes and crates filled with bills from five years ago and aging photographs, letters and diaries and notebooks, recipes and children's fourth-grade math tests and old grocery lists that had been saved by accident like fossil remnants preserved between the layers of paper strata, all the clutter of a long life. Yet she had known immediately where and how to put her hands on this one scrap out of all of them; this had not been buried or forgotten.

The paper was old, yellow at the edges, and the remnants of creases and crumplings long smoothed over showed in the texture of the page like old scars. It was almost completely blank, the third page of what had been a three-page document and all that it contained was the last two lines of some sort of authorization form. Below were two signatures, the name *Rebecca Tilton* written in clean and still-legible script, followed by the brief scribble of some official person and the date, July 7, 1966. The only other mark on the page was a stamp, slightly diagonal, faded to begin with and impossible to decipher.

"What is it?" I asked.

She shook her head. "I don't know. I don't think that she cared about the particular piece of paper, about whatever it had been for or where it was from. I think that the thing that made it important to her was just the fact that it had her signature. Her last signature using that name. She gave it to me, I guess, because she wanted to make me the keeper of her past self, the self she was giving up."

"She wanted to make sure that you were not going to say anything about her past, now that she was living nearby. She wanted your silence."

Alice gave me a hard look. "She already had it."

"But she wanted to see you, to know it was true. She went to see her sister, and a woman she had known, Miriam Beauclaire. She was careful. She had to come and look at you so that she could know for sure."

"She already had it. She must have known that." We sat there, old woman and young man, glaring at each other in the light from the lamps. "I will admit it. She was changed when I saw her that last time, and when I saw her at Mary's house. When she was a girl, she was hungry. She wanted so desperately to find a way out. I would have done anything to help her, not for thanks or reward but just to see her ascend and triumph, except that she had set the terms of her struggle and to accept my help beyond that one first step, asking me to help her find a job, would have hurt her pride, I think. But when she came back those years later, it was not hunger anymore. As I said to you already, something had changed in her. She was willing to do whatever it took to get what she wanted. So maybe you are right and she wanted my silence, maybe she didn't care about me or anyone else at all. I will accept any indignity, any slighting of myself. But I will not accept murder. I will not believe it. And what about Brewstead? She had him killed, too, her former employer?"

"It could have been a mistake," I said, looking away out the blank windows. "Brewstead was just in the wrong place at the wrong time. Or maybe she just didn't care. You won't like that idea, but I wonder. Maybe if an innocent man had to die to prevent her plans from dissolving away and keep her secrets safe, then that was a price she was willing to pay."

She shook her head at me with slow deliberation. "I will not have it. No. I don't expect you to understand. You are young, a young man, and I don't expect you to understand what she means to me, because she could never mean the same to you, could never mean as much. I will say it. I am *proud* of her. It would never mean anything to her for me to say it, or for her to know it, so it is my feeling alone, but it is that, at least. It is mine.

"Don't you see what she has done? Remade herself, out of nothing. Remade the world in the image she wants for it, not caring what she had to do to accomplish that feat. Because if she had cared, it could never have been accomplished. It is hard for a woman not to care, and it seems to be so easy for men, to take and take and act as though it is only right that the world should be there for them to take. So I have watched her all these years with *pride*, not because she owes anything to me, but because she doesn't, because she made and took and had the strength and the determination to find a place in the heart of the edifice that was built to exclude her. And I have been privileged to watch it happen, to understand her well enough to watch and to share vicariously in her success. Women spend so much time tearing each other down. You are a man and not old enough to have seen that, because you do not see women, not to understand them. But they do. Tear each other down and resent the women who succeed or accomplish because they think they are diminished by the other's achievement. So maybe I have not achieved much, but I have been here to watch her and to feel proud."

"Wait a minute. Wait. What exactly has she done besides marry a wealthy man? What kind of accomplishment is that?"

"Her *life* is the accomplishment. Her self. Nothing is impressive in itself, not until you consider the alternatives. Making a statue from clay is difficult enough even if you have the training.

She built hers from quicksilver, untutored, and held it together through force of will."

"But if it is murder. Will you condone that too?" I asked stubbornly, doggedly. Whatever resources of body and mind had been sustaining me this far were fading rapidly. I could feel it, as if each cell of me was winking out, leaving all the many rooms inside me dark.

"I tell you, I will not have it!" She was almost shouting it now, maybe she was closer to shouting than she had ever been before, leaning forward and looking fiercely at me. "If there is nothing else I can say to explain, at least let me say this. Let me say it again. No matter what happens, no matter what has happened, for me she is always that young girl from a summer day long ago, in a shapeless ragged dress, looking boldly at me and asking about my shoes. So even if she betrays the memory of that girl, even if she forgets her, I will always be true to her. I will remember."

Soon it would be time for me to go. I was exhausted and chilled, my eyes going unfocused, the lamps just blurs of yellow. We were not glaring, now, but still facing each other over the low table and the upturned bucket, Alice still fixing me with that intense gaze from behind her glasses. I was holding the old piece of paper in my hand with its signature out of the past, a mark made once by a hand, looping continuous, the visible sign and imprint of official identity. Once a hand had shaped the letters, the name. Maybe it had even known that it was putting the name on paper for the last time and from then on neither the signature nor the writer would ever be the same. I handed the page back to Alice.

"What are you going to do now, Kesey?" she asked. She spoke slowly, but there was iron in her voice and it did not shake.

"I don't know," I said. "Right now I'm going to go home and get some sleep."

33.

They were disappointed that it was not more different. It was the South here, no question, but there were still the twisting narrow rural roads, the trailers and shacks sharing the land with large houses, old and creaking under the weight of history. They had traveled, but they had not gone away.

They had come to stay with a cousin of Aline's on her father's side of the family, a woman she had met only once before. Nita lived in a small cabin that she shared with a boyfriend, and she was not pleased to see the three girls when they arrived, but she gave the living room to them for sleeping and told them all to get a job. The boyfriend smiled broadly and looked them up and down and rolled himself a cigarette at the kitchen table, orgy dreams an open secret in his faraway eyes.

Nita was in her twenties and she worked waitressing at a diner on the highway a few miles away, came home after her shifts smelling of coffee and grease. Her place was part of a collection of cabins, trailers, and small houses clustered around the perimeter of a large pond that was calling itself Summers Lake. The neighborhood itself was called Summersedge, although over the years the name had been shortened to Summers. The lake was a few miles outside the Qualla, where those Cherokee who were spared the trail of tears and exile to unthinkable Oklahoma still lived, and many of those who lived in Summers were Indian in part or whole, though there were white people interspersed and intermarried there. Some black families, too, but although some of them were part Cherokee as well, their houses were clustered separately along the southwest bank of the lake.

The girls got to know their neighbors to say hello to when they saw them on the road, and they would gladly have taken a week to settle into their new surroundings and look back fondly on the trip they had taken to get here. But Nita frowned at their torpor and their inability to clean up after themselves and wanted them out of her place as soon as possible, for any number of reasons.

They spent a few days drinking coffee and reading the want ads in the paper, looking for secretary or waitress work, making calls to prospective employers on Nita's party line, and evading the boyfriend's unsubtle innuendos. One day he took Miriam aside while she was brewing a pot. She put a hard look in her eyes, ready to discourage with a word, or even shove a knee in his balls and ask questions later, but it wasn't that, not exactly.

You know Bobby, the kid down the street?

Guy with the bike? Sure.

Looks to me like he's lost it for your friend there.

Becky? Not hard to believe.

She Indian?

Not that I know of. Why?

He spends all his time mooning over her and she won't give him a look. Wondered if she was, you know. Prejudiced. Or just stuck up.

You sure it's Bobby you're concerned about?

Seriously, girl. He's a sweet kid. I'd just hate to see him get hurt.

It was true. Miriam began to notice the excuses Bobby devised to be in Becky's vicinity, the time he spent hanging around on the street, tossing a ball to himself or making obscure adjustments to his bicycle in order to be in position to see anyone coming or going from Nita's place. She watched the curious dance of looks and body language that played out between the two when they were in any kind of proximity, he moving closer to her or trying to catch her eye, she resolutely unconscious—not wallflowerish or playing some deep coquette's game, but reserved, determined to hold herself apart from him.

Miriam, too, began to wonder if she thought she was too good for Bobby. He was good-looking, with a wiry build, straight dark hair that was creeping toward his shoulders, and an appealing openness that made the whole business all the more pathetic, since every emotion was broadcast immediately through the transparent medium of his face. Not that any of that compelled Becky to be interested, but still there was something in the quality of her disinterest that invited interpretation, something about her poised self-containment that seemed to say that she was holding out for something better, that she had ideas about where she was going and an Indian boy whose father landscaped other people's yards for a living was not that destination.

Maybe it was true. Certainly she must have known that this place was not where she intended to end her explorations. She would have had her eyes focused on an unknown future whose actual contours she could not yet see. There was no room to grow here, no place for her to expand into whatever the thing was that she would become, nothing to learn that she hadn't learned already.

But you couldn't say that the place itself was not a temptation, an invitation to imagine abandoning the future she had imagined, however vaguely, for herself. Whatever else it was, Summers was a pleasant place, comfortable, a broken-in shoe, a thing you could settle into for a good long while if you didn't need to go anywhere formal. The neighbors greeted each other on the street and gossiped about each other when the doors were closed, the stray dogs got fat at the backdoor of the eccentric woman who lived in a house full of cats and dogs and God knows what else, and it had that indefinable air of good nature that settled over certain neighborhoods without anyone ever being able to really explain how it had happened. She had heard Miriam and Aline talking about it, had noticed their animation when they toyed with the idea of finding a place of their own on the street to rent out. Maybe the two of them would settle here, stay here, raise families or find jobs or lovers, or take over for the woman with the pets and end up as those oddball old lady sisters down the street whom everyone whispered about and no one disliked.

Maybe, but her path lay in a different direction from the one that Miriam and Aline would follow. Their threesome was always accidental and bound to be temporary, and even if it turned out to be a taste of freedom for all of them, it was also unstable, unsustainable. Miri and Ali would always be a pair, even if life separated them, and Charlotte Lenoir would always have to go her own way.

Yet she stayed on, looking for work and knowing that she would not find it and did not want to. Maybe she wanted to hang on for one last week or month to the small delay she was allowing herself, the moment of closeness to the other girls, the companionable feeling that was like nothing she had ever had before. But that couldn't have been the only reason, because she wasn't sentimental enough to hold on to something that had no real practical value for her. There was one other thing that she had to take care of before she moved on.

It came to a head one evening when the girls were coming home. They had handed in their applications at three different secretarial agencies, although none of them could type well enough even to fake it. Seeing them park, Bobby walked over, abandoning his bike and wiping grease from his hands with a rag. The girls got out of the car and stretched in the cooling air, the dusky orange light dimming from the surface of the lake. Becky didn't look in his direction, but while the others stayed to greet him and complain about their day, she separated cleanly from them and went to Nita's cabin, not hurrying, but rather as if she and Bobby were magnets polarized to repel and his approach was pushing her irresistibly away.

Miriam watched disappointment bloom in his eyes and watched him tighten his face to try to disguise it, too, and she felt a sudden rush of righteous indignation. Leaving Aline and Bobby, she followed Becky and caught her just inside the door, the two girls facing each other, Miriam frowning and Becky meeting her eyes with a gaze not defiant, but just flat and unyielding.

What's wrong with Bobby?

Nothing's wrong with him.

Is it because he's Indian?

No.

What, then?

The sunlight faded and the cabin went dark in one swift

moment. The lightest breath of wind swelled the screens in the windows. The two girls faced each other.

Miriam. I need to see a doctor.

What?

I might be pregnant.

Oh man. You miss a period?

Yes. Maybe. I don't know.

Jesus, girl. Don't you even know about Griswold?

Who?

Happened just last year, girl. You can get the pill now, get a rubber at the drugstore. It's legal and everything. Man. I didn't even know you had a boyfriend back home or anything like that.

I need to know.

All right. I guess you do.

They went, all three together, to the clinic a few miles away. Nita had looked sharply at Aline when she asked for information about local clinics with services for women, but nonetheless Aline had got the information from her without explaining exactly why she wanted it. And it seemed important that the three of them should all go together. Becky couldn't have driven herself, of course, but also Miriam and Aline both felt the imperative for them to provide solidarity and support for the quiet and stoical girl who seemed to be incapable of confidences and who despite this, or because of it, seemed especially to deserve whatever comfort their company could provide.

They arrived, finally, at a large gray one-story building set on a flat patch of land surrounded by scrubby forested hills. Inside, the two sisters waited while Becky met with the doctor, but before she saw him, the receptionist who had verified her appointment and taken her information directed her to the office of a counselor.

That's how it must have happened.

Right there. That man, that room. That must have been the way it began to happen.

Maybe she even hesitated there, with some impossible foreknowledge of what was to come, the tiniest twinge of irritation, self-admonishment: why did I not foresee that giving myself over to a doctor would be accompanied by other indignities? I wanted only to see a man in a white coat in an office one time, to learn the truth and then to be gone, but there are always other men in other offices, other doors opening endlessly in a tightening circle of knowledge that has nothing to do with me.

The counselor sat behind his desk, read over the information she had provided, asked her questions and looked at her across the neat piles of paper arrayed in front of him. She held herself completely still, answered briefly or just nodded, watchful in case he came to one of the questions to which she had given a false or half-true response. Her age, for example. She had given it as eighteen, fearing that they might not give the test if she was too young or that they might want to contact her parents, which was not just impractical but unthinkable and would also give the lie to the local address she was claiming as her own. She sat still, giving up as little of herself as possible, emptying herself out and offering only her blank inscrutable gaze.

While he asked his questions he was taking note of her sullen and taciturn manner, her dark eyes and black hair, her address out on Summers Lake, her clothes. He was asking questions, talking about the pregnancy test, telling her to come back in three weeks, asking her to sign a piece of paper. Maybe he lied to her, made alterations and omissions when he spoke, he must have. Because she wasn't stupid, far from it, whatever this man might have thought. She was just young and inexperienced, and the only shield she had against the world in those days was to close herself off, to withdraw into silence and separateness. Yes, he would have lied to her, without compunction and all in a day's work. And maybe some of the things he was saying sounded strange to her, but it was all strange to her and she wanted so badly to be out of that room, out of that building, so that even if she had to come back one more time at least now she would be one step closer to the end of having to be there ever again. She signed the piece of paper, and then she could leave the counselor's office and a woman in a nurse's uniform walked her down the hall and around a bend to the doctor's office for the pregnancy test.

I see her walking down the hall and I imagine that in that moment she is surprised to find herself thinking about Summers, the neighborhood she will soon be leaving. Not even thinking about it, really, but just seeing it, a tableau in her mind's eye. The road that winds around the lake comes into focus, all the houses and trailers visible as if from a helicopter hovering above, hovering and rising, the houses becoming smaller and smaller the more she notices and concentrates on the details, the neighbors going about their business, oblivious; the gardens and weedy yards and the trucks tucked in against thick banks of bushes, all receding, the crooked rocky border dipping into the water, visible all the way around. The sun on the lake gives a last wink and flash, and then the image is gone for good.

34.

It was only when I pulled up and parked in front of the garage, well after midnight, that I thought, *I should have come here first.* Frederick was alone in the house, and it occurred to me for the first time, with a sharp pang of guilt, that the men who had beaten me at the casino could have come looking for me here.

Moving as quietly as I could, I opened the garage and took a flashlight, then walked all the way around the house looking for signs of damage. The doors were all locked, the windows and screens intact. There was no sign that anyone had even come near the house. I breathed out a long sigh. My shoes soaked again now from the wet grass, I replaced the flashlight and then I reached up into the darkness over the inside frame of the door to the garage, slipping the house key off the nail that was concealed there.

Inside, the house was dark and still. I turned on the lamp that hung over the kitchen table. Arranged there were the old man's sunglasses, the paperback copy of *Farewell, My Lovely* that we had been reading, several orange prescription bottles, a pack of cigarettes and disposable lighter, and the ashtray, carefully emptied and wiped although the table itself had a thin gray film of ash adhering to its surface.

I went to the cabinets over the sink and rummaged inside until I found a bottle of aspirin. I washed my face, grimacing when my hands touched a sore spot, and then walked back to the table with the pills and a glass of water and sat down heavily. I sat there with my eyes half-closed, empty of all thinking, finally letting myself feel the ache and weariness of my body. The room was blurry and I made no effort to pull it into focus. I swallowed the chalky pills and drank the water and sat in the pool of light in the dim kitchen.

There was a sound from somewhere in the house off to my left and then a creaking in the hallway. I sat and listened to it. The creaking became a shuffling, and then Frederick appeared in the hall, framed in the doorway, completely naked. He stood there for several seconds, his face bruised with sleep, and we regarded each other in silence. His old man's body was thick and saggy, almost hairless, swaying slightly, cock and balls hanging like ugly fruit. Then he turned slowly and went back the way he had come. I sat without moving, too exhausted to move. I heard more creaking and other noises for a couple of minutes. Then a toilet flushed, padding feet came back along the hallway, and he entered the kitchen dressed in loose khakis and a sweatshirt, his sparse hair disarranged and wiry, and sat at the table across from me. He put on the dark glasses, tapped out a cigarette on the table, and lit it before speaking.

"What'd you, get in a fight?" His voice was guttural, phlegmy.

"Something like that." I didn't see the point in telling the story, and it would have required far too much effort anyway.

He inhaled deeply, nodding. "Serves you right. What, you went to some fucking swamper bar and got yourself beat up? It figures. You get any punches in?"

I shook my head.

"Figures. Hey, how about a sandwich, huh? Got to keep my blood sugar up."

I dragged myself to my feet and headed for the refrigerator. Not such a bad idea, if I could keep the food down. I made two ham sandwiches and sat back down at the table. He stubbed out his smoke and we ate in silence for a few minutes. It was still and quiet and the light shone down yellow on the table, a bright circle surrounded by shadow in the dark heart of nighttime. Finally I cleared my throat and spoke.

"Frederick, have you ever been over to the casino?"

"That fucking place? I've got no interest in sitting around with a bunch of assholes just to gamble my money." He paused, thinking, and then looked at me. "So that's where you were tonight. Bet you lost a bundle."

"I wasn't gambling," I said. Another minute went by in silence. "But I spent some time looking at the old Indian artifacts they have on display there. It made me think of Frank West. You think that's really a piece of the *Mayflower* he's got in that case next door?"

"Who the hell cares? It's a goddamn cult, that business with the *Mayflower* and the bloodlines and all that. Like it means something who your great-great-grandfather or whatever was."

"The Original Americans cult."

"Well, you think that's some kind of joke, but that's really what it is. And West over there is a goddamn idiot, but he's got one thing right—you need to know a few things about history if you want to understand anything about this place. Do you even know who those characters on the *Mayflower* were?"

"Pilgrims?" I said. It sounded stupid coming out, the way it conjured a mental image of a man in a buckled hat and black culottes serving turkey dinner to a friendly Wampanoag.

"*Pilgrims.* Jesus." His thick fingers fumbled another smoke out, lit it, and waved it in my face. "What they were is Puritans running away from the king and the fucking church. You know anything about American Puritans? I mean, have you even read any of their sermons?"

Surprise yanked me partway out of my semiconscious stupor. The old man's fierce hatred of churches and his rants against religion made my own mild agnosticism pale by comparison. "Are you telling me you read Puritan sermons?"

He tapped out a length of ash and leaned back with lips pursed. His most dangerous pose, it said: time to teach the moron a thing or two that only a moron wouldn't have understood long ago. "Look. You've got to understand the way these guys think. Once you get inside their heads, then when they come at you with some bullshit, you can see where the bullshit is coming from."

"What does that have to do with you reading sermons?"

"You're not listening. This has got nothing to do with believing in anything. You don't have to spend all your time reading that shit about saints and sinners. But you have to understand the way these assholes thought. It's just like I keep telling you. You shouldn't be allowed to drive a car if you don't understand how a goddamn engine works. Especially with that shitbox hatchback you drive. You break down somewhere, you're not going to have any idea what to do, so what are you doing, driving the thing in the first place? It's the same thing with those sermons. They're like the engine of the whole shitbox country. You shouldn't be allowed to call yourself an American if you haven't read up on the Puritans. Because they're the original Assholes."

He was frowning hard at me, a sure sign that he was enjoying himself, just getting warmed up. All I could think was how good it would feel to drag my body up over the garage and into bed and sleep for the next week or two, but I could see it was going to be a while yet, so I forced my eyes open and plowed forward. Better to get it over with.

"All right. Tell me. Tell me about the Puritans," I said.

"You snide little fuck. The problem with the Puritans is that they thought they were the *elect*. The pure. Because they had that idea that came down from Calvin, everybody's fate is decided by God already, before anyone was even born, and everybody's a sinner, and so most people are going to Hell. They were very big into Hell. And the people who God decided are going to be saved, he's not telling who it's going to be, see? The only way to show that you might be one of the winners is to get religion, the *right* religion, so that way you can look down on everybody else, the big mass of losers out there. So they come to this country, they figure this is the place for the elect. It's the New World and all that crap, a place where they can start making the world over the way they want it to be. They're special people, get it? And this is a special country, the one that God *wanted* them to come to so that they could create it and make it perfect and pure, so that everyone else could look at it, all the sinners, and see how fucking virtuous it was."

"But people don't believe that anymore," I said. "That's a long time ago."

"Huh. You think so. But the idea is still the same. Look at this country. It's still the same old bullshit, it's the thing people in this country *want* to believe. The politicians know it. All you have to do is tell these assholes a story about how fucking pure they are and tell them someone else is damned because they don't work hard enough or their morals are bad or their race is lousy or they're goddamn Reds, tell them that and they'll vote for you. Every time. Because they want to think they're better than someone else, and you can always find the proof afterwards. You've got a house, a lawn, a couple of cars, your life means something, it's part of the big American project, you're moving forward, you're part of it. The ones who aren't part of the big project, who needs them. They're not going anywhere, they're just dragging us all down, giving the promised land a bad name. Be better if we could just get rid of them. See, look at them, they failed. God meant them to fail. Maybe they don't say God anymore, not all of them, but it's the same fucking logic. Puritan thinking. American thinking."

"Like calling someone a swamper."

"Swampers are swampers. Fuck them."

I was thinking of the casino I had been to earlier that night, though it seemed an impossibly distant memory—the artifacts and images, preserving something of the Pequots, who had been displaced so completely that to the extent that their living heirs continued on the earth even morphology had been lost to them. Thinking of segregated urban neighborhoods I had seen and passed through and felt uneasy in, growing up in the suburbs of the nation's capital decades after segregation's legal demise, thinking of streets I had seen where windows were blasted and boarded, blocks away from high-rise hotels and corporate offices, men in stained ragged sweatshirts holding out rough hands for money in the winter, in the chilly shadows of the gray stone buildings where the business of the government goes on. Was it possible that it all began that long ago, the Christian mission of the *Mayflower* exiles and all their fellows containing invisibly the seed of the world I knew, like the smallpox microbe nestled in the folds of a warming blanket?

The old man was looking at me, crushing his cigarette in the ashtray. "Welcome to America," he said, as if answering my thought. "Looks like you've been living here all along and didn't know it."

I frowned back at him. "But why is it *American* logic? Frederick, you came here from Germany, for god's sake. I know that was when you were a kid, a long time ago. But after that. Hitler, the Nazis. Mass killing in the name of purity."

I was expecting him to be belligerent, bracing myself for it, in fact, but he just looked away, into a distance that was not there, and shook his head. He looked as close to sad as I had ever seen. "Yeah. Well, that's where it ends up, huh? What can you say." He lapsed into a long silence.

Finally he roused himself. "I'll tell you what. I don't make any excuses for those genocidal assholes, but the only thing that ever surprised me is not that it happened in Germany, but that it didn't happen here, because there's no idea any Nazi ever had that someone right here didn't have first."

We sat in silence, the old man's hand toying with an unlit cigarette while he frowned into the dark kitchen. In the pause I heard the distant thump of the screen door above the garage, blown by the wind. It was time to wind things down so I could get out of here and get to bed. Maybe after one more smoke I could make my escape.

The old man's gaze was distant. "I was seven years old when we moved here, Ma and me. Yeah, so we came to the big promised land. It was a hell of a lot better than what we left behind, but even then I knew all that business about America was garbage."

He barked out a laugh. "Jesus, you know, I was watching this stupid movie on the television tonight, and this guy, he's narrating, talking about coming through Ellis Island, and he's saying in his cute little immigrant accent, 'When I feerst come to America, I theenk, is most bee-ootiful place in the whole world.'" Frederick was laughing now—actually, alarmingly, giggling—with the harsh hint of a smoker's cough breaking through from underneath. "'When I feerst—'" he said, his voice rising between pauses to catch his breath for laughing, "'When I feerst—come to A-mer-ee-ka—I theenk—it is—like *sheet!*'"

The kitchen door slammed open behind me.

The crash when it hit the wall was huge, shocking in the still-ness of the house, the night. The laughter stopped and the old man stared. I jumped and turned in my chair. Ellie West stood in the doorway.

She was out of breath, her eyes bright and desperate, red from tears, and for the briefest of moments we were frozen there in our places, in the still instant before everything happens, and be-fore I could even rise she said, sobbed almost, "Kese, I need you. Some men came to the house tonight to talk to my mother, to—" she was speaking fast, gulping her breaths, "to talk to her alone and she—now—I've never seen her like this and I don't know what to do but maybe you can—just, *please*, come now, will you?"

Then I was up and moving toward the door, pausing to turn back and say, quickly, "It's all right. Frederick, I'll see you in the morning," and he was opening his mouth to speak but I was already pulling the door closed behind me, Ellie ahead and mov-ing through the shadows at the top of the driveway where the garage light shone, having bolted again as soon as she had seen that I was coming, running fast into the dark, down the blacktop ribbon that wound invisibly through the trees.

I followed, trying to run but feeling dizzy, hobbled by an ugly stitch in my side, so I slowed to a jog that still jolted painfully, each hard footfall feeling like a vicious blow to the body. She was well ahead of me now and I could only just hear the slap of her feet on the wet driveway over the rushing of my own blood and my own ragged breathing. Rounding the corner that put me out on the short stretch of road, in the strange isolation of the dark and the straining against my body's inertia and the tunneling forward thrust of adrenaline, I thought, barely even in words, *I have been here before*, running after Ellie down this street toward her house, although then it had been day, but both times in the rush of uncertainty and desperation, and then before that, too, there had been the walk here on my first night, fresh from the highway and stumbling on the buckled asphalt in the dark, all the brief disoriented trips blurring together, and the doubling made the run dreamlike, time stretching and collapsing into timeless duration, as if I would always and forever be running this same path, repeating it over, and when I woke from the dream of running there would be no knowledge, no meaning, but only the sense of pounding and directionless pursuit without end.

But the end was in sight now. I could see the glow of the West house and it seemed that all the lights were blazing, every window lit up, making the dripping trees and wet shining grass visible in yellow patches as I ran by, moving faster now but still painfully, and I saw Ellie's form ahead, casting a long shifting shadow, running to the front door and yanking at it, leaving it open behind her as she disappeared into the house. I cut across the grass, my shoes squelching, watching the ground to avoid holes or tree roots, and then I was on the stone pathway and dashing up the step of the entryway, a creature of momentum, then through the door that Ellie had left open, toward the lights burning inside, where I was suddenly stopped as sudden and hard as if I had run into a wall.

Standing directly in my path was Charlotte West, her body still and tense, holding a gun that was pointed at my chest.

35.

There are two other girls in the car and she is not driving. Watching the world going by, going away. The things to see are different here. Trees, but different kinds. The car has seen better days, it has got them this far but then maybe this is not far enough after all. They are all young but there are no high spirits today, this evening, no one is speaking and the noise of the engine and the air through the windows are the only sounds. They have been here before, the route is the same, but it does not feel the same. It feels like behind all the things of the world there is another world, waiting to reveal itself, waiting for something. She tells herself that she does not know what is going to happen. She knows that something is going to happen to her.

Trees and houses glide by, they go away. Houses with round-faced children playing in front, with women sitting on front porches, bars with neon beer signs and stretches of dusty road like a lonely song on a jukebox some night a long time ago. Trees with twisted branches, branches hanging down heavy with unknown flowers, unknown fruit. What will the world look like on the last day. Like this, like nothing? Like everyone just going about their business, sitting on porches or getting dinner ready or driving down the road on some errand that could easily be put off, getting some milk at the store, while the world gathers itself toward some unimaginable ending and no one has time to pray or speak or grasp a hand for comfort? It happens all the time. Someone in one of those houses somewhere along the way is dying right now, and they are still popping the caps off bottles of beer at the bar on the roadside, this one, right now.

The neon beer sign in the bar is the same neon sign she has seen in a bar near her home. Memory and recognition fire, a stone skipped across the surface of knowing, sinking, lost. How far you can go and still find that your home is with you, how hard it is to escape, get out. Like a haunted house in the movies where you run blindly screaming for the door and the door is impossibly locked, there is no door, the house is your world and there is no way out and wherever you run you will still be there, standing at a door that only leads back the way you came when you thought it was the way out forever.

The car is moving. It is not a long drive and soon the drive will be over and they will arrive, they will get out of the car and walk and then. It has seen better days but there are no better days, nothing to look back to or go back to and if they are moving toward the end that's because it is the only place to go. The world is ordinary and completely familiar and it is a trap because whether you look forward or backward they've got you and so all you can do is ride in the back seat until you get there. The car is moving and the three girls in it are quiet and she watches the world going by and then they are there.

In the parking lot they open the doors and there is wind this time. It blows down over the hills, making patterns in the grass that she cannot read. Each blade of grass has a back and a front, dark green and pale green, on and off like flashcard pictures, sending messages. If she could read them, maybe she would know what to do. The wind blows clouds across the sky and the evening sun and the shadows of clouds are patterns on the grass too. If she could understand it all then maybe she could know how she came to be here now, walking across this parking lot to this building; if she could look down on her life in all its moments like looking down from an airplane flying high outside of time then maybe she could see the pattern and the meaning. Maybe then she would know what to do.

There is a waiting room, because things have to be hidden. There is a line between out here and in there, and that makes all the difference, and so what goes on in there is not for us to see until we are there and it is happening to us. Being there is knowing what it is and there is no knowing before the being there, that is why there is a waiting room. The woman behind the counter, behind the wall, does not look up. The nurse or receptionist, the gatekeeper. The two other girls sit in their chairs against the wall and she sits at a right angle to them, watching a spider. It is small and dark, spinning a web that connects the bottom of the low table to one of the table legs, a triangle with a spiraling circle built inside it, a beautiful thing tucked into a corner and the spider working and working at it.

The girls steal glances at one another but they do not speak. The lights are fluorescent, they make surfaces flat and awful and they glare on the shiny covers of the magazines on the low table. A picture of the president of the United States of America, a picture of a woman staring straight ahead through narrow eyes wearing a beret and not smiling, her hair glossy and strong, a picture of a tank on a street in another country, a picture of a woman wearing makeup and bending her body to be sexy, and all the pictures framed by words, words running over the pictures and under them, saying things.

The covers of the magazines are curling and wrinkled in places. That is why the spider is there, to remind her that this room should be spotless and antiseptic but it is not. It is dingy in the harsh dim lights and there is dust in the corners and a spider spinning a web under the table and the woman behind the wall speaks her words strangely, like everyone here. The magazines have the thumbprints of all the people who have sat here before, the room is greasy with their memory, and everything in the room is worn and tired except for the crisp pamphlets on the table with descriptions of diseases and complications.

The woman behind the wall took the filled-out forms and now she has them. That means that she has to go in there. She watches the spider while she waits in the waiting room, watches for a long time until she is thinking that she is inside the web, trapped in some spider's web that is not her own, stuck on the sticky strand with nothing to see except the terrible receding spiral lines stretched out in every direction and nothing to do but wait. And then the woman behind the wall comes into the room and says her name and it is time to leave the waiting room and go from out here to in there.

It can happen that in the moment it takes to walk through a doorway and find yourself on the other side, everything in your life is changed absolutely. The person that you thought you were is forever lost, and how many years and choices and how much scraping along, raw and ragged and exposed, it will take to build another, better one, like a fine house you can look forward to living in but while the building is going on there is no shelter for you when the cold comes and wind blows through the glassless windows and all the world's curious eyes can look in and watch you with their terrible searching pity while the years are long and go by slow and you want to scream all the while.

But in the moment, it's easy. You just keep walking.

On the other side of the partition, behind the desk that stands beside the door, she can see the shoes of the receptionist or nurse. They are white and scuffed, with thick soles. Her nails are long and red, they tap on the wood. She has her papers in front of her, she has her work to do. She does not look up as the other nurse, the other woman, leads the patient past the partition and through the door that leads to the rooms beyond. Three women close together in that moment of passing, and two in the waiting room still. What makes them women? The nurse at the desk has bright red nails. She wears stockings that whisper when she crosses her legs. The patient wants her to look up as she passes, wants her to say, it's all right, go home, but she does not look up. The nurses are efficient and firm and they give her looks that she does not understand, as if there is a mystery or a surprise party and everyone is looking at each other and putting fingers to their lips to say hush, hush now, don't spoil the fun, she doesn't know yet and then afterwards when we tell her she'll be so surprised that she'll just die.

As she crosses the threshold, the nurse holding the door open for her, the light different on the other side, she looks back at the two other girls in the waiting room. They are not in on the joke and they look small and dark and maybe scared, too. They do not look up as she looks back and the door begins to close. Maybe if they had looked up and their eyes met then there would be a different kind of conspiracy there, a strength they might share if they shared it together. Maybe she would discover that she could turn and go, could run even, into the fading light outside, late afternoon, summer heat in waves on the parking lot.

But the girls do not look up, and it is easy to keep walking, while the door begins to close, so easy to do what the nurse tells you to do, what the doctor tells you to do. It is so easy to keep walking, while the door closes and you find yourself in the place where the music stops and the lights go on and the masks can all come off and everyone says surprise, surprise.

She tells herself that she does not know what is going to happen.

Something is going to happen to her and she does not want to be there when it does.

36.

Charlotte West held the gun steady and she did not move or flinch.

I stopped running, my body arrested at the threshold so absolutely that it was as if another part of me was still running, carried forward by a momentum not of matter but of mind or purpose, moving fast and invisible through the woman and the gun and crashing into the bright room beyond like running through a sheet of glass, seeing the scene behind it as still and posed as a shop window—Ellie turned toward us with her mouth open and Franklin West further back with a stunned look as if he could not comprehend what he was seeing and around and between them the furniture, the couch and chairs and tables with lamps brightly lit, and then that other phantom me crashing through it all, the loud shattering leaving nothing behind of the scene at all, no light or staring figures or even the room itself, nothing left except for me standing in the sudden emptiness.

She stood still while endless moments passed, holding the gun pointed at me and not flinching or lowering it, long after she had had time to recognize who I was and maybe even to understand that Ellie had brought me there. I stood, wet and bruised and panting, holding myself still, like a boy who sees a poisonous snake ready to strike, watching the pistol that she held in both hands, watching the dark opening of the barrel and beyond it the unblinking dark eyes that looked forward without looking at me. Ellie was saying something now, maybe even shouting, but she could not shout loud enough for me to hear. Her mother did not turn or speak or lower the gun, maybe hoping that if she held it there long enough I would simply vanish without her having to pull the trigger.

I could feel a small stone that had worked its way into my shoe while I had been running and now was dug painfully into my heel. Shifting my foot I felt the squish of the sole and a sharp ache in my hip where it had rested, a few hours past, on something poking out from a garbage bag while I was sprawled unconscious beside the dumpster. All the small injuries and irritations of the long night, which still seemed to stretch ahead without any end in sight. Shifting back, I put all my weight on that one heel, focused my attention on the stone and the pain. Then I took a breath.

"Becky," I said. "You didn't need a gun to kill Eddie Slope."

No one moved and her face did not even show surprise. Ellie was not shouting now. We stood suspended, tense, waiting.

Finally, slowly, she lowered the gun and turned away, walking slowly back into the room and putting the gun down on the bar next to a half-full bottle of scotch. I watched the gun's progress and when she set it down, I breathed.

Then I walked across the threshold, trembling and unsteady.

Frank West was standing behind the couch, still with that baffled look clouding his handsome face. There were a lot of questions he could have asked then, about why I looked like something chewed up and discarded, about what I had said to his wife, about why she was looking like she wanted to shoot me in the first place, but he said nothing. Which was fine, because I did not want to answer any questions. Long past exhaustion now, I felt like the living dead come back to haunt, and I was going to have my say before anyone thought to put a stake through my heart and kill me again.

As I went by, Ellie looked at me uncertainly. She spoke my name, a question, but I walked past her. Charlotte West was standing with her back to the wall. She was not looking at me, but she was waiting.

"A car accident," I said. "Seventeen years ago, on the Boston Post Road. There's a sharp turn as the road goes past a pasture. You've driven past it dozens of times, maybe hundreds of times, you must have. There's a guardrail there now, in front of the telephone pole, before the grassy hill dips down in between the road and the farm. Maybe the rail was there then, too, I don't know.

But it's a dangerous curve, especially in the dark, and back then there probably weren't any lights out there either. It wouldn't be surprising if someone missed it, one way or another. Two men were found dead there in a destroyed car that night. One of them was named Eddie Slope."

I could feel Frank West's attention on me, but I didn't care about him, he was going to have to figure it out for himself. I wanted those dark eyes to look at me. "Your cousin's husband. The husband of the cousin of a girl named Becky Tilton. You, Becky."

"I wasn't there," she said. There was something strange in her voice, detached, as if she was not actually listening or speaking to me.

"No, you weren't there. Of course you weren't. I don't know how you arranged it, but you had them killed, and it was done well enough that no one ever suspected and not even the police asked any questions, apparently. But don't tell me you weren't there. I don't know what you think you mean by that, unless maybe you mean that you weren't ever anywhere. But I know that once there was a girl named Becky Tilton. There was, even if there isn't anymore. She grew up right around here, and she didn't like the way things were arranged for her so she left, headed south with a couple of other girls who wanted to get out of town. Then she left them, too. Maybe she figured she had to leave everybody and everything behind, start all over with a new name and new everything if she was going to get what she wanted. So she did. Got married and got to live in a nice house with a fancy family tree on the wall and a piece of wood that might be from an old ship everybody has heard of.

"But before that she had to take care of a couple of things. Because I know about—your sister's child," I said, carefully not turning, not letting my eyes stray over to where Ellie was standing. I did not want to know what her face looked like, or how much she understood. "That's why you did it, right? Isn't that it? Because you couldn't have anyone finding out who you were and who she was? Eddie might have known. Maybe he even told you he knew, and you were scared, or at least you were careful, and that's why you had him killed."

I stopped, still breathing hard in the silence, still watching her face that was not surprised or downcast or resigned, just far away, as if she was studying something that I could not see. Its beauty was undimmed, still affecting, maybe more than ever.

"I can't tell you because I wasn't there," she said, her voice low. "No one was, and that was why I had to kill him. Because he was the only one who could be held responsible."

There was a small anguished moan from Frank West, but no one could spare him any attention. He was beside the point. I was absolutely focused on her, and she did look at me now, and despite everything I was unprepared for the brief intensity of her gaze before she turned away again.

"I was sixteen." She said it with amazement, not just as if it was impossible to recall ever having been that young, but as if it was something she had never imagined she would ever admit to anyone. "I had been working at a job, cleaning houses, for over a year, trying to make the money that I would need to leave home and do some of the things that I wanted to do. Then one day, I was working at a house I had never been to before and the owner offered me a job working there full time."

"Brewstead," I said.

"What did you say?" Frank West asked. Again I could feel him staring, but I kept on ignoring him.

Charlotte did not nod or respond to either of us. "He offered me a job as a maid. He said he and his wife didn't like the intrusion of the cleaning girls, but they needed someone to keep the place clean, to arrange things when there was company. They never had any company, as it turned out. They did not seem to like company. But even if they had thrown parties every night, I would have taken the job.

"They had a little cottage in the back where I would live. That was good because I would be out of my parents' house, and because then I would have my room and board paid for and I could save my money. They were reserved people and they didn't expect me to talk to them much, so that was good, too. Her health was bad. It was bad the way you can afford it to be when you are rich. Often she stayed in bed all day, reading books. Sometimes she would loan me books so that I could *improve my mind*, but it was mostly romance novels that she read and I do not think the few I read were likely to have improved anyone's mind very much. He owned his family business, I don't know what it was, and sometimes he went to an office but many days he was at home working in his study. It was a big house, but even so there was not much for me to do. So I spent a fair amount of time in my little one-room house improving my mind by not reading Mrs. Brewstead's novels, and day to day I would only see the two of them and the man they employed part-time to keep the grounds."

"Eddie Slope," I said.

This time she did answer me. "No," she said. "It was a different man then. I think his name was Greeley. I worked there for a few months, through the spring and into the beginning of summer, and then one day he came to my little room."

"Greeley."

"No. Mr. William Brewstead," she said, enunciating each syllable flat and hard like she was slapping them down on the table, like she was showing a poker hand that was going to win even though she did not want it to. "He had never come out there before. Usually if they needed me for something they had a bell that they could ring, but they did not ring it often, and it was evening and the dinner things had all been washed up two hours since. He knocked and came in and he locked the door behind him."

"No," I said. "Wait a minute. Wait."

"He was talking to me, but I had seen him lock that door, I had heard the click. All of a sudden I could feel the whole expanse of empty space around us, and my mind rushed out past him through the locked door and into the yard that stretched for acres and the next nearest house down the road, so far away, and all the empty rooms of the house with Mrs. Brewstead in it probably napping in the bedroom way around on the far side of the house, and all the world beyond with no one in it who would hear me shout. All that space out there, all the space that money could buy, so that it was just him and me there in the quiet room, him who could buy a house with an extra little house for a maid to live in and could buy the maid, too, and put her in the house where no one would hear her.

"So it happened to me. I fought him, but it happened. He wasn't young but he was big enough and strong enough for that."

She paused. I did not tell her to wait again, because it was already too late, it was already all wrong. Her voice never faltered while she was telling it, and there were no tears in her eyes, but still I looked at Frank West, thinking, *Do something! Say something or hold her or whatever you can think to do, because you're supposed to be her husband* but maybe he didn't know who she was or what he was to her anymore, because he just stood there with a look of absolute shock and dismay on his face, as if the look could never be erased, looking like he thought that whatever was happening was happening to him.

Finally I said, "So it was him."

I don't know if she understood, but she said, "It was him." Her voice was flat.

I said, "So that was why."

She said, "No, that was not why."

We stood there for a few long moments before she spoke again.

"He left me there and I don't know what he meant to do next, what he expected me to do, what he thought would happen the next day or the next. But I knew that I was leaving right then, right away. I didn't spend ten minutes more in that little house. I packed and left and went to see a girl who had a car and who was going away soon with her cousin and told her that I wanted to go too. Then I just had to wait a week or so. I would not go back to my parents' house so I went to where one of my mother's cousins lived, not far away, and asked if I could stay in her backyard. There was a tent there and it was June, so that was fine. I lived there for a week, staying in the tent at night. There were lots of Japanese beetles that year, and they buzzed around and landed on the tent while I lay inside and thought about what I would do next, thinking that I was going to make it so that I never had to ask anyone for anything and so that no one would ever take anything from me again. I still didn't understand then, though I should have. I was going to go as far away as I could, I was going to find a place for myself and I was never going to come back. But I did not want to make any mistakes or let anything prevent me, and so first there was one thing I had to find out.

"I went south with the two other girls and when we stopped I knew it was time to go my own way. But it was easy to stay there, and I thought that I might need help for this one last time, before I said goodbye to asking for anyone's help ever again. So I told them that I needed to find out if I was pregnant."

For the first time she seemed to hesitate. But not for long. When she resumed, she spoke deliberately, her eyes staring past me and past her husband and daughter into darkness and distance. She sank down against the wall and crouched there, speaking steadily and quietly into the hushed room, staring past all of us.

"The first time we went to the clinic, I talked to a man behind a desk. He asked me questions and looked at my answers on a piece of paper, a form, and then he asked me more questions and had me sign my name on some of the papers and I signed my real name but I lied about my age. I think he said that I needed to sign the paper so that they could do the test to determine pregnancy. He wanted to talk to Miriam and Aline, too. They were in the waiting room, just waiting for me to come out, but the man went out and asked them to come in and talk to him, and then he sent me down the hall to the doctor's office where there was a doctor and a nurse, too. They took what they needed for the test and they told me to come back in three weeks for the results.

"So we left and then there were the three weeks to wait. I wasn't nervous, just like I was waiting for something to happen to me. And Miri and Ali, too, we were all waiting and I don't even remember what it was like, it was just a suspension, like we were hanging on the end of a rope and waiting for it to break. That's what I remember, hanging there and waiting for whatever it was to happen, no one talking very much, and where before they had been talking and making plans now it seemed like we just had to find out what was going to happen when the rope frayed away and we found out where we would all be when we fell, like afterwards we might pick ourselves up and look at each other and we would all have different faces and names and we would say Who are you, I think I used to know you, didn't I, and then walk away in three different directions.

"And then the waiting was over and we drove to the clinic again, and you will want to know what it was like. But I can't tell you because I wasn't there. They sat down in the waiting room and I went in and this time there was just the doctor and he said no I was not pregnant, I was not going to have a baby and wasn't that a relief, and now it was time to get ready so could I please go with the nurse. She took me to a room where I took off my clothes and put on a smock and my feet were cold. She took my things and put them away and I followed her into the room that was all white and black with the lamps above a metal table with a pad and a white sheet and I lay down and the nurse went out and I waited until she came back with the doctor and another man and they were all wearing masks and talking to one another and not to me. They turned on lights, moved them around and made sure everything was in its proper place and then they were all looking at me, the eyes above the masks. And maybe you will want to know what it felt like, but I can't tell you. I can't tell you. Because I wasn't there."

She stopped, the voice fading away in the large room, drifting away to the high ceiling. But now I could see it, the logic of it emerging, inescapable, taking shape as it had to, as it had to be. She was speaking again, saying, "He was the one who could be held responsible, he was the only one, and besides he was part of the whole problem, part of the edifice. And now I knew that I couldn't go away. I would have to come back and make my place in that edifice. I would have to take it. So when I took it and had the resources I needed, the first thing I had to do was to make him responsible, even if he was never going to know who had ended his life, just as he would never be able to know the consequences his actions had led to, so he died ignorant. I had the money to do it. I made the arrangements and paid the men. I made him responsible and they made him dead. That was better than nothing."

But I could see it now, I was seeing her through the eyes that were looking at her there in the clinic, the doctors, the nurse, the social worker with his papers and files—*the dark girl with the Summers address who barely answered if you asked her a question and didn't speak at all if you didn't ask; a good-looking girl, too—too pretty and too young, teenaged and without visible means of support so who would do the supporting when she did have a child? Or how many more, how long could it be now, for this honey pot to start attracting all the wrong bees, all the right ones? Because it had started already of course, obviously; teenaged and already sexually active, precociously deviant, and we can only wonder if that dangerous body of hers has already done what it thinks it was made to do and started populating the hills with more of her kind, with more dark silent girls to produce more like them, too; all of them living on us, not bright enough apparently to know how to keep her dress buttoned and no boyfriend even in sight, so running around maybe with every boy slick enough to get her in bed or the back seat of a car, a time-bomb body unregulated by intelligence and impervious to morality, to any thought of consequences, of economics, the cost of babies, generations of her kind producing more of their kind like weeds choking out the healthy plants and so what's needed is a gardener, to prune and distinguish, to choose and discard, to act in the best interests of the girl and the best interests of all of us, to determine what is best for all or else God knows what.*

There would have to have been approval from somewhere, a piece of paper stamped and authorized by someone in addition to the social worker and her own signature on the form, because otherwise why the three-week wait. So the authorization would have arrived and then they could go ahead and arrange for the surgeon and then it was a simple procedure and everybody would be better off forever and ever and all the generations afterwards.

When would she have realized, when would she have understood? Maybe she didn't know what was going to happen beforehand, but afterwards she would have understood. And she must have realized then that there was nowhere she could go, nowhere that would be different enough; she would have realized that there was nothing they could not take away from her. Now she knew.

And then the rest of it, William Brewstead and Mary Wood-house and Alice Pickett and Franklin West. And Ellie. Ellie, whom she took without apology because she wanted a child, and because she was through now with being taken from. Everything Charlotte had done had been done to put herself in a place where she need not ever ask for anything, where she could take what she wanted, and whatever it might be she had paid for it already. Maybe, too, she took Ellie because it was her own blood, her sister's child, that she would gather up and take with her, who would never have children of her own, to the sheltered place she had made for herself. So that even if she never loved the girl, even if the girl never loved her, at least it would be her blood relation and so there would not just be her after all to enjoy whatever triumph she had won. And all the better because the daughter would not know what had gone into the making of her, which was best for her and the sister and the daughter after all.

Charlotte West was still crouched leaning against the wall where she had dropped. Silent, expressionless, her eyes fixed on a distant corner where the walls met the ceiling. An old spider web hung there, worn and abandoned but too strong still to loosen its grip, gray strands swaying and swelling in an invisible breeze.

I turned, dazed and suddenly exhausted again, a weariness not of the body, which had long since given up, but of will and of comprehension, too, the night spreading like a vast fever dream before and behind me and I the hallucination at its center. The furniture was still there, strangely undisturbed, as if the world had not changed at all. Frank West had left the room. I had not heard him go. How much of what Charlotte had said had he heard and understood? Enough, surely, to have learned that the things he had valued all his life had been revealed as worthless. Enough that he had decided he could not hear any more.

"Ellie—?" I turned to her. She was staring at me, her face a mask of hatred.

I did not wait to hear what she had to say. Whatever it was, I surely deserved it, and I felt with keen self-reproach how terribly I had got everything wrong. Whatever had been right, too much had been wrong and all I could feel was how ugly and empty it was to learn the truth, how useless it was to know it. I crossed the room, leaving Ellie staring at me and her mother staring at the ceiling, leaving the long night's wreckage, passing the family tree that I did not need to read anymore because I knew what it said and what it did not say, and closing the door behind me.

Outside the air was cool. I felt the stone against my foot again, slipped the damp shoe off and shook it out, then started walking toward the road.

I stopped when I heard the shot.

Standing still in the darkness, looking back, I heard the scream that followed, muffled by distance and timber, a dying wail. The light at the front door cast a yellow pool over the lawn, and the house was still brightly lit at every window, so that it seemed I could see in my mind's eye a vision of the house ablaze, burning wildly, the loud hungry flames pushing out the windows and licking at the wood, and that I could see, at the same time, the aftermath and wreckage of that inferno, the house a black cinder.

But I did not go back. I turned and kept walking, hidden even from myself in the shadows of the dark driveway.

37.

For the next week I stayed in my little room as much as possible. I was stiff and bruised, but no bones were fractured, and the real ache was in the stories and images that stayed with me from that last night, all of them ugly, broken, and unfixable. I did not want to see anyone, did not want anyone looking at me. The first morning, Frederick pounded on the roof of the garage to wake me. I lay in bed staring at the ceiling and let the room shake and shake again until finally he gave up.

The days were gray and wet, full of drizzle, and when it did not rain it was overcast and a dirty breeze was blowing. It roused the smell of mildew out of closets and corners until it pervaded everywhere, hanging musty in the air and making furniture and sheets feel sticky and dank. I spent hours reading to the old man. There was nothing else to do, and it was all I was good for anyway. I could let my mind go blank, the words conveyed from the page and through my lips without any comprehension or curiosity on my part. Frederick would grunt occasionally in agreement, lifting his weights or smoking and watching the rain.

It was in the papers, of course. The death of Franklin Bradley West, local citizen and businessman, heir to West Maritime, Inc., recognized for his philanthropic work, from a family whose history was entwined with that of the local community, who had taken his own life with a handgun registered in his name, leaving no suicide note or other explanation, survived by wife and daughter, and so on.

There was no escaping from that. People talked at the post office, the business office, the diner, and the old man sought out anything printed in the papers and made me read the articles slowly while he bent forward attentively, not upset so much as fascinated, working to understand it, to find the detail that would allow him to put it in a box with a label on it like everything else. But my name never came up in the papers, and the police never came to ask me anything. The old man asked me questions and I lied, said I was as shocked as anyone, I had gone over there and Charlotte West was a little bit upset, I didn't know why, but she calmed down and I told them I was very tired and had to get to bed and that was all. Frank West? He had seemed like he always did, I hadn't noticed anything out of the ordinary. He seemed concerned about his wife, but then she was all right and everyone seemed to be all right. That was all. I was relieved that Frederick did not suggest that I go to the police.

I heard that Charlotte and Ellie had already moved out of the house, that their things were being packed up by a moving company and the place would be put up for sale by an out-of-town real estate agent. In the meantime nobody knew where they were. Ellie would be going away to school soon, if in fact she was still going. I thought about them and did not know what to think or to wish for them. I thought about the two of them, what on earth they might talk about now, if anything, and about the tattoo. Would Charlotte ever explain its meaning to her daughter, or would Ellie ever explain it to her mother, and if they didn't, would it matter?

I never saw them or heard anything about them again. There was a memorial service and funeral for Frank West a few days later, but neither the old man nor I went.

Surely Alice did. I even sought her out—almost the only thing I did that week that I actually willed, that required me to make a decision or an act of any kind. I could have gone to her house, but instead I drove downtown and went to the church on the night of her painting class. A gray rain was falling and I took shelter in the entryway to the basement, standing there and peering out into the gloom while a few other elderly painters came down the stairs. Turning to look behind me, I could just see around a corner into a room with fluorescent lights and easels set up. Then I turned back and Alice did appear, stopping to collapse her umbrella and looking up to see me. There were drops of rain on her glasses.

She blinked, then nodded. I nodded back.

"Well, Kesey."

"I came to say goodbye. I'll be leaving next week."

She nodded again. Then she looked at me keenly, sticking her head forward. "You were there," she said. It was not a question.

"Yes."

"And you are going to tell me that I am better off not knowing."

"Yes."

"Because I am an old woman and you don't want to upset me."

"No," I said. There was a moment's silence, and then I looked away, down. "All right, yes. But not because you are old. Just because—because—I guess I don't want you to feel how I feel. Or maybe that's not even it. I just can't explain it all to you. I can't tell it. Not yet."

She looked at me for what seemed a long time, a look in which annoyance and sadness were strangely mixed. "Well, I will not ask any more for now," she said finally. "But you will have to come and see me, tell me, before you go. I deserve that much."

I promised to do that. She was right. She deserved that much, and more.

She sighed, pausing to shake rainwater from the umbrella. "You know," she said, "some days it is harder than others to get out of bed and keep going."

"Why do you do it?"

She started to walk down the hall toward the lighted room. She stopped, turned, and cocked her head for a moment.

"Because," she said, "I want to see what happens next."

I nodded. "Goodbye, Alice."

She waved the umbrella, already walking away again down the hall.

38.

Two days later the weather cleared, the sun broke through the haze, and that morning when we pulled out of the garage to get breakfast, steam rose in slow white curls from the blacktop of the driveway.

Duke had just arrived in mud-stained boots and jeans to work on the soggy grounds, and he was moving aside a tarpaulin that was covering the tools in the back of his truck. He waved, walking toward us as we were turning around, and I rolled down the window. The new weather had done nothing for my mood. I squinted into the sun like a man with a hangover. Duke was talking to Frederick about the yard and I was watching the last threads of steam as they lifted and faded, so absorbed in watching them, while my mind drifted in desultory circles, that Duke had to repeat my name twice before I understood that he was talking to me. He asked if I could come by his place the following day after lunch, and I said sure, why not, and then we drove away.

Going out to Duke's place again, it was all repetition. The clearing was the same, appearing at the end of the crunching gravel drive, the sun the same, though perhaps the slant of its light through the trees was more faint and more oblique now that the summer was almost over.

As I closed the car door and walked toward the front door I heard the discreet leafy scuttling of cats as they took cover, crouching in the shadows beneath vines and bushes to watch my progress. Next to the house I saw the two battered pans that they ate from, one empty of food and the other with an inch of water still, its surface catching a glint of sunlight as I passed. I registered it all dully, wondering without enthusiasm what it was that Duke wanted to see me about. It was not until I was on the steps in front of the screen and the voice that was not Duke's was telling me to come in that I noticed that the truck was not there, and the shiny black car parked against the edge of the woods was the same one that had been there last time, its presence inserted so neatly into the repetitions of the day that it had seemed the only possible thing. So I opened the door and there was Clinton, his back to me, rummaging through the cupboards.

He was wearing a pale blue dress shirt and dark pants, neatly creased, shoes a shiny black. His suit jacket was draped over one of the kitchen chairs, a patterned tie hanging on top of it. In Duke's neat kitchen the cupboard doors were all open and several containers and cans and boxes were out on the counters.

"Want some coffee?" He turned and caught my eye briefly before sticking his head back behind a worn cabinet door, emerging again with a mug in each hand. He pulled the pot out of the coffee maker and filled the mugs while a drop fell and sizzled on the plate where the pot had been. "Got some I just brewed up. Hope you like it unsweetened, though, 'cause we have got a can marked *Sugar* here but it seems to be full of nothing but weed."

I took the mug he handed to me, the worn white ceramic stained with use, faded letters reading *World's Greatest Dad*. Clinton's said *Keep on Truckin'*. He held it at arm's length for a moment, then took a sip, grimacing at the lack of sugar, and gestured to the kitchen table. We sat down across from each other. The tame cat, Mutt, was settled on another of the chairs. She raised her head to gaze at me when I sat down, on the lookout for a head scratch, then after a few seconds curled into herself and went back to sleep.

"All right," Clinton said. "I wanted to talk to you, just us, someplace where we could have a little privacy, and this seemed like the place. I asked Duke not to fill you in beforehand. Didn't mean to be all secretive, but I did want to be careful. Hope you don't mind."

I took a sip of burnt coffee, shrugged. "I'm here."

He leaned forward over his mug and looked at me steadily. "What I have for you is a sort of apology. A *very* unofficial apology."

Despite myself, I sat up a little in the chair, listening.

"Like I told you before, there's been a lot of action around the reservation these last couple years. Busy times. The casino's pulling in money like nobody's business, which means a lot of things are happening all at once. For one, the tribe has to deal with all these new Indians keep showing up. Like me, for instance. Sort of like the old American problem. The tribe needs immigrants, too. Every new Pequot enlarges the tribe, helps to make it legitimate. New blood. But then the more come in, the more the tribe worries about keeping its identity, whatever it thinks that might be, the more it starts thinking it needs to find a way to control that flow of people into the tribe. Set some limits, make sure it's the right people, you know how that goes. Growing pains. Big new houses going up, big old houses getting bought, seems like at the tribal council meetings you can't spit without hitting somebody's this-year's-model BMW in the parking lot. So as you might figure, real estate prices in the area are, let us say, volatile. There are a lot of people who would like to get a piece of the action, and they'll do whatever it takes to grab what they can, while they can."

He paused, still keeping his steady gaze on me. "I heard recently, never mind how, that you got beaten up pretty badly by some gentlemen in the casino parking lot. Looking at you now, I'd have to say that was the truth. I don't know what all they might have said to you that night, whether they threatened you or anything."

It was a question. "No," I said. "They didn't say much at all." I rubbed at the back of my head where it was still tender.

"Well, I also happen to know why you got beat up. Not that the casino or the tribe had anything to do with it, of course. But you might say it was a kind of side effect. It happened because somehow you managed to get on the wrong side of some of the more unscrupulous individuals who are trying to get their hands on that real estate money."

I was staring at him, suddenly understanding.

"Harrison Adams," I said, almost whispering. In the back of my mind I tallied yet another wrong deduction I had made, one more thing I hadn't been able to see because I was so busy watching Charlotte West.

Clinton did not blink or move at all. *I can neither confirm nor deny.* Then his face became a wry question. "Now, here's a curious thing. I understand that somehow these—individuals got the idea that you were some sort of—investigative reporter?"

I sighed. It felt so long ago. "All right, yes. I may have said something like that." He raised his eyebrows, looking almost amused. "Duke had told me about Adams buying up land around the reservation and inflating prices, about him trying to scare people with rumors about organized crime—Adams even said something like that to me, the one time I met him. Besides, I just didn't like him and—well, I don't know exactly what I was thinking. Maybe I thought I could find out something, that people would be more likely to talk to me if I said I was a writer, a real journalist. It was only the lawyer, Payne, who I gave that story to, but I guess it got back to Adams through him. Maybe some part of me was even hoping that the lie *would* get back to Adams, the part of me that wanted to make him worried, make him think someone was on to him."

Now Clinton did smile briefly, nodding, his mouth still wry. "Yeah. See? Do-gooder. I knew it first thing." He shook his head. "Well, that's fine. This *individual* we are talking about here, he's a straight-up asshole, no question. Someone wants to kick him in the balls, I'll be the first one in line to buy a ticket and some popcorn for the show."

He paused for a moment as if picturing the scene in his mind, then shook his head again and went on. "But you should understand, too, that there aren't any innocent victims needing protection here. This isn't like a Movie of the Week or something where a big bad white man does nasty things to the poor helpless Indians. What it really is, it's a story about a white man who wishes he were big, one who's so desperate to get a piece of the Indians' pie that he does some bad, stupid things. End of the day, he's an annoyance, because he can be bought, and the tribe has got the money to do it. So really it's not even a story about him, it's just another story about money. The casino, it's not operating in any big noble cause. It does raise the profile of some Indian causes, and it's going to help keep the Pequot traditions alive. But even with all that, the casino, it's a business, a successful one. And sometimes assholes are just the cost of doing business. In fact they may be what business is all about—but you didn't hear that from me."

But I was thinking now, rusted gears creaking slowly to life. "Wait," I said. "So the men who beat me up, they were trying to get me to stop asking questions about whatever shady real estate deals were going on around the reservation."

Clinton nodded.

"And would these men maybe have then gone to Franklin West's house? Adams was trying hard to get West to sell him some land, and West was holding back, hesitating, because that's the kind of person he was, a guy who didn't like change and really didn't like to give up anything that belonged to his family. So what if," I paused, trying to think it through. "What if Adams had found out something about West's wife, a piece of information that she would not have wanted anyone to know or to make public. I don't know how he would have found out, but he could have. So he sent someone to their house, maybe even the guys who got me in the parking lot, sent them to have a private conversation with her, to strike a deal: you persuade your husband to sell the land and we will keep this particular piece of information to ourselves, and everybody's happy. That could have happened, couldn't it?"

He stared in open bafflement. "Hold on. Hold on there. I'm not following you at all. Because what kind of information are we talking about here?"

I shut my eyes tight, opened them, blinking. Maybe it would be a relief to tell someone. Maybe. "How much time have you got?" I asked.

Still looking puzzled, he glanced at his watch. "You got me for an hour if you want me. What is it, Kese?"

So I told him, all of it.

It took a while, sitting in the kitchen in the afternoon light with no steam rising anymore from the coffee and the cat sleeping in a little box of sun and a light wind moving the shadows of trees around on the floor. But I told all that I could remember as best I could, and he sat and listened with thoughtful attention and did not interrupt. The words poured out, and with them everything I had thought and felt the whole summer long, and I knew that I could not stop until I reached the end because I had to say it all together and complete at least once, and if I stopped before the end then the story would never cease and it would always be there waiting to end and never going away.

When I stopped speaking at last, there was a long pause, as if the silence had been waiting and waiting for me to stop and now could finally rush in to fill the room. Maybe it was the coffee, but I was trembling, feeling cold in the heart of summer's warmth.

Clinton was rubbing his chin and looking at the table. After a while he said, "An operation. Goddamn. I wouldn't even have thought they were still doing that in—what, the sixties?" He paused. "I've heard about it, of course. A lot of poor black folks, lot of Indians, too, for that matter. I wonder if they thought she was—or if she was just—" He trailed off there, his eyes roving around as if moved by thinking. "Well. I guess it doesn't matter. They did it."

He took a sip of cold coffee. "So you think that maybe a certain *individual* found out somehow that Charlotte West was really this Becky person. And that maybe he decided to blackmail her just a little bit, just enough to put some pressure on her husband to sell his piece of land. And that his friends paid her a visit that night, but that after they left, when she saw clearly that someone had her secret and was willing to tell it, she freaked out, gave her daughter a fright, so she went and got you—and that's when everything went down."

I nodded. "It would explain a few things."

"I suppose it would. And maybe you've got a future as a reporter after all." A month ago, those words would have given me a rush of pride, but they did nothing for me now.

Clinton frowned, gazing out the window. "You know, the part of the whole thing that I don't get is why she ever came back here in the first place all those years ago."

"She had to. I think she was going to go away, before, after Brewstead raped her—she wanted to get as far away as possible, start a new life. But then after the operation, she decided she had to come back here. Like she wasn't free to go away anymore, because she had to make somebody responsible. And the thing that was responsible wasn't just Brewstead, it was bigger than him. I think I understand. I just wish I had understood more of it in the first place. Maybe I wouldn't have fucked it up so badly."

"Kese. You seem to be taking this all on yourself, you know? You tell it like you're responsible for everything."

"I got it all wrong," I said.

"It was wrong a long time before you got there. I understand how you feel, sure. You've got this story, all about things that happened in the past, somebody else's past, and now you feel like you're responsible for all of it. That's fine, but none of it is your doing."

"It still feels wrong. It feels like I should have been able to do something, should have done it better. And there's one other thing, too. Something I can't figure out."

"What's that?"

"Way back at the beginning of the summer. Did I tell you this? The man who walked into the diner, asking for Eddie Slope, a man who's been dead for almost twenty years. It seems awfully strange that anyone who knew the guy well enough to want to see him wouldn't have known that, found it out sometime. Who was this guy?"

"Who knows? Maybe he was a ghost."

I looked up sharply, but he looked serious, not like he was laughing at me.

"You believe in ghosts?"

"Not the way my grandma did, but sure. Ghost. It's like another way of saying that the past doesn't ever go away. Might as well get used to that."

"Or another word for unfinished business."

"What kind of business you have in mind?"

"The kind I let happen when I didn't go to the police, or do anything else. That's the other thing I can't seem to let go. She sacrificed him, you see? She decided she had to kill Brewstead, and Eddie Slope was just collateral damage, he was the innocent who just happened to be in the wrong place, wrong time, and so he got killed, too. I don't know how she felt about that, and it doesn't matter. But I sacrificed him, too. All I did was stir up a lot of ugliness from the past, because I thought you were supposed to bring that stuff into the light. And what right did I have to do it, what right did I have to know her secrets, if there wasn't some justice at the end of it all? But then I let his death go unpunished. Maybe I let Brewstead's death go just the same way, too. That equation's too complicated for me to solve, what's justice and what isn't. But Eddie Slope died for no reason and no one remembers him and I let him disappear, too."

"Maybe it wasn't your responsibility," Clinton said.

"Whose was it?" I said, but I knew the inevitable answer: no one's. And if no one's, then who was responsible for anything? What was there to be gleaned from the whole dark unraveling history?

Clinton was frowning, looking down into whatever was left in his mug. He looked at it for what seemed like a long while. Finally he began to speak.

"My grandmother," he said. "She grew up right around here. Part white, part Indian. Pequot and some Narraganset, too. Her family moved down to Providence when she was a teenager and they lived in a neighborhood that was mostly black and Puerto Rican. Her parents didn't like it there and they sure didn't like having to live around black folks, but her father had a job and that was the Depression so they didn't have much choice. No landlord was going to rent to them in any white neighborhood. They knew that, 'cause they'd tried every single one they could find. White people with places to rent out took one look at them and figured they were just some kind of weird Puerto Ricans who didn't like to speak Spanish.

"I think her parents mostly just kept to themselves as much as possible. But my grandma, she was in school every day, out on the stoops with the other girls every chance she could get, she wasn't keeping to herself. Long story short, she started dating a black boy. Her parents found out, they went through the roof. Kicked her out, said she wasn't any daughter of theirs if she wanted to mess around with the coloreds, and that was the end of that. The boyfriend ditched her pretty quick after that and she dropped out of school, so now she was alone and living on the street. I've heard her tell the story, but I still don't know how she survived, a teenage girl on her own in the city. Tell the truth she kind of skips over that part. I've always wondered if maybe she turned prostitute for a while. There's always a market for that, but if she did she managed to get out of the racket somehow, which most don't. Whatever happened, it was something she wasn't ever going to mention to her grandkids.

"She got herself down to New York somehow and got a job sewing in a sweatshop, and I guess you can imagine what that was like, but it was better than starving. She took up with another black man, that was my grandfather this time, and together they got married, moved out to Detroit, started a family. My granddad went off to Europe for the war and got himself killed. So then she was all by herself again, except now she was a maybe-white woman, without a whole lot of money, raising a couple of black kids on her own. There wasn't any neighborhood, white or black or anything else, that liked the looks of that. She moved seven times in the first two years after her husband died, and no one ever helped her, unless you count wishing her gone as a kind of help.

"She still says there's no place she ever feels like she's at home, even though she's been living in the same house for the last forty-five years. I told her she ought to come out here and live on the reservation or somewhere nearby, it's as good a place as anywhere to not feel at home. But most of the family's still out in Michigan so I guess she'll stay there."

He paused, uncertain maybe whether he was done talking, letting the story hang in the air, looking thoughtfully at Mutt, who looked back at him with an expression of polite and absolute unconcern, green eyes half closed against the sunlight. "Well," he said, still looking at her, "guess it's time I was on my way."

He stood and took the two mugs to the sink, then flipped up his collar, deftly knotted his tie, and shrugged on his suit jacket. I watched him.

"Do you have a meeting at the reservation?" I asked.

He tugged his shirt cuffs out of his jacket. "You're wondering why I'm all dressed up? Well now, don't spread it around next time you file one of your investigative reports, but I'm planning to get myself into politics, become an elected official, and I figure it's time to start looking the part. One thing I've noticed these past few months is just how much you can get done in politics if you've got some money. Guess it's time I took some of that cash the white folks have been spending at the casino and put it to good use, use it to sell them something they definitely had no idea that they needed. A black Indian politician." He flashed a grin, wicked and infectious. "After all, I've got a namesake in the oval office these days. Must be a good omen."

We headed outside, watched by the large eyes of the feral cats in the undergrowth. Clinton walked around to the side of his car. I walked to mine, then hesitated, fiddling with my keys.

"You really feel it, don't you?" I said. "Your connection to all this. To being an Indian. A Pequot."

"Yeah," he said. "I feel it. Blood isn't everything, but then again nothing is everything. We're making ourselves all the time. Out of what we've got." He paused, looking at me thoughtfully. "Kese," he said finally. "You know what you said about how the old lady, Alice, how despite everything she had a kind of, how would you say—*admiration* for that West woman?"

"Yes."

"I think I understand how she feels," he said.

"Yes."

Then we both drove away.

39.

My bags were packed and waiting in the car. The apartment above the garage was cleared out and ready for the cleaners, the room empty and anonymous again, its surfaces washed in latticed light that set the dust motes floating weightless in the air aglow.

I had opened my eyes in the bed there that morning and lain there for a few minutes in the deep and fragile warmth of waking. Half dreaming, I had found myself remembering my last morning in my own bed at home on the day I had driven up here, the suburban soundtrack playing, a lawn mower trundling somewhere, indistinct voices, the huge quiet humming of the populous world, and me lying there, thinking of the trip ahead. Here at the old man's house we were insulated by trees and acreage from the sounds of the neighbors, so there were only the birds to listen to while I lay in bed and let my mind wander ahead to the next journey.

Then there had been breakfast, of course, at our accustomed booth in the diner, the Greek proprietor smiling and giving me a mechanical wink as I slid onto my seat. The waitress set the coffee in front of us and Frederick tapped out a cigarette while I poured cream from the cold metal pitcher and scanned the day's headlines. When I looked up, he was smoking with his face tipped upward in thought.

"Why do you think he did it?" he asked.

"Why did who do what?"

"You know. Frank West. Why do you think he did it?"

I had thought about that, had spent plenty of time thinking it over during the past week. Had he assumed the guilt, the culpability for the two men's deaths that his wife had refused, or had he maybe been shocked beyond reason to learn that he had been married to a murderer for twenty years? Or was it her story; had it been too awful to have to know what she had lived through, and to discover that he had never really known her at all in all those years they were supposedly together? Maybe it was the simple matter of what she had been, not the murder but just the offense to his family's lineage that she represented—an offense that was compounded by learning what a man of good family like William Brewstead had done to Charlotte. The lineage. That idea into which he had placed so much of himself that when it crumbled, he did too, the bank failing and his assets gone with it and him left standing at the window high above the street staring down at the welcoming pavement below. Was it one of those things, or all of them together, or maybe even something else that I had not known about or imagined?

That is what I was thinking. But what I said was, "Maybe he couldn't stand to see what was going to come next." Alice's phrase, and once I said the words, they seemed fine. They seemed like they would do.

The old man considered this.

"Okay," he said. "Sure. A guy like that."

And then the bags were packed and waiting in the car and I was standing in the driveway. Duke had contrived to be working at Frederick's place that day, although he was mowing sections of the lawn that looked smooth and close-cropped already. When he saw me, he stopped the mower and came walking across the sloping yard, wiping his hands on his jeans and then holding one out for me to shake.

While I was thanking him for everything, the old man came out of the house carrying something. He had already given me my last month's wages—though he wasn't paying me much, and it had been understood at the start that room and board was to be the larger part of my compensation.

"All right," he said. "I found this in the closet upstairs last night." He handed me an old-fashioned wool overcoat, dark gray and worn. "When you go back to school one of these days, there's going to be some place there, some bar where the guys all get together and they're going to be drinking and talking about books and bullshitting, wearing overcoats and scarves. I figure you're going to need this."

I held up the overcoat. It was desperately out of fashion and it had the musty smell of old houses and old men. I had spent enough time in bars and other college hangouts to know that, even if I ever did go back to school, there was no place anywhere in America that was anything like what he was describing.

I was making plans to throw the overcoat away at the first highway rest stop, but then I thought, maybe I should give it to my father instead. My inheritance.

"You're going to need these, too," he said. He handed me a paper bag. I reached in and pulled out a carton of cigarettes.

I looked at it blankly. "I don't smoke."

"You just wait. They'll start looking good when you're sitting around in that bar with those fucking guys talking about Kierkegaard."

Duke raised his pale red eyebrows at me, deadpan, and I almost wanted to laugh. He said, "I thought maybe I'd come by today and do a little of that reading you've been doing. So Frederick doesn't have to go cold turkey."

We said our goodbyes and I got in the car, put the overcoat and the carton in the back seat, rolling down my window to wave as I drove away. In the rearview mirror I could see them standing in front of the garage, Duke standing at ease with his hands in his pockets, the old man with his hand raised in front of him in a stiff mock salute of farewell.

Out of sight, at the bottom of the long driveway where it met the road, I stopped the car and idled in neutral, leaning forward over the steering wheel.

Along the road on either side the low dry-stacked stone walls stretched, rising and sinking with swells in the land, marking property, marking borders. The devil's own stones. Shaded beneath the trees, a few of the huge moss-covered boulders were immovably planted, hulking in their permanence, older than the walls, signifying only their own ancient mass.

By borders and boundaries we divide the land and burrow into it, trying to plant ourselves, to make a home in the rock, but the wind drives us out and blows us helplessly down the old land's endless paths. You do not have to be an immigrant to find yourself out on the road in this country, to find yourself looking for a home, a shelter, something you can hold on to, something that can hold you together when the wind comes to pull you apart. Charlotte Lenoir was out there somewhere, and Ellie West, too. Maybe together, maybe not, living their lives in the shadow of a past that reaches back far beyond their own lifetimes, a shadow at evening, stretched impossibly over the landscape to an unseen vanishing. They were out there. And so were Miriam Beauclaire, and Jerry Tilton, and Mary Woodhouse, maybe, and all of us. I was thinking of Clinton, telling me the story of his grandmother, putting it alongside the story I had told him as if maybe, if you held them both together up to the light, some previously unseen color or pattern might emerge and flicker into meaningfulness for a moment. I felt, just then, that he had been saying the same thing the old man had said to me that night, sitting under the yellow kitchen lamp. Welcome to America. If you don't see that the place is full of stories like this then you haven't been paying attention. And if you don't have a story of your own, you're just lucky. For now.

I said aloud, "So what are you going to do about it?"

The late summer sun filtered weakly through the canopy of leaves and here and there a clearing in the branches left a bright patch burning on the road's surface. I put the car back in gear and let out a breath that I did not even know I had been holding. I was ready to follow the signs back to the highway.

ACKNOWLEDGMENTS

This is the place where I pretend that thanks are possible, for all the large and small contributions, the acts of support and friendship and collegiality and everything else—all the many and various reminders that, however solitary the process may sometimes feel, no book is written without a whole lot of help.

Thanks first of all to my excellent readers. Stephanie Hartman read the first fifty pages and told me that I might as well keep on writing, so I did. Glenn Moomau, Tanya Agathocleous, and Dave Zirin all offered generous, invaluable readings and detailed suggestions. To paraphrase the Beach Boys, God only knows what this book would have been without them.

David Keplinger consistently offered his help and expertise as I started the process of trying to publish the book. Really, all of my colleagues in the Literature Department at American University deserve a big shout-out, too—what luck to be part of a supportive intellectual community like this one—and the university made this project possible by giving me the sabbatical year during which the book was written. At Regal House, Jaynie Royal has somehow always remained patient with me, and has been immensely helpful in guiding the book through the publication process.

My brother Michael and his wife Nikki kindly shared their experiences and impressions of Connecticut casinos, and I even took a few notes myself. I cannot claim to have done a great deal of research for this project, but I did consult a few sources: Kim Isaac Eisler's *Revenge of the Pequots*; Brett Duval Fromson's *Hitting the Jackpot*; John Bodinger de Uriarte's *Casino and Museum*; and also *Better for All the World* by Harry Bruinius, and the collection *A Century of Eugenics in America*, edited by Paul Lombardo. There are, too, a few writers whose work I have been reading so much for so long that they exert an inevitable influence here, in particular William Faulkner, Toni Morrison, James Baldwin, and Raymond Chandler. While we're at it, let's not forget some of the musicians who made the albums that I listened to over and over while writing, like Juana Molina, Yo La Tengo, Patrick Watson, Fela Kuti, and Talk Talk.

I had better take this opportunity to remember my maternal grandmother, Ellen Noyes Woodhead Mueller, and her husband Walt Mueller—because without them this book really would not exist.

So now we come to the part where thanks are truly and forever unequal to the task. Everything I do is possible because of my parents—Sally Dougherty Dussere (who knows her way around a family tree) and Paul Dussere (who knows his way around a Stennes Book)—and my brother Michael (who has put in his time reading aloud). And one last and loudest hurrah for Stephanie and Liv, who make everything worthwhile, who create the future every day.